
★

A sharp crack. Gunshot. Oh, Jesus.

Grabbing the Smith & Wesson from her shoulder bag, she ran past Debra to the inner door and slammed it open against the wall. The hallway went straight back, offices on each side.

Two doors before the hallway turned off to the right, Jen lay sprawled on the floor. Susan knelt beside her. The girl had fallen forward, partially on her side, one arm flung out beside her head, the other tucked under her body. No pulse. Breathing in short, agonized rasps. Small bloodstain on the blouse, left side of chest.

Beyond Jen, just outside the open office door on the left, Dorothy Barrington lay in a pool of blood. Dead almost before she fell, Susan thought.

★

"[Weir]...keeps the tension level high, the heroine likable, and the puzzle's solution both ingenious and believable; the best of the author's outings so far."

—*Kirkus Reviews*

"Great characterization and topnotch plotting... a wonderful read."

—*TeleGraphics*, Baldwin, KS

Charlene WEIR

FAMILY PRACTICE

WORLDWIDE.

TORONTO • NEW YORK • LONDON
AMSTERDAM • PARIS • SYDNEY • HAMBURG
STOCKHOLM • ATHENS • TOKYO • MILAN
MADRID • WARSAW • BUDAPEST • AUCKLAND

To Jackie and Ariana and Jake

FAMILY PRACTICE

A Worldwide Mystery/May 1997

First published by St. Martin's Press, Incorporated.

ISBN 0-373-26236-1

Acknowledgments

Thanks are owed to Detective David Peres of the Daly City, California, Police Department and Sergeant David Hubbel of the Lawrence, Kansas, Police Department.
Special thanks go to all the wonderful people at Alta Bates Hospital.
Any errors are mine alone.

ONE

WHOEVER IT WAS won't get away with it. Dorothy strode into the relative gloom of the open garage behind the medical building and ran the back of her hand across her forehead. March may have come in like a lion, but it went out like a drenched cat. All the rain left the air so sticky with humidity it felt like flypaper. The heat was getting to her; she felt a little sick. Or maybe it was because she was so angry. Fingers spread, she pushed at the blond hair that clung damply to her face.

Snapping the folded newspaper under one arm, she lifted the lid of the trash can near the rear door, dropped in something, and carried the remains of her lunch inside.

The air-conditioning raised bumps on her sweaty, bare arms. She took a moment to smooth the skirt of her tan dress, adjust the navy belt, and compose her face, before walking along the carpeted corridor to the waiting room. One elderly lady sat in a brown tweed armchair.

"Oh, Doctor, there you are." Debra Cole, a young woman with soft brown hair and doelike eyes, looked up from the reception desk with a worried frown. She plucked at the cuff of the long-sleeved white blouse she wore with her green skirt. "Mrs. Clinkenbeard's been waiting, and there was—"

"I need to make some phone calls," Dorothy said, "before I see her."

"But Doctor—" Debra looked startled.

And no wonder, Dorothy thought, glancing at the clock on the wall. I'm late, and on top of that I'm going to keep a patient waiting. Not the way things are run around here. This time it's necessary. I'll be as quick as I can.

In her office, Dorothy tapped the folded edge of the newspaper against the desk, then smacked it down hard on a corner and sat rigidly upright in the swivel chair. Oak, old and scarred, the chair had been her mother's, as had the desk, the ancient wooden file cabinets, and the medical practice. She slid open the bottom desk drawer to stash her purse and realized she was shoving in the paper bag with her lunch.

Where was her purse?

Oh, for heaven's sake. Abruptly, she stood up, headed for the door. Maybe I'm getting old. Forty-six. She lifted the trash can lid, fished out her purse, brushed off a few coffee grounds, and dumped the sack. Nonsense. Forty-six wasn't old.

At her desk, she snatched up the phone. "Come to the house this evening," she said when Carl answered.

"Not tonight. Sorry. I've got plans."

She'd meant that as an order, not a suggestion. "You think I don't? That I wouldn't like to spend an evening with my husband?"

"Hey, live it up. Play out your dreams."

As usual, he was going to fight her. Depression draped itself around her like a heavy shawl. She was living her mother's dream. Where would she be if she'd followed her own? Mama's plan was that all five of her children would attend medical school and then practice in a family clinic. When she died, it was Dorothy's responsibility as the eldest to see the program was carried out. She brushed damp strands of hair off her forehead. What if she hadn't promised? "This is important."

"Isn't it always? Where would we all be without you?"

Willis had always wanted to be a doctor, but Marlitta was going to be a movie star. And Carl— "Huh, you wanted to be a cowboy, as I recall. You'd be drifting nowhere."

"With no focus for my misery."

"Save the sarcasm. I've got patients waiting. Be there at eight." When she hung up, tiredness rolled over her. How would it be simply to go home and play Chopin nocturnes on the piano?

Deep down any little smidgen of depression terrified her, because of Daddy. She shook herself to throw it off. Get those calls made. Picking up the phone again, she punched in Ellen's number.

Mama always worried about Ellen. Because Ellen looked like Daddy, Mama was afraid she would turn out to be like him.

And then, after all, it was Daddy who was responsible for the money. Well, now Dorothy was responsible for that too, and if whichever one of them did this thought he—she—could get away with it, he—she—they were wrong.

APRIL FOOLS' DAY. Very funny, God. Ellen, standing at the kitchen sink full of dirty dishes, stared out the window at the lush green hills, leafy trees, and a sky with such a huge mass of black clouds it looked painted in. A speck of white in all the green caught her eye, and she watched a bald eagle take off, spread its wings, and bank in a lazy arc. Usually a sight so beautiful it made her teeth ache; lack of a morning shower made life take a sour turn.

She felt sticky, hot, and grumpy, and only half-awake. With all ten fingers she scratched her itchy scalp through her short, dark curls. Try to think of the heat as a good omen, predicting a good growing season.

Sure thing, Pollyanna. You won't even plant for another two months, and God knows what the weather will be then. All those clouds out there? They're working up for more rain. Get a grip. Well, at least my crops haven't washed out, unlike others around here.

She loved this little house, nestled up against the shallow hills. Built in 1865 of native limestone, it had walls eighteen inches thick. The most exciting day of her life—the day she'd signed her name on the deed. Owner of a house and twenty-five acres of land.

A knock at the open kitchen door made her turn from the window. A stocky, red-haired man in blue work pants and short-sleeved blue shirt with the name "Winslow" stitched above the pocket obliterated the light coming in, then treaded carefully across the old, scuffed linoleum floor like the bearer of bad news and handed her a grubby sheet of paper.

Averting his eyes, he stepped back. She didn't know if it was the cutoffs she wore, which had unraveled more than they should have in the laundry, the skimpy red T-shirt with glittery gold letters that read "Good Gourd!" or if she smelled bad because she'd missed a shower.

While he self-consciously looked around her cheery kitchen—white wood cabinets, striped gray wallpaper with tiny, pale-yellow flowers, bright-yellow curtains, plain pine table, and hanging baskets with an assortment of varicolored gourds—she zeroed in on the figure at the bottom of a column of numbers. It loomed up like total disaster.

"Seven thousand dollars?" She looked at him. "For plumbing?"

"It's an extensive repair. Your whole sewer line has collapsed. All them pipes need to be dug up and replaced—wrong kind of pipes in the first place—and the new ones laid in. You can see there on—"

"My ex-boyfriend put in that sewer."

Winslow the plumber treated that with the scorn it deserved.

Well, the ex-boyfriend hadn't been good at anything else; why should he be good at plumbing?

"I'm sorry, Miss—uh—Barrington. You're welcome to get another estimate, but—"

She waved that away. Seven thousand dollars was seven thousand dollars no matter who wrote it at the bottom of digging, pipe fitting, joins, and corners. Oh dear God, where was she going to get seven thousand dollars? She was barely scraping by, the business was just beginning to take off and she probably had all of three hundred in her checking account.

Winslow shifted from one foot to the other as she gazed with horror at the paper quivering in her hand. She had no shower, no flushing toilet, no clean dishes, no usable washing machine. She couldn't even brush her teeth; just the thought made them feel fuzzier.

"Well—" She cleared her throat and tried again. "I don't know—"

He nodded, giving her time to work up to it. He had her and knew it. She could live without washing dishes, but she couldn't live without a shower. Fine. All you have to do is figure how to pay for it.

When the phone rang, she grabbed the receiver with a stranglehold. "Yes?"

"It's Dorothy. I want you to come to the house this evening. Eight o'clock."

How like her oldest sister to dispense with the nonessentials. No hello, how are you, what's new. Just, I want you to. "Why?"

"There's something that needs— Well, it's very important. I want everybody there."

Important? What was so important that Dorothy wanted *her* there? Ellen, youngest of the five siblings and twenty-three years younger than Dorothy, was the only failure in this family of overachievers. Half the time she felt they forgot about her, and the other half tended to treat her like a poor, unfortunate retard.

"Okay." She threaded her fingers through the phone cord. "Dorothy, something important has come up for me too. I wonder if—"

Winslow the plumber stood with his back to her, gazing out the open door at the empty fields and pretending not to listen.

"Later, dear. I have patients waiting."

"Right. But Dorothy, is it okay if I come over sooner, like in an hour or so, and stay—uh, for a few days?"

"Of course. It's your home. Your room is always ready." There was a click and then the dial tone.

Ellen grimaced and hung up. She'd wanted to ask to borrow the money, even though she was pretty sure Dorothy wouldn't lend it. Dorothy had been against her buying the property in the first place and strongly insisted the only thing was for Ellen to move back home. And after that, what? Live with Dorothy forever as the never-amounted-to-anything sister?

Ellen slapped the sheet of paper on the pine table, signed on the dotted line, and handed it to Winslow the plumber before her mind could tell her what she was about. "Do it," she told him. She could always rob a bank. Or steal a painting. "How long will it take?"

"Big job. All them pipes have to be dug up and the new ones laid and fitted, and then there's—"

"How long?"

"Oh, I'd say—" he studied the ceiling as though it might have the answer "—maybe seven to ten days. Working days," he added ominously.

Ten days? "Good. Fine. Just get it done." She'd stay with Dorothy until all those expensive new pipes were in working order. Dorothy would be pleased; plenty of time to get in lots of I-told-you-sos, with little jabs of here's-what-you-should-do.

Winslow the plumber folded the paper carefully, tucked it into his shirt pocket, lumbered out, and took off in a pickup with "Ackerbaugh Plumbing" painted on the side.

She watched it jounce down the road. And that could use another truckload of gravel too.

Nadine's station wagon, bouncing along, coming this way, pulled aside to let the pickup pass and trundled up to the house. "What's happening?" Nadine asked as she slid from the car.

"Well, for one thing, you're fired."

Nadine grinned. "You can't fire me. You haven't paid me in two months." She'd squeezed her plump body into jeans—hers reached all the way to the knee—and a white T-shirt with the same glitzy lettering as Ellen's. Nadine, blond hair coiled into one thick cord and pinned in a circle on the top of her head, opened the rear car door and leaned in to collect three-month-old Bobby complete with carry cot. Slinging a diaper bag over her shoulder and propping the carry contraption on one hip, she kicked the door shut and trudged to the house.

"So what is it now?" She plopped Bobby and carrier on a wooden chair. He slept serenely on; he might have Nadine's round face, blue eyes, and pale coloring, but he also had his father's phlegmatic disposition. She pulled out another chair and slumped into it with her short legs stuck under the table.

"Bankruptcy," Ellen said.

"Oh, boy, we better have some coffee."

"I can make it, but you'll have to drink it all. I have no drainage." She relayed the bad news.

"*Oh, no.* Ellen, what are you going to do?"

Ellen spooned grounds into the coffee maker and poured in bottled water. "Maybe I should just give up and sell out to Harlen Dietz."

"Do you think he did it?"

"Made the sewer collapse?" Ellen laughed. "Not unless he paid that jerk to put in the wrong kind of pipes."

"Well, I wouldn't put it past him. He wants this place and you won't sell. I still think you should have gone to the police. There have been weird things going on around here."

When the coffee dripped through, Ellen poured two mugs and set them on the table.

"If I had it," Nadine said tentatively, "you know I'd lend it to you."

"I know. I couldn't have done any of it without you."

Three years ago, when she'd decided to go into the business of raising decorative gourds, Nadine had been the only person who'd thought it was a good idea, and the only permanent employee. At harvest time, fifteen or so people were hired temporarily; the rest of the time, she and Nadine struggled with it all. Nadine worked like a plow horse, sometimes waiting months to get paid.

Ellen dropped into a chair, rested her elbows on the table, and blew out a breath. "Just when things were starting to go."

"It'll be all right."

"I feel much better for those words of comfort."

"I'm being sensitive and understanding," Nadine said. "Another loan?"

Ellen took a sip of coffee. "The last time I tried, the loan officer could hardly stand up for laughing."

"Well, I'm not giving up. This is the only job I've got. If you think I'm going to find a tender for Bobby and expose myself to sexual harassment in some business office, you've got another think coming. We'll get through this. Somehow."

"I'm trying to wallow in the depths of despair here. Do you have to be so upbeat?"

"Despair is useful."

"I'm tired of this. I really am. I want to live like the rest of my family. Successful. Respected. Loan officers overflowing with obsequiousness. Flushing toilets," Ellen added darkly.

"Oh, that's why you're so down? Something happen with your family?"

"My sister called."

"Marlitta or Dorothy?"

"Dorothy."

"What did she want?"

What had she wanted? A mind filled up with sewer lines didn't leave room for real sharp. Dorothy's usual brisk, I'm-in-control voice had held an odd note of uncertainty.

"Now you mention it, I don't know." Something to do with the clinic? That wouldn't require *her* presence. With a little squiggle of uneasiness, she picked up the coffee mug.

"You think she might lend you the money?" Nadine asked.

"I suppose I'll have to ask. She disapproves, you know. Raising gourds is not at all a suitable occupation for a Barrington."

"What about Marlitta? Or one of your brothers?"

"It's Dorothy who has money. The rest do very well, managing to live just beyond their means."

"You have a really weird family, you know that?"

Ellen smiled. She truly did. Nadine came from a large, extended family of hearty, affectionate people who squabbled and hugged and genuinely liked to spend time together. She'd never understood the reserved, repressed Barringtons, who lived within a few miles of each other and barely spoke. They were all strangers. Ellen sometimes wondered if they even liked each other; other times the whole thing just seemed sad.

Nadine's family used to astound Ellen when she was a kid, the joking and teasing, the general feeling of people living together with interaction. Ellen's family might have resided in the same house, but they all lived separately.

She'd always thought she felt isolated because she was so much younger than the rest of them, but over the years she came to realize every one of them felt isolated. The really sad part was they probably wanted to like each other but didn't know how.

"I guess," Ellen said, "you get to take a few days' vacation. At least until we have functioning pipes."

"What will you do? You want to stay with us?"

"Thanks." Nadine had a tiny one-bedroom apartment, a large husband, and a baby. "I'll stay with Dorothy. That'll give her something to be pleased about."

No matter how hard she struggled, they always pulled her back. Home, money, family, security. Odd, even though she felt like a barely tolerated stranger in their midst, the thought of going home made her feel better.

Nadine fiddled with her spoon, swirled it through the coffee, then lifted a spoonful to her mouth and sucked it in. "Have you talked to Adam since he's been back?"

"No." Ellen sat her cup down with a clunk. "Don't intend to, either."

"You're bound to run into him, don't you think?"

"Not if I can help it." Adam had been her own true love. Except it turned out he wasn't. The bastard. It was after Adam that she'd taken up with the jerk who couldn't even put in sewer pipes.

"I just wondered," Nadine said, "whether Dorothy's snit has, you know, anything to do with Adam."

"I don't see how. She never liked him. Made it clear to him if he married me, I'd never see any of the Barrington money."

And, Ellen thought, Willis, Marlitta, and Carl wouldn't be called to attend for that. What could it be that was so important? Ah well, she'd find out soon enough. In the bosom of her family. Ha. If one of them put poison in Dorothy's sun tea, all Ellen's troubles would be over.

TWO

SUSAN WREN POURED a glass of orange juice, dropped in two ice cubes—orange juice had to be good for a sick kid—and took it upstairs, where eleven-year-old Jen in blue-and-white-striped pajamas, looking small and miserable, lay in the big bed.

"How you feeling, Jen?" Susan put the glass on the side table and sat on the edge of the bed.

"I'm okay." Jen jammed the extra pillow behind her head, scooted herself higher, and brought up her knees. The pajama legs slid along her thighs, exposing bony kneecaps.

"I can see that." The kid's face was about the color of the rosy flowers on the pillowcase. Susan laid a hand on Jen's forehead. Hot. Very hot. Oh shit. Call Jen's mom?

It's only a fever. Kids have fevers. Nothing to worry about. Oh, yes? What did she know? Nothing about kids. Fevers could mean something serious. Her first thought was to call her own mother. Mothers know about this stuff. Oh, yeah, real helpful. Susan's mother lived halfway across the country in San Francisco.

Let us not panic here. I'm a cop. We're trained to handle crisis situations. She smoothed Jen's brown hair, usually braided tight into one long plait, now falling loose across the pillow, away from her flushed face. "Do you hurt anywhere?"

"No."

Susan raised her eyebrows.

"Well—maybe I've kinda got a sore throat."

Fever. Sore throat. What did that mean? Some kind of flu?

"I'm all right," Jen insisted. Her beautiful yellow-green eyes were too bright.

Susan didn't even have a thermometer. Why not, for God's sake? Every well-ordered household had a thermometer. "It doesn't look like you're all right. It looks like you're sick. I think maybe we better get you to a doctor." Saturday afternoon. Were they all out playing golf? Didn't matter. She'd pull one in.

"It's just a sore throat," Jen said. "I've had that lots of times."

At least I had sense enough to get the doctor's name, Susan thought, before Jen's mother went off on her blissful weekend. Should I call her? She'd been nervous about leaving her daughter anyway; this would really freak her.

Perissa, the kitten, climbed laboriously up the bedsheets and poked her chocolate-brown face in Jen's ear, then licked her cheek. Jen laughed—Susan could hear the rasp in her throat—and raised a shoulder to rub against her cheek. Perissa clambered over to Jen's stomach, crouched, and tucked brown paws under her beige chest.

"I'm really okay." Jen scratched the kitten's head and Perissa purred loudly, blue eyes narrowed to slits.

"I'm sure you are, sweetie, but I'm new at this. You'll have to make allowances. To avoid frantic worry, let's just have a doctor take a look at you."

Jen sighed, a forlorn sound.

Susan patted a bony knee and stood up. "Try to drink a little orange juice. I'll be right back."

Downstairs in the small room off the living room that she used as a home office—being chief of police meant work spilled over into off-duty hours—she retrieved the note from under a glass paperweight. Dr. Barrington. Sliding open the bottom desk drawer, she pulled out the phone book and looked up physicians. Four Barringtons were listed under "Barrington Medical Group." She punched in the number and gazed out the window as she listened to the ringing. The sky was menacing, like a movie shot just before a thunderclap and God started talking to Abraham. Somewhat to her surprise, the phone was answered by a receptionist who said Dr. Dorothy Barrington was in the office today and could see Jenifer Bryant at two.

All right. Susan looked at her watch—one-ten—and trotted back upstairs.

"I suppose I have to go," Jen grumbled, and sat cross-legged in the middle of the bed.

"'Fraid so." Susan found a yellow raincoat in the neatly packed duffel Jen had brought from home the evening before and held it out for Jen to slip her arms into.

Jen was aghast. "I can't go in my pajamas."

Despite Susan's half-hearted murmurs, Jen was insistent, and she pulled on a pair of white shorts with an elastic waistband and buttoned up a shirt patterned in armor-bearing knights.

"I'm not helpless," she said when Susan knelt to tie her Reeboks.

"Right." She left Jen to her own laces and discarded her sloppy jeans and too-large man's shirt for blue linen pants and a tailored blue blouse.

IN THE WAITING ROOM, Jen listlessly paged through an ancient *National Geographic* and scuffed the toe of one shoe against the oatmeal-colored carpet. Outside, rain poured down, relentlessly pounding against the window. Except for Debra Cole behind a counter in the reception area, they were the only ones here, and the building had the empty feel of a Saturday afternoon. Pictures on the walls showed green meadows, leafy trees, and idyllic streams. In one corner stood a metal sculpture with myriad spillways, and water trickled through it in a never-ending cycle.

"She'll probably say I have to stay in bed," Jen muttered.

Susan had to lean forward to her through the crash and

rumble of thunder. "Sick people are supposed to be in bed."

Jen closed the magazine and dropped it on a stack on the table next to her chair. "We won't get to go to the ballet."

Susan gave her a sympathetic smile. Disappointment came with thorns when you were eleven. Weeks ago, when Susan had asked her what she wanted to do this weekend, Jen, in a don't-dare-to-hope voice, had said what she really really wanted was to see a ballet. She'd never seen one. Somewhat surprised at her choice, Susan had readily agreed. They had a special day planned: drive to Kansas City, have dinner in the fanciest restaurant they could find, and then take in *The Sleeping Beauty*.

"We will go," Susan promised. "If we can't go this evening, we'll do the whole thing another time."

Jen, wrapping herself in indifference, nodded. Her parents were divorced and much absorbed in creating new lives for themselves. Jen often got lost in the shuffle, and too many times promises weren't all they were cracked up to be. Slumping back in the chair, she closed her eyes.

Susan looked at her with worry. What was the holdup here? Shouldn't they be getting some attention? She was about to ask Debra how much longer they'd have to wait, when Dr. Barrington came through the door that led into a hallway. An angular woman with a high forehead and light hair that fell straight along her thin face and curved in just below her jawline, she wore a tan dress with navy piping and navy buttons.

She glanced briefly at the folder in her hands, then bent to smile at Jen. The smile softened the severity of her appearance. "Well, Miss Jenifer, what have you been doing to yourself? Let's take a look at you." With a hand behind one shoulder, she guided Jen toward the door.

Susan stood up to follow.

"You can wait here," the doctor said in a voice that left no room for argument. "I'll let you know what I find."

Slowly, Susan lowered herself back onto the chair; she was seriously reluctant to let Jen out of her sight. She picked up an elderly *New Yorker* and perused the cartoons, dropped it and watched the water ripple endlessly through the metal sculpture, listened to the rain beating against the building, picked up another elderly magazine, and read an article on the artistic corruption of the coloring of old black-and-white films. Not a subject she'd ever felt hot about.

Thunder crashed, making her jump. Why was it taking so long? Jen had something life-threatening. Bubonic plague.

She lived a few houses from Susan on Walnut Street. A great kid: bright, thoughtful, a lively interest in everything, a touch of hero worship for Susan. Jen had gotten in the habit of dropping in at Susan's when things got too heavy at home. Three weeks ago, she'd come by in a grumpy mood. Mom was planning a weekend away, and Jen would be staying with a babysitter.

"I'm not a baby," she had groused. "And Mrs. Hoffsteader doesn't like me."

"I can't believe that," Susan said. "How could anybody not like you?"

"Mrs. Hoffsteader doesn't like *kids.*"

"Well, what would you think about staying with me?" Jen's face lit up with her sunshine grin.

"We'll have to ask your mom," Susan cautioned.

Jen's mother wasn't so thrilled with the idea, nor did she like Susan all that much—Jen's admiration roused some maternal jealousy—but she had, after Jen's pleading, finally agreed.

Susan had arranged her schedule to be off duty the entire weekend. The big plans she and Jen had made didn't include sitting in a doctor's office.

Thunder rumbled. Behind it was a pop. She jerked her head up and listened intently. She caught a puzzled look from Debra. Four, five seconds passed.

A sharp crack. Gunshot. Oh, Jesus.

Grabbing the Smith and Wesson from her shoulder bag, she ran past Debra to the inner door and slammed it open against the wall.

The hallway went straight back, offices on each side. As she dashed down it, a frantic buzzing started up in her mind.

Two doors before the hallway turned off to the right, Jen lay sprawled on the floor. Susan knelt beside her. The girl had fallen forward, partially on her side, one arm flung out beside her head, the other tucked under her body.

No pulse. Breathing in short, agonized rasps. Small blood stain on the blouse, left side of chest.

Beyond Jen, just outside the open office door on the left, Dorothy Barrington lay in a pool of blood. Susan stood and took several steps closer. Chest wound, left side. Shot at close range. Dropped as soon as she'd been hit. Dead almost before she fell, Susan thought.

She heard mewling whimpers and looked up at Debra, whose gaze was fixed on Jen.

"Is there another physician here?"

Debra continued to whimper.

Susan got in her face. "Another doctor!"

Debra tore her glance from Jen and stared at Susan, eyes wide with shock. "Only Dr. Dorothy. She's the only one—" Her eyes rolled up and her knees started to buckle.

Susan caught her, eased her to the floor, and left her propped against the wall.

Using the phone in the empty office across from the one where Dorothy Barrington's body lay, Susan called the police department. "Chief Wren," she said to Hazel, the dispatcher. "Shooting. Two victims. One fatality. Send an ambulance." In a voice so tight it didn't even sound like hers, she gave the address. "Round up Parkhurst and Osey."

"On the way," Hazel said.

Susan hurried back to Jen. Still making horrifying noises in her struggle for air. Again, Susan could find no pulse. How could she be breathing and have no pulse?

Susan was trained in CPR, but CPR was used on victims with no respiration.

Abruptly, the noises stopped. The silence was even more horrifying.

Hand under neck. Four quick puffs. Check for pulse. Five pushes on chest.

The ambulance screamed up outside. Three paramedics came in at a run. Susan got out of their way. Both victims got attention, but they immediately focused on Jen. Two young males zipped her into trauma trousers, strapped her to a backboard, and hoisted her to a gurney. They raced toward the door, the third rushing alongside rhythmically pushing down on her chest.

The ambulance tore off, siren wailing, and swayed around the corner.

The driver grabbed the radio mike. "Medic One. Brookvale."

"This is Brookvale. Go ahead."

"En route. Eleven-year-old girl, gunshot wound left chest, no pulse, CPR in progress. ETA two minutes."

"I read you, Medic One. Two minutes. We're ready."

THREE

DR. ADAM SHEFFIELD hung-up the phone and set off for ER at a flat-out run. He had about sixty seconds before the patient arrived to assemble a team and check for needed supplies.

"Set up the thoracic tray," he told the nurse, then turned to his assistant. "Cutdowns. Don't piss around with IV's. Use the largest tubes you got."

A cutdown was an open door into the circulatory system. Slice through muscle, isolate the biggest vein available and shove a tube in it. Enough cutdowns and, no matter how massive, hemorrhaging can be compensated for.

"We got blood?"

"Two units," the nurse said. "More coming."

Two paramedics slammed the gurney through the doors hard enough that it bumped against the table.

"No pulse," the third paramedic said, never pausing in his rhythmic pressure on the girl's chest. "None."

The backboard bounced as the patient was half-shoved, half-slid onto the table.

"Stay with CPR," Adam told the paramedic as he looked at the girl; her chest jerked spasmodically.

From the head of the table, the anesthesiologist slapped two heart monitors onto the exposed chest. The bullet wound was a small hole, dark and puckered, very little blood. Adam glanced at him. "Ready to intubate?"

The anesthesiologist nodded and reached for a laryngoscope. Adam cast a glance over his team. The paramedic continued the pressure on the girl's chest. The assistant was probing the right groin with a scalpel in search of the saphenous vein.

Adam studied the heart monitor; electrical activity moved across it, but no pulse, no regular heartbeat.

A pulse that disappeared so fast meant only one thing; the bullet had penetrated the heart. The membrane around the heart filled with blood and prevented the heart from beating. Cardiac tamponade. Only one thing to do. Cut. Fast.

No time for anesthetic. Didn't matter. The girl was unconscious, for all practical purposes dead.

Adam grabbed a bottle of reddish-brown antiseptic liquid and sloshed it over the girl's chest, clamped gauze pads in a hemostat, and swabbed the liquid around.

The nurse held out a latex glove. Adam jammed his hand in, other hand in the second glove. No time to prep the patient, drape her, or scrub. Aw shit.

If the kid had any chance at all, he had to move. He sloshed around more antiseptic and grabbed a scalpel. Leaning into it as hard as he could, he sliced through muscle and gristle between the fifth and sixth ribs.

Not surgery, he thought. More like butchery.

No blood; the kid had no blood pressure.

A lab tech rushed in with two more units of blood. The assistant snatched a unit, attached it to a cutdown, and handed it over to the nurse. "Squeeze," he ordered.

Adam kept cutting deeper through layers of muscle until he reached the chest cavity. Blood gushed. As he worked the incision wider more dark blood, partially clotted, splashed over the table, soaking into his pants and shoes.

"Jesus," the assistant said, and hooked up another unit.

Adam stuck three fingers in the incision, couldn't get his hand inside. "Scissors." He held out a hand, palm up.

The nurse smacked heavy shears in his palm. He started snipping. When he ran into a rib, he wrapped both hands on the shears and gripped down hard, felt the rib snap. He stuck his hand in the incision, let it slip through, and took a breath. Okay.

"When I yell," he told the paramedic, "stop CPR."

He squatted, peered in the incision, and saw the pericardium. Dark blue, swollen with blood. Oh boy. He needed to cut into it and let that blood out. And he'd damn well better not cut heart tissue when he did.

"Give me better forceps. With teeth."

The nurse smacked a hemostat in his waiting palm. He tried to nip the pericardium with the hemostat; it kept slipping free. "Damn it."

After several frustrating attempts, he felt the teeth grip and hold. Yes. Gently, he tugged the membrane up to create a small pocket and snipped it open. Blood poured out.

All right, kid. This is it. Hang in there for me.

"Now," he said to the paramedic. "Stop CPR."

The paramedic stepped back, sweating, breathing hard.

Quickly, Adam extended the cut in the pericardium, stuck his hand through, and curled his fingers around the heart. It quivered.

Yes! Now, let's be very careful here. Slowly and with great care, he tightened his fingers, relaxed them, tightened, relaxed.

The heart made a spontaneous contraction. Yes! All right! Hooray, kid!

He felt blood trickle against his palm and with his fingertips explored the heart's surface. There it is. Right near the top. He slid his thumb over it and began a fingertip feel toward the back of the heart. Yep. Exit wound. Back of the heart. He moved his middle finger over it. The heart made another beat.

"Pulse!" the anesthesiologist said. "There's a pulse!"

"Don't celebrate yet," Adam said. "I've got my fingers in two holes." He looked at the clock on the wall. Five minutes had elapsed from the time the kid was brought in until her heart had started beating on its own. Her blood pressure had started to rise, dark blood oozed up in the incision.

He was forced to stoop in an awkward position to keep his thumb and middle finger over the holes in the left ventricle. Already his shoulder ached. He tried to relieve it by moving slightly. Didn't help. Great. He couldn't hold this position for long, and he dared not move either.

Mentally, he pictured the anatomy of the heart. The entrance wound was awful, goddamn close to one of the major blood vessels. He eased his forefinger across the surface of the pulsing muscle, searching for the vein. Christ, if the bullet ripped it, my finger is stopping blood to that area of the heart. The kid, as near as made no difference, would be undergoing a heart attack.

Second attack actually. First one when the bullet ripped into it. A treacherous thought sneaked into his mind. Could she make it?

"Pupils," he asked the anesthesiologist.

"None. Fixed and dilated."

Was he going to lose her? He'd lost a patient once. Torn open a chest and felt the heart die, right in his hands.

This sure looked like measuring up to another one. CPR didn't stack up to normal heartbeat. Hell, she could be brain dead already.

What odds for survival? This ain't no super-sterile OR. What we have here is an emergency room, full of bacteria, viruses, old blood, old sepsis, just a few feet away from a door to the big, dirty world.

The heart beat strongly in his hand. He ordered the nurse to give the kid a whopping slug of antibiotics. As long as there's any hope, sweetheart, I'm hanging in there. You've got all I can give you.

Easy enough to say, but the hardest part was still ahead. A beating heart moved all the time. Made suturing a bitch. As soon as he removed a finger to plant a stitch, blood spurted, obscuring anatomical signboards. Heart muscle was delicate; a misplaced suture that tore loose would not bear thinking about.

He asked for pledgets, tiny plugs of felt. Once in place, they soaked up blood, which then formed a clot and closed off bleeding.

Cautiously, he removed a finger, slapped a pledget over the hole, and held it in place while he carefully attached it with running sutures.

The back of the heart was sturdier, but the exit wound was larger, and he was forced to lift the heart and turn it in order to see the hole. If he lifted too high or turned too far, he'd risk pinching a vital blood vessel. That sure as hell wouldn't do the kid any good.

Back aching, he bent over the open chest, carefully dropped a pledget in place, and, working as fast as he dared, managed the sutures.

Finally, he straightened, flexed his shoulder muscles, and glanced at the wall clock. Twenty minutes from the first cut. A lifetime.

He looked down at the heart beating strong and steady. The sutures strained, but by God they held. He grinned at the nurse. She grinned back.

"We can take care of the rest in OR." He peeled off his gloves and dropped them.

SUSAN PACED OUTSIDE the emergency-room doors and looked at her watch again. Thirty seconds later than the last time she'd looked. They were still working in there. That must mean something. Oh, God. Jen. Please be alive. Please, God, let her be alive.

In her mind, she saw Jen's inert form being tossed on the gurney and sped to the waiting ambulance. At least they'd moved fast. Jen was alive then.

In California, if a minor child was injured and a parent or guardian wasn't available, the child was automatically made a ward of the state. It was similar in Kansas. Susan had notified Social Rehabilitation Services, and papers had been drawn up.

Lieutenant Ben Parkhurst and Detective Osey Pickett had arrived in the wake of the paramedics. Susan had left them to get on with it and taken herself to the hospital. Since she'd driven to the doctor's office in her little brown Fiat instead of the pickup, she had no police radio, no way to keep in touch. This enhanced her sense of numbness, left her less able to pull in thoughts through her anxiety over Jen.

A muscular man with a pugnacious jaw, in green surgical garb, came out the emergency-room door, covered with blood from the waist down. His shoes squished when he walked.

"Dr. Sheffield." She trotted over to him. "How is she?"

He stopped, turned, and looked at her. "You a relative?"

"Chief Wren. I've not yet been able to reach her mother. What can you tell me?"

"We've patched up the holes in the heart. She's alive, that's about all I can say. We're not done yet, by any means. The bullet tore into her left lung. We're bringing her upstairs to take care of that now."

"What are her chances?"

The doctor gave a wry smile. "Don't bet on them. If she makes it—and that's a big if—no telling what kind of life she might have. The insult to the body was great. Could be more than any eleven-year-old can survive. Maybe I can tell you more after we get the bullet out of her lung."

"I'll need the bullet."

He nodded and took off at a fast trot, leaving a trail of bloody footprints.

The emergency-room doors popped open, and the assistant and nurse trundled the gurney toward the elevator, IV bag swaying on a stand. Jen was covered with a sheet; tubes and wires curled away from every part of her.

Susan followed onto the elevator, eyes on Jen's waxy face. The elevator rose. Susan's knees felt rubbery; she hoped she wouldn't faint.

The doors hissed open. The gurney was shoved out. Susan plodded along behind to the operating room and watched Jen disappear inside. Dr. Sheffield, in clean scrub greens, hurried in.

What was it like to hold somebody's life in your hands? She leaned against the wall, closed her eyes, and took a few deep breaths. Time seemed to stop. She waited, resting her weight on one foot, then the other. The waiting went on.

She might scream if she had to wait much longer.

Finally, the operating room doors opened. A nurse came out with an emesis basin. She handed it to Susan.

The bullet lay on a gauze pad. Behind the misery that hung over her like nerve gas, her mind noted it was bent at the tip, slightly flattened on one side. Only a little misshapen, easy to recognize the five lands and five grooves and right-hand twist. A .38 Smith and Wesson.

Routine came through; automatic action made her bag it and label it, have the nurse sign the tag. Downstairs in the emergency room, she gathered Jen's cut-up white shorts and the shirt with fighting knights—a surprisingly small amount of blood—from the emergency-room nurse. She made her way past the lobby and around to the public phone, checked in with Hazel, the dispatcher at the department. Still no word from Jen's mother. By the time Terry Bryant was reached, would the news be of Jen's death?

She told Hazel to send Officer White hotfooting it to the hospital. He was to stick like glue outside Jen's door when she got out of surgery. She replaced the receiver, slumped against the wall, and stared hard at the floor. People walking by looked at her, and she straightened her shoulders. Better get it together. She couldn't see Jen again until Jen was out of surgery; an hour, minimum. She couldn't simply hang out here with worry chewing up her mind, getting in everyone's way, and not being of any help to Jen. Much as she did not want to leave the hospital, she had a case to work. It wasn't routine, it had the deep-reaching effects of personal tragedy, but it was imperative she get on it.

FOUR

AFTER OFFICER WHITE arrived to guard-dog Jen, Susan dropped off the bullet at the lab, then stopped in at the police department and spread out Jen's clothes in the interview room—because there was no other place—to dry before they could be bagged and given to the lab. The white shorts, scissored down the front, looked pathetically small; one of the armor-bearing knights on the shirt had a bullet hole in his shield.

She saw Jen sprawled on the floor, clamped her teeth, and swallowed. She informed Hazel she was headed back to the medical offices and if Jen's mother called, let her know immediately.

Across the street from the office building, a crowd had clustered; they stood, some with umbrellas, and watched and watched, sober and quiet. The rain had stopped, but somber gray clouds hung overhead. Trees dripped. Several police cars, Parkhurst's Bronco, and the ambulance were angled near the entrance. She was irritated, but not surprised, to see the van from the local radio station nearby. The reporter was talking with the onlookers.

Officer Yancy, posted at the door, was keeping people back. She parked, then noticed in the side mirror that she'd been spotted and the reporter was bearing down on her. With firm determination in her step, she set off for the entrance. Yancy gave her a nod and smartly blocked the reporter.

"Chief Wren," the reporter called. A stocky kid in khaki pants and short-sleeved brown shirt, he looked more like a clean-cheeked high school wrestler than a real-life radio news reporter. "Can you tell us what's going on?"

Yancy said, "You'll have to stay back, Gary; this is a crime scene."

"Give me a break."

Susan ducked inside before she heard Yancy's response. The same paramedics who had sped off with Jen were now trundling the covered body of Dorothy Barrington along the corridor. She stepped aside to let them pass. Dr. Fisher, obviously, had already come and gone.

Kick in, she told her mind. Don't think about Jen. Concentrate.

Just outside the murdered woman's office, Detective Osey Pickett, wearing latex gloves, squatted to collect a sample from the blood soaked into the oatmeal carpet. At her approach, he leaped to his feet in uncoordinated spasms and tossed a hank of straw-colored hair from his guileless blue eyes. "Ma'am." He jerked to attention. Built along the lines of a scarecrow, he was young, with a prominent Adam's apple and enormous hands and feet that he never seemed to quite get the knack of managing. In blue jeans and white shirt with the sleeves rolled up, he looked like a hick and acted like one, but underneath the drawling speech and country-boy smile he had a quick mind.

"How's it going?"

"Haven't found anything like a murder weapon. Why do you reckon anybody'd want this pale carpet in a doctor's office?"

"Maybe she saw only clean patients."

The desktop, with a leather-edged blotter, held a stack of medical books, blank prescriptions used as bookmarks, AMA journals, various slips of paper with jotted notes, and a folded newspaper in the corner. In the center above the blotter was a marble pen holder with two pens. A gooseneck lamp with a fluorescent bulb added to the grayish daylight coming from the window and shined down into the dregs of a pale, clear liquid that looked like tea. Next to the phone, a small glass vase held one lavender tulip.

With her hands clasped behind her back so she wouldn't touch anything, Susan leaned over the desk. What she could see of the blotter had ink squiggles and scratches, nothing legible beyond the odd letter here and there. The slips of paper said things like CAT scan, Lowe's, gasometry, lipid screen, and glycohemoglobin, protoporphyrin—erythrocytes, plasmas, feces. Notes the doctor had scribbled to herself. None of it meant anything to her, but she would examine them more closely when Osey had finished in here.

At a right angle to the desk sat a credenza with four neatly cantilevered file folders; next to the files was a typed list of the times and names for today's appointments.

Beneath the appointment list was another sheet of paper. With the end of her pen, she eased the top page aside. The paper below had four names printed on it in black ink: Willis, Marlitta, Carl, Ellen. Beside each name was a check; apparently the doctor had gone down the names and ticked them off one at a time. Across the bottom was written "eight p.m."

"The receptionist still here?" she asked Osey.

"Yeah. Ben thought you might want to talk to her. Next office down."

Officer Demarco, arms crossed, had taken a stance by the closed door. She tapped on it, then opened it and went in.

Debra Cole, eyes and nose red from crying, streaks of mascara on her pale cheeks, huddled in an armchair beside a desk with haphazard piles of books and folders; message slips lay scattered around amid a clutter of pens and pencils.

"Miss Cole, I'd like to ask you a few questions, if you feel up to it." Susan pulled out the desk chair and sat facing her, leaning slightly forward.

"I've already told you," Debra said without looking up. "The other one. The lieutenant." Her hands clutched a soggy tissue.

"I know you have," Susan said quietly. "But it would help me if you could go over it again."

"It's Mrs., actually. Not that it matters. It's Ed's name. Cole, you know."

"Ed is your husband?"

Debra raised her eyes. She reminded Susan of a deer: soft brown eyes, frightened and defenseless. "Most people take their husband's names," she said as though Susan had questioned her integrity. "Except Dr. Dorothy. Well, Marlitta too. She's married to Dr. Wakeley. Like Barrington was better."

Debra was obviously in shock, mind skittering around from one extraneous thought to another. Susan had seen this often. Individuals caught up in homicide tended to skate around on the edges of nonessentials. What lay in the center was too horrid to approach.

"Do you always work on Saturdays?"

"Oh, God, it's all my fault." Tears filled her eyes. She doubled over and buried her face in her hands; her shoulders shook.

"Your fault?"

"Twice a month," she said dully.

"Excuse me?"

"On Saturday. Two Saturdays a month." She looked at Susan directly, her manner changed, so slightly as to be almost imperceptible, just enough that Susan caught it.

"Dr. Barrington was the only physician working today. Was that usual?"

"They're all Barringtons." Debra looked away, then down at her lap, and twisted her hands together. "They took turns. They didn't really want to. Work on Saturday, the rest of them, but Dr. Dorothy said so. They all did what she told them. If I worked Saturday, I got another day off. During the week?" Debra made it a question to see if Susan was following.

"Same with Faith. She's the other receptionist. Usually

we both worked. They're really busy, you know? It takes two of us. Just the two days. Saturday and one other during the week. Not always the same day."

"I understand," Susan said. "Why did you say it was your fault?"

"I should have been here." The response came a touch too quickly.

"When?"

"At noon."

"Where did you go?"

"Home. For lunch."

"Where is home?"

Debra gave her an address in Riverside trailer park.

"Was the office usually closed during the lunch hour?" Debra nodded.

"Was Dorothy here when you left?"

"She had already gone."

"Did you lock the doors?"

"Of course—" Debra paused. "I mean, I must have. I don't remember exactly doing it, but I always do. I always lock the doors."

"Was the door locked when you came back? Did you have to use a key to get in?"

Debra nodded, but not with any decisiveness.

"Tell me what happened today."

A faint tint of color had come back to her face, but it faded suddenly. Susan wondered if Debra was cut out for this line of work. In a physician's office, emergencies must arise every now and then. A serious career evaluation might be in order here. "What time did you come in this morning?"

"Nine o'clock. I'm always careful about that, so I'm sure to be here five minutes before. Unless there's a blizzard or something. Dr. Dorothy gets—upset if anybody's late."

"Did anything happen this morning that was different from any other Saturday?"

"Well, there was Dr. Sheffield." Debra stared at her hands clasped in her lap.

"Adam Sheffield?" The doctor who was slicing up Jen? "What about him?"

"He came to see her."

"That was unusual?"

"He didn't have an appointment or anything. He just came."

"And Dorothy saw him?"

"I don't think she was real pleased. Her mouth got all tight, like it does."

"How long did he stay?"

"Maybe ten minutes or like that. She had a patient, and she doesn't like to keep them waiting."

"Why did he come to see her?"

"I don't know."

"Is there anything else you can tell me?"

"She was late." Debra's eyes widened with the enormity of it. "Coming back from lunch. She's never late. I was starting to get worried. And then, when she got here, she was mad about something."

"About what?"

"I don't know. She just was. Her face was all pinched, and she had a newspaper she kept tapping against her palm. She was snippy. And then she said she had to make some phone calls before she could see the patient. She kept a patient waiting. I wanted to tell her about the unscheduled patient she didn't know about. That would have been Jenifer Bryant." Tears spilled again. "How is Jenifer? Is she going to be all right?"

"That's not certain. Who did Dorothy call?"

Debra rubbed at her face with the shredded tissue. Susan reached for a box on the desk and placed it on the arm of the chair.

Debra ripped out a fresh one. "I don't know who she

called. Except Dr. Willis. I heard her talking to him when I brought in Jenifer's chart.''

"What did she say?''

"Something about being at the house this evening. I really was only there a minute. Just to bring in the chart and put it on her desk, you know.''

"Willis is her brother.'' Susan turned a page in her notebook. "Marlitta and Carl are also siblings?''

"They're all doctors.''

"And Ellen? A sibling and a physician?''

"Just a sister. I mean, she's not a doctor.''

"Where did Dorothy have lunch?''

Debra sniffled into the tissue. A bright ray of sunshine suddenly teased hints of gold from her brown hair, then disappeared as a cloud passed over. "I don't know.''

"Where did she usually eat lunch?''

"Sometimes here. I mean, she'd just eat it at her desk. Something she brought or went out to buy and bring back. Some days she liked to go to the park.'' Debra blew her nose. "Who would kill Dr. Dorothy?''

"You have no idea?''

"People don't kill doctors. Doctors make them well.''

"Dissatisfied patients?''

"The patients are all going to be really upset.'' Debra gulped and held the tissue against her mouth. "I can't seem to think. I don't know anything.''

"I know this has been very upsetting,'' Susan said. "Thank you for your help. I'll have somebody see that you get home.''

Susan told Officer Demarco to take care of Mrs. Cole and watched as he guided her toward the door.

Debra had been evasive when asked why she thought she was at fault, and Susan wondered why. Stumbling on a homicide victim was traumatic for the ordinary citizen; it made thought processes disorganized and unreliable. Lies were just as likely the result of shock as deliberate false-hoods.

In the dead woman's office, Osey was lifting prints. Susan didn't have to worry whether he'd miss anything. He always dusted everything that could take prints and many that could not. To Osey, collecting prints was right up there with singing in the church choir for having a good time. The voice of her former boss in San Francisco sounded in her head. You will never lose a case by collecting and preserving too much evidence. You can lose—badly—by making a premature decision that a certain article or mark is unimportant or unworthy of your attention.

She wanted every article and every mark noted and examined; she wanted no mistakes, nothing overlooked, no foul-ups that could allow the bastard to get away with it.

"Where's Parkhurst?" she asked.

"Out scouting the garage."

Across the hall, she stood in the doorway of an examining room and looked around. From the crumpled paper drape on the table, this was obviously where Dr. Barrington had taken Jen. The doctor must have left the room, walked toward her office, and been shot. Why had she left? Someone called to her? She heard something? And Jen? Did she hear the shot and run out?

Just past Dorothy's office, the hallway turned right and led to an outside door.

The shooter, standing at the right-angle turn, could have fired twice and been out that door in three or four seconds.

The door opened to a parking garage, small, with space available for about ten cars, empty except for the white Buick near the door. Dorothy Barrington's, most likely.

Ben Parkhurst, a compact man with a hard face and dark hair, stood at the far end of the garage, fingertips in the back pockets of his jeans. He'd been off today too, until the phone call rousted him, and he'd come in with a light-weight sports jacket thrown on over a blue knit shirt. He was talking with another man, but when he noticed her he gave a nod, and both men walked over to her.

"This is Murray Kreps," he said, and introduced her to the slight man with thinning gray hair, wearing tan pants and a brightly flowered shirt.

"Ma'am." Murray nodded at her. "Terrible thing. What's this world coming to? Drug addicts all over the place. Nobody safe anywheres. That what it was? Some addict thinking a doctor's office is a good place to find drugs?"

"Murray takes care of maintenance for the building," Parkhurst said.

"Was Dr. Barrington a good person to work for?" she asked.

"Dr. Dorothy, you mean? They're all Barringtons. Except for that Wakeley fellow. Pretty good bunch. Dr. Dorothy was the head of things." He nodded firmly. "You might say she was good to work for. Long as things went smooth. Fair. Can't say better than that, can you? Could get all riled if anything went wrong."

"How long have you worked here?"

He wrinkled his forehead. "Must be going on for fourteen years now."

"Any trouble lately?"

"Trouble?"

"Violent patients," Parkhurst said. "People hiding in the building after hours. Break-ins."

"Just the one time."

"What happened?" she asked when he didn't seem inclined to elaborate.

"Intruder, I guess you'd call it. Would have been last week." Murray scratched his scalp through his sparse gray hair. "Maybe the week before. Working late, she was. Dr. Dorothy. Did that sometimes. Door was still unlocked. That one right there." He nodded toward the garage entrance.

"Who was it?"

"Can't say I got a look at him."

"It was a man?"

"Well, now you ask, I'm not right sure of that. She was just finishing up, getting ready to leave, and there was this somebody coming along the hallway. She shouted at him. I was way off on the other side of the building, and I came running. Course he was long gone by the time I got there."

"You didn't get a look at him?"

"Didn't, at that. Out the door and just gone."

"Dr. Barrington—Dorothy—did she know him?"

"Said she didn't. Didn't get much of a look at him herself."

"Did she report the incident?" Parkhurst asked.

Murray shook his head. "I kinda mentioned it like maybe we should, but she said no harm done. Figured it was somebody thought the place was empty, everybody gone home, and had come in to see what he could steal. She said she'd be more careful about locking up when she was here after closing time. You all about finished in there? I should get in and start cleaning up."

"Not yet," Parkhurst said. "We'll let you know."

"Why wouldn't she report an intruder?" Susan said after Murray had gone. She walked from the garage to the open parking area behind and squinted in a sudden burst of sunlight. The sky was a vivid blue beyond the huge puffy clouds; wisps of steam rose from the wet pavement. Parkhurst, at her side, paced in the lithe, economical manner of a predator.

She looked across at the large maple trees lining Tennessee Street, trees that had been planted the day Lincoln was assassinated. It was a commercial street with an entry into the parking lot. Office buildings sat on both sides of the lot. Across the street, old stone two- or three-story buildings with fancy cornices: the Rademacher Pipe Organ Company, Mayes Mercantile, Timely Creations. On the corner, the beautiful old Episcopal church, massive and impressive, with stained-glass windows, a heavy steeple, and clusters of bright-yellow daffodils in front. Old-fashioned, gas-lantern-shaped street lights. Traffic, not much, but moving in both directions.

"Anybody see anything?" she asked.

"I've got Ellis and Zawislak canvassing the area and taking down license numbers."

The license numbers of any cars parked in the area would be noted, the numbers run through DMV, and the owners tracked down and questioned.

"How's the kid?"

"Not good. Still alive when I left the hospital. This is a Saturday afternoon. Somebody must have seen something."

"Rain was slamming down like a son of a bitch. Very few people out. Any who were would be concerned only with getting in."

From the garage, Officer Yancy called, "Chief Wren? Hazel on the phone. She's gotten hold of the girl's mother."

FIVE

THE BARRINGTON HOUSE, on Indiana Street only a few blocks from the medical clinic, had been built on the original site of the stagecoach depot. The house dated from the early nineteen-hundreds: Italianate style, white, three-story, with dormers, many-paned windows, a columned porch across the front, and a wide expanse of lush green lawn.

The three-car garage was a strictly modern addition. Behind it, Susan could see part of a gazebo with a latticed top.

Parkhurst at her side, Officer Yancy following, she climbed steps onto the porch and poked the doorbell. Discreet chimes tinkled away inside. She hated this part of being a cop: bringing bad news. Wading into the midst of family or loved ones of a victim meant getting mired in an emotional swamp. Survivors reacted differently according to character; some got hysterical, some froze. A few attacked: kill the messenger. Several years ago in San Francisco, the wife of a young man killed in a drive-by shooting had come at her with a knife.

Double all that for homicide. Add in that the cop knew, odds on, one of the grieving was the killer. Most murder victims were killed by someone they knew.

A young woman opened the door. She had a piquant little face with short dark curls and was wearing cutoff jeans and a red T-shirt with "Good Gourd!" in gold letters.

"Police officers. Chief Wren and Lieutenant Parkhurst." Susan held out her ID, but the young woman ignored it.

"Is something wrong?"

At first glance she looked like a teenager, but a closer look showed her to be early twenties. "Your name?"

"Ellen."

"Ellen—?"

"Barrington."

Ah. The youngest of the siblings. "May we come in? We'd like to speak with Mr. Talmidge."

"Taylor?" Something skittered behind the dark eyes, but was gone too fast for Susan to get a fix on it.

"Is he here?"

"Yes. Come in."

They stepped into a wide foyer with pink floral wallpaper, a padded bench covered in pale-green-striped silk, and a writing desk with a potted plant; just inside the door was a bright-green umbrella stand. They followed Ellen into the living room, large and high-ceilinged, with a row of windows that looked out onto a back garden. Despite the late-afternoon sunlight slanting through the windows, the room seemed dark: heavy dark-rose draperies, velvet Victorian sofas in the same dark color, wing chairs and upright wooden chairs with carved legs and backs, and padded pale-pink seats. Small tables of dark, carved wood sat by the sofas and chairs and between the windows, holding vases, plants, and cutglass bowls. A somber painting hung above the fireplace of a stream overshadowed by menacing trees. Through an archway, Susan saw a Queen Anne dining table and a tall, glass-fronted cupboard filled with china.

"Ellen?" A tall man, smooth, polished, with straight, dark hair silvering at the temples, prominent nose, and strong jaw, came through the archway. "Was that the door?" He wore a white dress shirt, subdued tie, and fashionably pleated brown trousers.

"Mr. Talmidge?" Susan said.

He looked at her with the deceptively amused expression that conceals contempt. "Yes? What can I do for you?"

"We'd like to have a word with you."

He flicked a glance at Ellen. "Certainly. What is this about?"

"It's about your wife."

The appraising look disappeared, and an opaque mask slipped over his face. "What about her?"

He had something to hide. Not necessarily that he'd shot his wife, but something.

"She's still at the office," Ellen said.

"I'm sorry," Susan said. She'd never figured out a way to say this. No matter how she tried to ease into it, she brought news of death, and it was devastating. "Dorothy Barrington was shot this afternoon." She watched Taylor Talmidge's face. The spouse, or any variation thereof, was immediately suspect in a homicide. "She died almost instantly."

He seemed to stagger, threw a look at Parkhurst, who nodded in confirmation. Talmidge turned and stared out a window at the sunlit grass. She felt momentarily sorry for him, for his loss and for what lay ahead. Even small-town gossip was nothing compared to being under the microscope of a homicide investigation. His whole life would be open to scrutiny.

Ellen, white-faced, took in air with a sharp gasp and then seemed to stop breathing entirely. She stumbled back onto a sofa, crossed her arms, and clutched them to her chest.

"Why?" Talmidge whispered hoarsely. "Why did this happen?"

"That's what we need to find out."

Leaning forward, he covered his face with his hands, and his shoulders shook with an attempt at control. He mumbled to himself, and she strained to make out the words.

"It couldn't have—" was all she could hear.

She and Parkhurst waited silently for him to regain his composure. Ellen sat frozen, her eyes blank.

"What do you want me to do?" Talmidge said dully. He took a handkerchief from a back pocket and wiped his face before turning toward them.

Parkhurst said, "If you could sit down, sir. We need to ask some questions."

"I don't understand." Talmidge slumped in a gold curved-back chair by the fireplace. "Who shot her?"

Susan sat in an identical chair on the other side of the fireplace. Parkhurst, making himself unobtrusive, leaned against a window ledge. Yancy stood stiffly in the archway. "Can you think of any reason why anyone would kill your wife?"

Talmidge shook his head, not so much in response to her query as in an attempt to readjust his thinking.

"Was anything bothering her? Did she mention any problems she was having? With the medical practice, for instance?"

"Sometimes she worries about her patients, but—she wouldn't discuss anything like that with me."

"Did she come home for lunch?"

"No—" He stopped, then said, "I'm not sure. She may have. At times she did."

"You weren't here between twelve and one?"

"Uh—no. No, I wasn't."

"Where were you?"

Ellen's dark eyes were fixed on his face.

"I was—" His manner seemed to sharpen, and he focused on Susan. "Why are you wasting all this time? Why aren't you out finding who killed her?"

Ellen got a startled look on her face and ticked a glance at Susan. Nothing slow about this one, Susan thought. She picked up right quick that we're treating her brother-in-law as a suspect.

"We're simply gathering information, Mr. Talmidge. You weren't here this afternoon? Can you tell me where you were?"

"I was here. Not at noon. I went—" He squeezed the bridge of his nose. "I'm thinking about a new car. I went to look—"

Ellen got her very mobile little face well in hand, no expression at all, but she was paying close attention. It may have been her way of putting off acceptance; it may have been the realization that she was also going to come in for her share of suspicion.

"What time did you get back?"

"Maybe two or two-thirty. From then on I was here."

"By yourself?"

"Yes."

"Did your wife phone you at any time?"

Talmidge shook his head.

"Miss Barrington," Parkhurst said, "did you get a call from your sister?"

Ellen jumped as though she'd forgotten he was there. "Yes. At home. My house."

"What did she say?"

"She wanted me here this evening."

"Just you?" After Susan's soft questions, Parkhurst sounded harsh and accusing.

"No. Everybody."

"Everybody being?"

"Willis and Marlitta and Carl."

"Why did she ask you to come here?" Susan took over the questioning again.

"Something that needed to be discussed."

"What?"

"She said we'd discuss it this evening. She had patients."

"No idea what this was about?"

"No."

"Where were you this afternoon?"

"My place." Ellen explained where she lived and told them about the plumbing. "I just got here a little while ago."

"Mr. Talmidge, do you know what this was about?"

"No. I didn't even know she'd called them."

"Does either of you own a gun?"

Talmidge said no, in a somewhat bewildered way. Ellen went totally still; when Parkhurst repeated the question, she shook her head.

"Mr. Talmidge," Susan said, "we need you to make a positive identification. If you feel up to it, Officer Yancy will take you to the hospital."

He nodded.

SUSAN LEFT PARKHURST to execute the search warrant. They were looking for the murder weapon; a handgun was small enough to enable them to search virtually everywhere in the house, grounds, and outbuildings. She was headed for Brookvale Hospital to meet Jen's mother.

Doubts nagged at the edges of her mind when she slid the Fiat into a parking space. Cops needed to stay objective, otherwise they didn't function efficiently. They had to build protective walls around their emotions and keep them neatly inside. Her emotions were exposed and raw. The worry was, did it affect her competency?

The hospital doors slid open as she hurried up. The seriousness of Jen's condition, which she'd tried to push aside while she concentrated on her job, came rushing back. Damaged heart still beating? An irrational thought zinged through her mind; concentrating on the crime scene, questioning suspects, had deprived Jen of some crucial life force.

She jabbed the elevator button. Jen's mother was upstairs. Terry Bryant had gone with a friend to Topeka for the weekend, boyfriend actually, silly word for an adult.

As a cop, she'd had occasion to inform a parent about the death of a child. Nothing was worse. She'd rather collect a floater three weeks in the water, bloated and reeking of putrefaction. With chunks falling off.

Jen is not dead.

She jabbed the button again, swore to herself when the

doors opened and the arrow pointed down. She took the stairs.

Terry Bryant stood by the high-railed bed where Jen lay with a sheet draped across her. Wires and tubes ran in all directions, a respirator hissed air into her lungs, peaked lines flickered and bleeped on the monitors above. Terry lifted her stricken face to look at Susan, and fury flashed in her eyes.

A nurse, rightly expecting an outburst, spoke up in a soft voice. "It's been five minutes."

Terry turned on the nurse as if she wanted to scream.

"You can come back every hour for five minutes," the nurse said calmly. "But really, there won't be any change for some time. You might want to go and get something to eat. Or even go home and get some rest. We're taking very good care of her."

Susan took Terry's elbow to draw her from the room. Terry jerked her arm away. She stomped across to a waiting area where three anxious-eyed people sat rigidly on vinyl and chrome chairs, sipping coffee from Styrofoam cups.

She strode four paces, sandals clacking on the tiled floor, spun with flowered skirt swirling, and strode back to plant herself, face lifted in front of Susan. "Don't worry! Have a good time! She'll be fine! *Fine!*" Terry looked far older than her thirty-two years. Usually twinkly and bubbly, her face was slack and gray, except for the two red spots of anger on her round cheeks. Mascara was smeared, lipstick was chewed off, brown hair that fell in waves to her shoulders was tangled.

"You call that fine? That's my baby in there! She's dying. Oh, my God, my baby is dying." Tears streamed down her cheeks. She buried her face in her hands.

The waiting trio avoided looking at them, faces drawn in what sympathy could be spared from the relief that at least my spouse, child, relative, friend isn't dying.

Susan clamped down hard on her back teeth; her throat

closed, and tears pushed at her own eyes. She wanted to offer comfort, put an arm around Terry, but knew that would simply make Terry angrier.

Terry rubbed the heels of her palms over her eyes, distorting her face. Susan offered a tissue.

Terry snatched it and blew her nose. "How could you let this happen? Shot! Jen! I don't— I can't—" Tears spilled over again.

"I'm sorry," Susan murmured. Stupidly inadequate. Throw out a few more meaningless phrases. Don't worry, everything's going to be all right.

Terry's anger was understandable. In her grief and despair, she needed someone to blame. Susan was handy for sloughing off guilt.

"She's still alive," Susan said softly. Another meaningless phrase. Stupid as it was, she felt they had to cling to it. If they didn't, she feared in that same irrational way, their despair would permeate through the air into the intensive-care unit and leach away the thin spark of life pulsing through Jen's inert body.

Rage burned in Susan's chest. Jen should have a life, she should have it all, the good things and maybe even some not so good, but not this. Not at eleven years old.

Murder investigations didn't afford the luxury of rage. Homicide demanded total focus and clear-thinking logic. Rage would have to wait. Right now, she'd better shove aside her personal import and start asking routine questions. Who killed Dorothy, and why.

"Tell me what happened," Terry demanded.

"Terry—"

"Tell me!"

Susan led her out to the hallway. Briefly and calmly, she explained Jen's sore throat, the fever, and the doctor's appointment.

Terry cried with gasping, choking sobs. Susan went in

search of a doctor. If Terry didn't get some kind of sedative, she was going to develop raving hysterics.

The nurse at the desk gave Susan a harried look. "I'm afraid there's no one available right now."

One glance at Susan's face and the nurse picked up the phone, spoke a few words, and hung up. "A doctor will be up in a few minutes."

"Thank you. Where can I find Dr. Sheffield?"

The nurse looked at her, then sighed and picked up the phone again. Dr. Sheffield was on the floor below.

He sat at the nurses' station, muscular shoulders and broad chest straining the seams of the scrub greens, making notations on a chart. His thick, curly, dark hair was in need of a trim. After a final scribble, he slapped the chart shut and shoved back the chair.

"I need to ask some questions," she said.

A hand rasped over a stubble of beard as he rubbed his heavy jaw. "Nothing I can tell you yet."

"I'll try not to take too long."

He stood up. "I could use a cup of coffee anyway."

In the cafeteria, he put two Styrofoam cups on the Formica table and sat down across from her. "Caffeine. Just what I need. With all the adrenaline rushing through my bloodstream, I probably won't sleep for two days as it is."

Although it was only six-fifteen, the cafeteria was nearly empty. A family group lingered over the remains of a meal, three nurses spoke quietly to each other, two or three people sat alone with a soft drink or cup of coffee in front of them.

Susan took a sip of hot, bitter liquid. "Does Jen have a chance?"

Picking up his cup, he looked at her carefully, as though judging her ability to handle what information he might feel like doling out. She put on her official expression: working cop. She could see he wasn't impressed. It must be too apparent she had more at stake here than professional interest.

"I don't know what her chances are," he said, "I'm not sure what kind of life she'll have even if she lives."

Susan felt suddenly cold. "What do you mean?"

"A piece of lead ripped through her heart, tore through a lung, and ended up embedded in the sternum. The insult to her body might have been too much."

Susan heard his words, but couldn't grasp meaning through the buzzing in her mind.

"She might be a cabbage," he said bluntly.

Jen. With her sunshine smile, quick mind, endless capacity for anything new. In the brightly lit, almost empty cafeteria, Susan started to shiver. She clenched her hands, digging fingernails into her palms. Don't lose it.

"There's a more immediate problem," he said.

"What problem?" Her voice sounded far away.

"She's running a fever. ER isn't the best place to slice open the human body. It's not exactly what you'd call a sterile environment."

"She had a fever. Before. That's why she was at the doctor's office."

He looked at her sharply. "Other symptoms?"

"Sore throat."

He took in a breath and shook his head.

"Makes it worse," she said.

"Sure doesn't help."

Do your job. "How well did you know Dorothy Barrington?"

"What?"

"She was also shot this afternoon. Fatally."

"I heard about that." He tilted the cup back and forth and studied the black liquid as it sloshed.

"How well did you know her?"

He was silent for a moment, then said, "It's complicated."

"Is it? If you speak slowly and use words of one syllable, I may be able to follow along."

His hazel eyes, warm and intelligent, regarded her with a hint of amusement. "Is there something I'm missing here? You implying I had something to do with her death?"

"Did you?"

"Not me. I only kill people with scalpels. Have you checked with her brothers and sister?"

"You think one of them killed her?"

"Now there you're beyond me. You need a shrink. Family ties. They're all bound up together and can't get loose. All of them want to."

"You sound like you know them very well."

"Maybe I do at that," he said with a wry smile.

Likable smile, pretty teeth, nice face; altogether a likable man. "Doesn't Dorothy have two sisters?"

"Yes."

"Which one did you leave out?"

He shot her a sharp look, then tipped the cup and swallowed the rest of the coffee. "Would you believe me if I told you I went to see Dorothy about a patient?"

"Did you?"

He chipped a small piece of Styrofoam from the cup. "She wanted to see me, actually."

"What about?"

With a thumbnail, he flicked the chip across the table. "Ellen."

"The youngest sister. What about her?"

"Dorothy announced that she wouldn't have me upsetting Ellen. I was to leave her alone."

"Were you upsetting Ellen?"

"I don't do well with orders. Played hell when I was in medical school. I pointed out that what I did was none of Dorothy's business and I'd do what I damn well wanted." He tipped his head and gave her another quick smile. "At the time it sounded right. Only in the retelling does it seem silly and childish." He suddenly sobered. "I'm sorry she was killed."

"How have you upset Ellen?"

"That's the complicated part. Ellen and I— Well, a few years ago we were all set to get married. Dorothy didn't approve of me. Happiness reigned when I left."

"Where did you go?"

"Back East. Broken heart. Surgical residency." He shrugged. "Now I've returned."

"To see Ellen? She's happy you're back?"

"Remains to be seen." His beeper went off and he stood up. "That Jen is still alive is a good sign. We'll know a lot more in the next day or two."

She watched him hurry off. I hope you're as good as you think you are. I want Jen in good hands.

SIX

At shortly before seven, Susan poked the doorbell of
Dr. Willis Barrington's house on Longhorn Drive, five
blocks from the victim's. Osey had already questioned him
when Willis was brought in to check the drug supply, but
as Dorothy's second-in-command he deserved close scrutiny, and she wanted a personal look at the man.

He lived in an expensive area: tall trees, hedges, large
homes, well maintained, with carefully tended gardens. But
even the largest and most expensive was only a fraction of
what the same house would cost in San Francisco's Pacific
Heights district.

This one was brick, two-story, in a French-country-home
sort of style, roof peaked in three or four places, shrubs
along the front, beds of flowers. The air was still sticky
with heat, but the sky was a deeper blue with the length-
ening rays of sun. The evening was quiet, only an occasional breeze, and filled with the sound of crickets and the
sweet scent of something blooming. Hyacinths maybe.
Flowers weren't her strong point.

Vicky Barrington, Willis's wife, opened the door, a slender blonde in a flowered dress with narrow shoulder straps
and a full skirt. Her makeup was expertly applied, and her
hair, shoulder length in a cascade of chestnut curls, looked
newly styled. Everything about her suggested a label that
read "outfitted by money."

She seemed startled to see Susan, and her manner was
awkward. "Yes?" she said uneasily. Behind all the
makeup, it was difficult to read her expression.

Susan asked if she could come in for a few minutes.

Vicky stepped back from the door and looked over her

shoulder uncertainly. "I'll get Willis." She tapped away in beige high-heeled sandals, leaving Susan standing on a bronze and apricot Oriental rug in the pale, parquet-floored entryway. On one side was a living room, on the other the dining room, the table still cluttered with dishes and glasses from dinner. Or maybe supper here; Susan never got that right. Whichever it was, the thought made her hungry. She hadn't eaten since the doughnuts shared with Jen for breakfast. Jen was lying in a railed bed being kept alive by a machine pumping air in and out of her lungs.

She took a few steps into the living room, and the overall impression was that nobody actually lived here. As in the entryway, the floor was parquet, covered by another, larger Oriental rug. The couch and two chairs were pale gray; the tables had marble pedestal bases and glass tops. There were no lamps anywhere; instead, recessed lights in the ceiling. Two watercolors hung above the couch, apparently chosen to blend with the color scheme: a bronze bowl of apricots, and orange poppies in a gray vase. It looked like a model home for some classy housing development. The only item even remotely personal was a framed photo on one of the glass-topped tables. She walked over and picked it up: a wedding picture, radiant Vicky in clouds of lace and smiling Willis. She was quite a bit younger than her husband.

"Chief Wren?"

She turned as Willis Barrington came into the room. From running backgrounds on all the Barringtons, she knew he was forty-four, but he looked years older and walked carefully, as though unsure of his footing. "Please sit down."

"Shall I make some coffee?" Vicky hesitated in the doorway.

"No thank you," Susan said.

"I wouldn't care for any either." He showed obvious signs of grief: his grayish-blue eyes were bloodshot and red-rimmed. His hands, square and blunt-fingered, shook slightly when he gestured toward a chair; his mouth was set in a tight line.

Approaching middle age had thickened his waist a little, put streaks of gray in his blond hair, and added lines to his forehead and around his eyes. Even dressed as he was, in a suit, white shirt, and tie, he seemed out of place in the carefully arranged room. Anybody—everybody—would seem out of place; the room was totally sterile.

"How can we help you?" His voice was slightly unsteady. "Tell me what we can do. He has to be found. I'll do whatever I can. To come in and just shoot her down—"

Susan sat in one of the gray chairs. He sat on the couch and held out a hand for Vicky to join him.

With his fingertips, he rubbed his eyes. "I can't believe she's dead."

Susan dropped her bag at her feet and settled further back in the chair. No matter how many times she'd seen the pain in the wake of a homicide, she always felt helpless in the face of naked grief. That's what she was seeing here. In her first homicide investigation, she'd stood before a woman whose daughter had been beaten to death by an abusive husband. Practice didn't make it easier.

"We're a very close family," Willis said.

Vicky folded her hands in her lap and studied them.

"But Dorothy and I—" He shook his head. "From the time we were children. Always the two of us." He seemed to be talking to the mantel clock. "I feel like half of me is missing. She was always so strong, so determined. Nothing could stop her. I can't believe it." He reached out blindly and grasped one of Vicky's hands.

She didn't move except to raise her eyes and look at Susan, then quickly away.

"I understand that Dorothy was almost a parent to the rest of you." Susan included Vicky in the comment.

"That's exactly what she was," Vicky said. "She was

in charge. Always——'' Vicky glanced uneasily at her husband.

"Did that cause you to feel resentment?"

"Why would I feel resentment?" Willis said.

"In your medical practice?"

"Of course not."

Vicky didn't seem to agree altogether, but all she did was take in a breath like a sigh.

Susan nodded as though she accepted his statement. "You were asked to check the supply of drugs and medications at the medical office a while earlier. Could you tell if anything was missing?"

"Nothing. As I told Osey. I can even say nothing looked disturbed. I can only conclude that whoever it was didn't have the opportunity to get that far."

Or Dorothy's death had nothing to do with the theft of drugs. It would be a pretty stupid druggie who tried to steal from an office where people were present. Stupid was possible—druggies often were—but she didn't think that's what had gone down here. Doctor's offices in general didn't have all that many drugs on the premises. Here again, a stupid thief might not have known.

"Have you had trouble with a patient? Someone who was upset about a treatment, perhaps, or felt it was incorrect or unnecessary? Dissatisfied with the results?" Patients had been known to hold a physician responsible for the death of a loved one.

"That is something I cannot discuss."

Vicky flicked her eyes at him. He didn't notice, but Susan did.

"We'll need to look at patient records. Especially those with appointments today."

"Not without a subpoena," he said firmly.

She had expected as much, and let it go. So far, they had no evidence needed to obtain court permission to peruse confidential files. She directed a question at Vicky. "Where were you between twelve and two this afternoon?"

"Shopping," Vicky blurted, a frightened look on her face.

What's this? Till now she'd been nearly impassive.

"Dr. Barrington?"

He puffed up like a snake. His face sharpened from sorrow to disbelief, and then anger, so quickly Susan wondered if the grief had been a convincing performance.

"What are you suggesting? You have the bald insensitivity to come in here and accuse—"

"I'm sorry, Dr. Barrington. I understand this is a difficult time. My job is to find out what happened. To do that, I need to ask questions. Some of which you'd rather not hear."

He stared at her a long moment, then slowly deflated. "Yes, of course. I apologize. This has been a dreadful shock. I'm having trouble accepting it. There are stages one goes through. Disbelief. Denial." He rubbed the tips of his fingers up and down his forehead. "I was here."

He was by himself, had made or received no phone calls beyond the one call from Dorothy. He had no idea why she had asked him over this evening and wouldn't speculate. She frequently called. The family frequently got together.

Throughout his discourse Vicky maintained a watchful quiet. Susan wished she knew what thoughts were going on behind the pretty, painted face. "Did Dorothy have any enemies?"

"Of course not. The very idea is absurd."

"There was the shelter," Vicky said.

"Shelter?"

"For battered women," Willis said, his voice as thin as winter light. "It was an interest of Dorothy's."

"Had that caused any problems?"

"Problems? Certainly not."

"No resentful husband ever threatened her?"

He got a worried expression as he tried to pick through a cluttered mind for something important. "Not to my knowledge. I suppose it's possible. None of them would have reason to harm her. It wasn't as though she were hiding these women, simply patching them up when the occasion made it necessary."

Susan asked Vicky, "You got along well with Dorothy?"

Before she could reply, Willis patted her hand and said, "Of course she did. I told you we were all very close. That includes Vicky."

One big, happy family, Susan thought, and made a mental note to question Vicky without her husband present. She kept an inquiring expression on her face and waited for an answer.

"We didn't have a whole lot in common," Vicky finally admitted.

"Nonsense." Willis patted her and again. "Dorothy loved you."

A shadow flashed across Vicky's smooth face, gone too quickly to read, but it definitely wasn't loving.

VICKY STOOD in the entryway as Willis opened the door for Chief Wren. After he closed it, he put his arms around her. She ought to feel sympathy or grief, or something. All she felt was sorry. Even in death, Dorothy was running their lives. She didn't know how to comfort Willis.

He gently kissed her forehead. "I think we'd better get ready to go. We're supposed to be there at eight."

She gave him a smile and a little push. Anybody but Willis would think they were already ready. "I'll be right along. Soon as I clear away the supper things."

She gathered dishes from the dining room table and carefully wiped crumbs from its perfect polished surface. She stacked the dishwasher, wiped down the cabinets, scrubbed the sink, and made sure everything was tucked away, swept up, smudges erased. As though wiping out any trace of her presence. A lump formed in her throat as she looked around the spotless kitchen: white appliances, dark wood cabinets, peach-veined tile flooring. Everybody thought it was her who wanted everything so neat, so clean, so untouched. She knew they sneered behind her back, felt superior and snide about her fluffy life. It wasn't her at all, it was Willis. He was the one who wanted everything so clean it had no life.

Tears came to her eyes as she compared this kitchen with the messy, disorganized one at home. Her mother cheerfully cooked huge meals, the washing-up often left until later if something more important needed tending to. The coffeepot was always hot on the stove, the sink filled with plates and cups from two brothers with appetites not satisfied by only three hefty meals a day.

Dust and mud got tracked in on the worn linoleum from working in the fields, tending the livestock. As often as not, there was a bunch of chicks or an orphaned kitten in a box by the stove.

For a moment, she wished she were back there, with her family, on the farm, in the kitchen. Except her parents had moved to Arizona to be near one of her brothers, and the farm had been sold. She knew there had been hard times, worry about money, anxiety about weather, and crops that were ruined, as they probably would be this year for anybody foolhardy enough to farm, but there'd been so many good times. Joyous times. She couldn't remember the last time she'd felt joy.

Her wedding day maybe. That had been joyous, all right. And she'd looked beautiful in the yards and yards of lace.

She'd met Willis one rainy night when she'd backed the old family station wagon into his fancy sports car in the parking lot of Erle's Market. It was all her fault; she'd been in a hurry, and with the rain so hard, she couldn't see clearly. So scared she was, when she realized whose car she'd hit: Dr. Willis Barrington. But he was so nice, so sweet. She was crying and saying how sorry. He tried to comfort her, saying only a dent, nothing to worry about, nobody hurt.

He'd taken her for coffee. And he'd talked. After that he'd started taking her out. He had a sweet smile and a sweet voice, and he'd talked and talked. It wasn't until sometime after their marriage that she realized he never said anything.

All her girlfriends had been ripe with envy. He was so handsome, an older man, and a Barrington. Her parents were so pleased when he asked her to marry him. "You can have pretty things," her mother said. Her mother had longed for pretty things all her life, but there was never money to buy them. "He's a good catch," her father said. Both her parents had beamed with pride at the wedding.

Not so any of the Barringtons. None of them thought she was good enough; they all thought she was stupid because she had no education and had this dumb idea that she could be a singer. Dorothy thoroughly disapproved and tried to talk Willis out of the marriage. It was probably the only time he had ever gone against her wishes.

Looking back, Vicky sometimes felt the wedding was the high point of her life and everything was downhill from there. Willis always wanted her to look perfect. Never a spot, never a wrinkle. Makeup from the moment she woke.

She sighed as she rinsed the dishcloth and hung it over the towel bar. Sometimes she felt so awful she just wanted to cry. Or scream. Or find a pen full of pigs and roll around in the mud. She knew what they thought about her, all those Barringtons, how they felt.

When she'd heard about Dorothy's death, she'd felt relieved, and then glad, and then hopeful. It was very unChristian of her. She could hear her mother's disapproving voice. She felt guilty for not feeling what she ought to feel, but with Dorothy gone, Vicky thought, maybe now we can have a life. Dorothy had always told them what to do. Willis had always done what she said. And the money Willis would get meant they could move away, far away from here.

She had a secret. She didn't know how Willis would feel if he knew.

And she was afraid. She really was.

SEVEN

At the police department, Susan sat at her desk reading through the reports in thus far on the Barrington shooting. Paperwork: everybody hated it, grumbled about it. She'd done her share of grumbling, but now she was on the receiving end, she had more appreciation. Nobody yet found who'd seen anything suspicious in or around the medical building. She thought of the general rule of twenty-four and twenty-four, the basic principle that the last twenty-four hours of a homicide victim's life and the first twenty-four hours of the investigation were crucial to nailing the perpetrator.

The department was quiet. Hazel had gone home, and Marilee Beaumont was working as dispatcher. Eight-thirty. Too early for Saturday night activities: the usual disorderly, driving under the influence, traffic offenses, disturbances. Not that there would be an abundance. Back in her rookie days in San Francisco, Saturday nights were known as spot 'em, scoop 'em, run 'em nights: get the injured party into an emergency vehicle and to a hospital.

At this point in an investigation, she'd be high on adrenaline and bad coffee, caught up in the crazy tension and energy of the team. Homicides averaged out to one every three days in San Francisco. She'd already have a backlog; a new one would feel like overload, and she'd want to wrap it up immediately and have it out of her way.

Dropping her pen, she leaned back and rubbed her eyes with a thumb and forefinger. When she opened her eyes, Parkhurst was sitting in the wooden armchair in front of the desk. She sat up straight. "Didn't your mother ever teach you to knock?"

"From her I learned it's never advisable to let your presence be known."

Whatever that meant. "You have anything for me?"

"Bits and pieces. Let's get something to eat, and I'll tell you."

Yes. Good. Why not? She hadn't eaten since breakfast. Build up a little blood sugar.

He stood. "Coffee Cup Café?"

She nodded and slung the strap of her bag across her shoulder. "I'll meet you there."

"What have you got?" she asked when they were seated in a booth in the rear.

"The patients, those scheduled in the morning, have all been questioned, and—" He broke off as the waitress handed them each a menu and continued when she left. "They saw the good doctor, got whatever it was attended to, and have nothing useful to say. Except for Mrs. Clinkenbeard, who's ninety-three and suffers from arthritis. She claims she had a feeling in her bones. Now, you might just put this down to arthritis flareup, but she knows it was a premonition of impending death."

When the waitress returned, Susan ordered a turkey sandwich and coleslaw. Parkhurst asked for chicken-fried steak.

Susan closed the menu and handed it back to the waitress. "No weapon?"

"Not yet. Not the right one, anyway. Carl owns a handgun. 9-mm Browning. It's not the murder weapon. Nothing useful in the Barrington house. Although that place is so large, it'd take a month and even then we couldn't be sure."

"Prints at the office?"

"Sure. Latents all over the place. Probably none of them helpful. You ever get a lock on a case with fingerprints?"

"Once. Made me feel like a real detective."

"According to Dr. Willis Barrington, no drugs missing."

"There wouldn't have been time. Couldn't have been

more than five seconds before I was chasing him, and then I found Jen. The shooter barely had time to scoot out that rear door."

The waitress brought the food, and Susan kept her eyes averted from the chicken-fried steak, a piece of midwestern cuisine that was right up there with fried brains when it came to appeal.

"None of the nearest and dearest have what you might call an alibi," Parkhurst said when the waitress left. "Dr. Willis was home alone most of the afternoon, although he did go out to the post office to pick up some stamps. Wife Vicky was shopping. We're tracking down clerks or whoever who saw her, but even so she could have nipped in, shot Dorothy, and rushed back to fingering lingerie." He cut a bite of steak.

Susan picked up a fork and poked at the coleslaw.

He chewed and swallowed. "That goes for all of them. Dr. Marlitta was home alone except for a trip to the grocery store. These people spend a lot of time home alone. Her husband—whose name is Brent Wakeley, by the way; Barringtons like to hold onto that name—claims he was at Emerson."

"Why at Emerson?"

"The brilliant physician is also a dedicated teacher."

"On Saturday?"

"Mostly dedicated to the pursuit of female students, if the rumors are correct. Dr. Carl, home alone. Except when he went out to run some errands. There's a man not happy with his life."

"If he's not happy, why doesn't he change it?"

"Something we might want to find out. The husband, Taylor, in his perusal of new cars could have slipped in and iced his wife between the BMW and Mercedes."

"Any motive for any of them?"

"Money." Parkhurst gave her a wolfish grin. "Always a good one. More on that when I get the scoop on wills.

As in last and testament." He speared a French fry, dipped it in catsup, and popped it into his mouth.

"Not one of them knows why she asked them all to come to the house this evening?"

"So they say, and not one would hazard a guess. I'll wager they've all thought on it. And come up with reasons. Maybe different for each one. And maybe none of them right. I'll set Osey on them. Maybe he'll ease out a speculation or two."

She nodded. Detective O. C. Pickett, slow-talking country boy with an engaging grin, was one of those loose, relaxed people whom everybody liked. He could walk up to a group of strangers and in ten minutes they'd all be joking and carrying on like he was an old buddy.

Parkhurst slid his plate to the corner of the table, set his coffee mug in front of him, and wrapped both hands around it. He studied her. "You all right?" he asked softly.

"Fine," she said, self-consciously aware of him: high-planed face, straight nose, penetrating brown eyes, thick dark hair, full lower lip, arched upper lip. Air of icy arrogance. Hard-edged, giving a sense of violence barely contained. When he softened, like now, she got nervous. They'd worked together for over a year, had started out with distrust and thrown barbed darts at each other, but had gradually moved toward a grudging respect; she'd become appreciative of his worth and learned to rely on him.

Then, while she wasn't paying attention, this stupid adolescent attraction popped up and slapped her in the face. After Daniel's death, she'd vowed, never again. Too much potential for pain. The trouble with love was the hole it left when it was gone. If she were so foolish as to get in an emotional entanglement, it wouldn't be with Parkhurst. That would be disaster. He wasn't her type. He had too many hard edges. She outranked him—hell, was top of the line in authority.

And there was her position as police chief. Hokey as it

sounded in today's social climate, the good citizens wouldn't take lying down—so to speak—their chief of police cavorting around without benefit of matrimony. Hampstead's climate was several degrees below the modern world.

She didn't like the awkwardness between them. Things floated around in it that made her twitch like a scared rabbit. She didn't know what to do about it. And right now she didn't want to think about it. She had all she could handle with Jen's precarious situation.

"It's not your fault." He smiled, which was itself unusual and put her on alert.

"I know that." Right about now, she and Jen should be settling in their seats after intermission, waiting for the ballet to continue. "If Jen doesn't recover, I'm going to resign."

He raised an eyebrow. "Susan—"

She shook her head, found bills in her wallet, tossed them on the table, and stood up.

Before going home, she stopped at the hospital to see Jen. No change.

When she snapped on the kitchen light, Perissa came in nattering pleasure at her arrival. Susan scooped up the little cat, who climbed onto her shoulder and bit her ear. She dumped the cat and squatted in front of a cabinet, found a flat can of liver, and stuck it under the can opener. Perissa waited patiently, sitting tall, tail curled around her front paws, while Susan spooned liver chunks into a bowl.

After a quick shower to wash away the sticky feeling, she pulled on one of Daniel's white T-shirts and opened the windows wide to encourage any stray breeze to wander in. It was just dusk; the air was like velvet, the trees made moving shadows in the soft wind. Fireflies glowed and winked out, glowed and winked out. Crickets sang. A dog barked.

She propped pillows against the headboard and stretched

out on the bed to study her notes. Maybe something would leap up at her. Perissa jumped on the bed and industriously kneaded Susan's hair. "Well, cat, we're left here with the night terrors and the dreams and the regrets. What do you think? We gonna get through this?"

Perissa gave her an inscrutable look.

HERE THEY ALL WERE, just as Dorothy had told them to be. Ellen toed off her cruddy Nikes, pulled up her socks, and leaned against the arm of the sofa to tuck her feet up under her.

"She must have said something to somebody." Willis, with a clink of bottles, slid the crowded tray onto the oak chest against the wall and poured out a splash of bourbon.

At least I've had a shower, Ellen thought. And washed my hair. Life is better, right? Sure. Everything's the same. I sit here like somebody else's dog, like I don't belong, like what am I doing here anyway. Life is the shits. Dorothy's dead. Nothing's the same.

They were in the music room, where they gathered to play Bach or Mozart or Strauss waltzes, Dorothy on piano, Willis with cello, Marlitta and Carl violins. Ellen played the flute, except she usually got kicked out because she never practiced enough.

The enormous room was crammed with furniture: upright piano against one wall, wing chairs, small tables, two Victorian sofas. Crystal lamps all over the place and all of them lit. The windows were open, and periodically a tepid breeze stirred the lace curtains.

It was easy to see they were all related: light hair, blue eyes, pale complexions and lookalike features, lookalike mannerisms. Except me. The cuckoo in the nest. Looking like Daddy with dark hair, dark eyes. All by myself too. The others came in pairs. Dorothy and Willis. Marlitta and Carl. Here's me, long time later, all alone.

"Taylor." Willis turned to Dorothy's husband. "Why

did she want us all here? She must have said something to you."

"She didn't." Taylor, in one of the wing chairs, sat leaning forward, elbows on his knees, chin propped in one hand. His face looked stiff and pale. If he resented Willis taking over as lord of the manor, he stomped on it.

He had to know what the family thought of him, figure he'd be tossed out as soon as decency allowed. He wasn't that much of a dimwit.

"I didn't even know she'd asked you to come," he said.

"Scotch, please, Willis," Marlitta said. She was a younger, softer version of Dorothy; like a photocopy that hadn't come out quite right. Even her voice was softer, giving an impression of uncertainty where Dorothy always sounded decisive. "And water. Make it weak. She must have wanted to discuss something about the practice."

Not so, Ellen thought. Or I wouldn't have been ordered to present myself.

"There is no trouble with the practice." Willis handed Marlitta a glass.

She took a sip, sat the glass on the side table, crossed her legs, and adjusted the pleated blue skirt over her knees.

Willis looked fit and prosperous in his summer-weight suit, white shirt and tie, freshly barbered, hair showing a little gray. Without asking Vicky what she wanted, he handed her a rum and Coke.

"There's Ackerbaugh fuming and threatening because the baby's not any better." Carl got up to fix himself a drink.

Winslow Ackerbaugh? He was the one putting in all her expensive new pipes. She hoped fumes and threats didn't seep through into leaky pipes.

In contrast to Willis, Carl looked rumpled in baggy brown pants and open-collared tan shirt with the shirttail hanging loose. Everything looked loose on Carl, because he was so thin. He had the narrow, ascetic face of a monk in an old book of medieval tales. Or a fanatic. "Whatever the reason, Dorothy was pissed about it," he said.

Willis frowned. Decorum, please. Let us not forget we're Barringtons. He was doing his best to take over as head of the family, but he didn't have the stuff of which Dorothy had been made. He'd managed to get them all here, but Ellen thought only because Dorothy'd already arranged it. They bitched and griped about Dorothy, but none of them quite knew what to do now she wasn't here to tell them.

Me too. I'm just like the rest. Such pride that I got away, did my own thing. Ha. How far did I get? A few miles out of town, where I get to lie awake all night worrying how I'm going to pay bills. And just how much of my ersatz escape was my determination? Maybe Dorothy just thought I wasn't real bright and not worth the effort, I'd end up like Daddy anyway.

"The police have been asking me questions," Willis said. "I don't like it. Obviously, it was someone who broke in, looking for drugs or items to steal."

"The police have talked to all of us," Carl said. "And it's going to get a lot worse before they're through."

"They should be chasing down suspects."

"They are," Carl said. "*We* are suspects."

"That's absurd." Willis glared at him. "What's the matter with you?"

"Tired, I guess. Makes me forget the rules and open my mouth. Communication! Good God. Haven't we all thought about it, big brother? Fantasize about what we could do if she wasn't standing over us holding the whip. And the money. Now we can add substance to dreams, right? What are you going to do, Willis?" Carl looked over at Vicky. "Go on to bigger and better things?"

Vicky smiled uncertainly at Carl. Automatic. Whenever anyone looked at Vicky, she smiled. In a sundress with narrow straps and gathered skirt, she'd been sitting quietly on a sofa with a pulled-tight look as though trying not to be visible. She held the glass Willis had handed her, but, Ellen just realized, had yet to take a sip. That wasn't like Vicky.

Ellen had to admit Vicky was decorative and assumed that was why Willis had married her. What other reason? As far as Ellen knew, all Vicky ever did was apply makeup and change clothes.

Barringtons weren't smart when it came to choosing a spouse. Marlitta's husband was total scum. Brent came in a great package: a visage to swoon over, dark hair drifting across his forehead just asking for feminine fingers to brush through, dark brown eyes that seemed compassionate and wise. Ha. He sat there in the wing chair looking as though every word everybody said had some deep significance and he was the oracle who understood all. Marlitta loved him. You didn't tell your sister her gorgeous husband was garbage and ought to be dumped over the side.

Taylor? They all thought he was a plain, old-fashioned fortune hunter when Dorothy married him. He was too slick, too smooth, and—in Ellen's opinion—not to be trusted an inch. He must have gotten a nasty shock when he found out the money wasn't all that easy to get at. Ellen uncoiled herself, padded over to the chest, and poured a glass of white wine.

"Don't talk nonsense," Willis said, flushed. "None of us killed Dorothy."

Carl stretched his mouth in a tired smile. "The cops are looking for motive, among other things. Every one of us benefits from Dorothy's death." He looked at Taylor and tossed off the remainder of his drink. "Except perhaps the grieving husband. But we don't know about that, do we?"

"I fully realize you'd all like to pin it on me." Taylor looked at them one by one, his slightly bloodshot eyes scornful. Had he been crying? His voice was level, but Ellen noticed dots of perspiration on his forehead. "All of you gain from her death. I don't. I've lost my wife. I just identified her body.''

His eyes were suddenly moist. Could he have loved her? Totally untried thought.

"Nicely done," Carl said dryly. "Although there is Dorothy's own money. Can we assume that goes to you? And we don't actually know she didn't do something sneaky about our mother's will."

"The ancestral home?" Taylor laughed. "You can bet that stays in the family. Willis has probably already started packing. And Vicky's making up schedules for remodeling."

"There's no need to throw around accusations," Marlitta said. "It's preposterous to think one of us killed her."

It might be preposterous, Ellen thought, but they all were sliding glances at one another and wondering.

Not a one of them mentioned the gun.

EIGHT

UPSTAIRS IN HER old room, Ellen spent a restless night with sleep lurking just around the corner and being chased back by memories.

"Ellen! Get up!" Dorothy was calling from the foot of the stairs. "Hurry up! You're going to be late."

Ellen woke, groggily rolled over, and was on her feet before she realized she'd been dreaming. Easing down on the side of the bed, she leaned forward and gripped the edge of the mattress with both hands. For a moment, she'd been fourteen and hearing Dorothy yelling at her to get up, she'd be late for school.

Oh, God. Just dump her back here and she was a kid again. The room hadn't even been changed. Heavy oak bed with carved posts, dresser, bookshelves with kids' books. Cripes, books she hadn't looked at since she was ten. Stuffed animals all over the place. Same quilted bedspread with squares of different kinds of flowers. Yeah, well, don't knock it. You lived in here. With Daddy away so much, Mama always working, and brothers and sisters so much older, she'd mostly been left to herself. Those old books were friends.

She crept to the window and slid aside the lace curtain to let in the pearly light of pre-dawn. The thin nightgown reached to her knees, and she tugged it up to kneel on the window seat, looked out at the backyard. There was not yet enough light to see the masses and masses of flowers her mother loved so much. A gardener took care of all that now, but not when Mama was alive. She was better with flowers than with children.

Ellen pulled on a robe, opened the door a crack, and

peered out. The house was silent. She wondered if Taylor had gotten any sleep. What had he thought about in the wee hours of the night? She padded across the hall to the bathroom and turned on the shower.

Dressed in jeans and a striped blouse neatly tucked in, she moved quietly along the wide hallway toward the stairs. At the doorway to the sunroom, she paused. The wall of windows reflected the rosy tint of sunrise and gave a ghostly cast to the white wicker loveseats. Daddy used to be wheeled in here, after his stroke. He'd sit slumped in the chair, face stiff and distorted on one side, unable to speak with any sense. Her throat tightened, and tears prickled her eyes.

Downstairs in the kitchen, she started a pot of coffee, found some bread, and dropped two slices in the toaster. She tried not to make any undue noise, just like when she was a kid and hoping not to attract Dorothy's attention. Waiting for the toaster to do its thing, she stood by the back door and watched the world get light. Except on schooldays, she always got up early. There was something secret and exciting about being the only one awake in a sleeping world.

She pressed her hands hard against the sides of her face, trying to get a grip on reality. Weird being back here. Right back into the same slot in the family, same patterns of thought, same habits. Like all those years in between hadn't happened. Maybe she could stay with one of the others.

When the toast popped, she jumped. She smeared on butter and forced herself to eat. No taste. Hard to swallow. She was putting off driving out to her place, afraid of what she'd find. Or not find. Putting off thinking about it too.

Like a good product of Dorothy's training, she stacked the dishes, brushed up the crumbs, and then found the small thermos in the corner cabinet, right where it had always been. Nothing ever changed. So go stay someplace else. Willis wouldn't mind, but what about Vicky? Marlitta? Ellen grimaced. Definitely not. Brent would probably paw at her in the living room with Marlitta in the kitchen. Carl, maybe. She could ask.

She poured coffee in the thermos, heard Taylor stirring around, quickly screwed on the cap, and left by the back door.

It was working up to another hot, humid day. The forecaster on the car radio predicted more rain. Too bad. There'd been too much already. Better pick up her raincoat while she was there. Past the old wooden water tower on the edge of town she speeded up.

The sky was early-morning blue, only one huge, cottony cloud streaked with pink. Behind barbed wire, the fields on both sides had standing water. A meadowlark sitting on a stone fence post sang a long trill of flutelike gurgles. She topped a rise and headed downhill. In the low-lying area on her right, part of the Kress farm, the field was nothing but a big lake. Tethered in the center was a gaudy, inflatable sea horse with enormous eyes and a dopey grin. She braked as she came to a hand-lettered sign: "Lock Kress Monster." She burst out laughing, took her foot from the brake, and pressed the accelerator.

From the crest of the next hill, she could see her stone house—her very own—the trees tall behind, the hills lush and green rising and falling away. Just seeing it helped restore her adult self. After a deep breath of woodsy-smelling air, she went inside, plonked the thermos on the pine table, and went around opening windows. It was almost chilly inside; the thick walls made the house nearly impervious to heat. She opened the kitchen door. Across a corner at the top of the frame, a large spiderweb, covered with dew, sparkled like diamonds.

The house wasn't large but had enough space to suit her: a good-sized kitchen; a living room with a stone fireplace; a bedroom and bath in the rear as well as the big room she used as an office; two small attic rooms with steep-pitched ceilings under the eaves. So far the upstairs rooms were empty, but she'd labored four hours refinishing the wide board floors.

Yanking open the bedroom closet door, she shoved boxes and clutter aside and grabbed the shoe box buried beneath. *Oh, shit.* The box was too light. She flipped off the lid. Empty. No no *no.*

Even though she knew it was useless, stupid, a waste of time, she searched every room, every little niche and hidey-hole. All she accomplished was a broken vase, nudged off the shelf while she was groping behind books. She kept thinking Willis, Marlitta, Carl. Willis, Marlitta, Carl. Oh, God, she needed to talk with someone.

NADINE, STALWART FRIEND, faithful employee, backbone of Good Gourd. She answered the door still wearing her robe, baby asleep against her shoulder, long blond hair hanging loose down her back instead of coiled on top of her head. She looked like a witch, a good, kind witch with endless compassion. Tears glistened in her eyes, and she put her arm around Ellen in a tight hug.

"Oh, Ellen, I'm so sorry about Dorothy."

Tears seeped into her own eyes. "I can't seem to really believe it. I'm sorry I'm so early." It wasn't yet seven o'clock. "I wasn't thinking. Did I wake you up?"

"With this guy?" Nadine nuzzled the baby's fuzzy head. "He just went back to sleep. I'll put him down."

The apartment was tiny, one of four in a boxy, fifties-style building in need of paint, furnished with donations from relatives and items picked up at flea markets. Ellen squeezed around the stroller and sat on the sagging brown couch with a jumble of freshly washed clothes on one end. She set the thermos on the glass-topped coffee table next to a stack of folded baby garments.

"He should sleep for a while." Nadine said when she returned. "I'll make some coffee."

"I brought some."

Nadine got cups from the cramped kitchen and filled them from the thermos. She set one on the coffee table, plopped into the overstuffed armchair, and, before taking a sip, eyed Ellen critically. "What's wrong?"

"Wrong?" Ellen laughed, heard the thin thread of hysteria. "Everything's wrong. Dorothy's dead. Somebody shot her. I can't find my raincoat. And—"

"I didn't mean it that way. You just seem—"

"I'm afraid." Ellen picked up her cup. "Nadine, that time you lost your keys."

"I didn't lose them. They were stolen."

"Yeah."

Nadine had claimed that at the time, but Ellen had been doubtful. Nadine always misplaced keys. She'd set them down and forget where. How she could be so meticulous about business and so careless with keys Ellen could never understand. "When?"

"I told you. At the crafts fair."

Ellen nodded. "Who was there?"

"Everybody."

"Willis? Marlitta? Carl?"

"Probably. Vicky, for sure, because she got a skirt I wanted to buy. And Marlitta. Maybe the others. Everybody was there."

Ellen shoved both hands, fingers spread wide, through her hair. "I don't know what to do."

"Hey now," Nadine said. "Try to hang on. It's terrible. It's tragic. You'll get through it."

"I thought it was my imagination."

"What was?"

"When I thought somebody'd been in the house. Stuff just a little bit different. Like whoever it was had been careful. I couldn't be sure."

"I told you we should have called the cops."

"Nothing was stolen. There's nothing to steal. Unless

somebody got an irresistible urge to have a few gourds. I didn't want to be treated like a nervous nut."

"What are you afraid of?"

Ellen picked up the cup and cradled it against her chest. "The gun is gone."

Nadine stared at her. "Somebody stole my keys to get the gun?"

"I don't know."

"Who knew you had it?"

"Nobody," Ellen said, and looked at Nadine. "Except my family."

WHEN ELLEN PULLED into Carl's driveway, she was relieved to see his car in the garage. The house was modest by Barrington standards: weathered wood, split level, a deck on one side above a gurgling creek, three towering walnut trees in front. If he hadn't been here, she would have thrown herself on his porch and howled. She banged on the door, and when he didn't answer right away, banged again. She heard thumping around inside and waited.

Carl, hair standing up in spikes, wearing only khaki shorts hastily pulled on, squinted at her with bloodshot eyes. "What the hell, Ellie?"

He plodded into the kitchen, looked blearily around, and rubbed a hand over his jaw. "Has something else happened? What time is it?"

He dumped leftover coffee in the sink, opened a cabinet, and gazed at the shelves as though he'd forgotten what he was searching for.

"I'll do it." She nudged him aside and moved around cans until she found the coffee.

He pulled out a chair and collapsed in it, legs stretched under the table. "What are you doing here at the crack of dawn?"

"I was up before dawn ever cracked. Did you get any sleep?"

"No."

She scraped the used grounds into the disposal and turned it on. He clapped his hands over his ears. Standing in the stream of sunshine pouring through the window, she washed the pot, spooned in fresh grounds, and poured in water. She didn't really want any more coffee, but the homey actions were comforting; they put a cushion of normalcy between her and events too awful to contemplate.

Sitting down across from him, she clasped her hands on the table and stared at them. "What's the matter with our family?"

With a wry smile, he reached over to ruffle her short, dark curls. "Oh, little Ellie, it would keep a herd of psychiatrists happily busy for years. Is that why you came rushing over here?"

He leaned back and hooked an elbow over the chair. "It probably has something to do with our crazy daddy and our mother who had to be so much in control she set things up to keep control long after she died."

Ellen got up, found two mugs in a cabinet, and set them on the counter, then stood watching the coffee drip through. The sunlight hitting the glass pot made the liquid look like warm molasses. "The gun is gone," she said.

"What gun?"

"Daddy's gun."

"He didn't have a gun."

"Yes he did." She felt like stamping her foot. Let her be around her siblings and she was right back to childhood. "I remember when he bought it."

"Oh. Yeah. Probably intended to do himself in. Mother took it away from him. What were you doing with it?"

"I don't know." She filled the mugs, carried them to the table, sat down, and pushed one across to him. "I just had it. After he died, I took it. I had this feeling that I wanted something of his, and— It doesn't matter. The point is, it's gone. And Dorothy was shot."

"How do you know it's gone?"

"Because I went out to my place this morning before six o'clock and I searched from top to bottom. It's gone! Will you drink some coffee and wake up?"

He took a sip.

"Do you think Dorothy's death was an accident?"

"Accident? Ellie, get a grip. She was shot through the heart. And it wasn't self-inflicted."

Ellen brushed hair back from her forehead. "I know that. I mean, do you think it was somebody who broke in, like Willis said, and she just happened to be there?"

"Let's just say I think that's the line we should stick to."

"But do you believe it?"

"Oh, Ellie—"

"Do you?"

He took a breath. "No."

"Neither do I." She got up, rummaged through the cabinet for the sugar bowl, and brought it back to the table. She stirred a spoonful in her mug. "That means one of us did it. With Daddy's gun."

"It doesn't mean any such thing. Anybody could have killed her. And there's more than one gun in this world. I've got one. Listen to me, Ellie, it's not a good idea to say stuff like that. Even here."

She lowered the spoon into the mug, let it fill with coffee, and raised it to her mouth. "They didn't like us very much, did they?"

"Who?"

"Our parents."

"Daddy might have, but he never got a chance to find out. Mother always kept us away from him. Like she was afraid what he had might be catching."

Especially afraid I might catch it.

"We got in her way," Carl said. "She resented us for taking up too much of her time. She did have the call, you know. The great Dr. Barrington, battler of diseases; beat them back, stamp them out, make the world safe for health.''

"Was she a great doctor?"

He lifted his mug and stared into it. "I think maybe she was," he said slowly. "She had healing in her fingers, our mother." He smiled and took a swig. "Which is a great deal more than I can say for the rest of us."

"What do you mean?"

"Oh, little Ellie, don't tell me you believe the myth about the eminent Doctors Barrington. It's a crock. Except for Dorothy, maybe. She's the only one who comes close. That's why Mother liked her, I guess." He plunked down the mug and tipped his head to one side. "Don't look so shocked. We're not any of us quacks. We're all well trained and competent, but we're not great. Some of us don't even know it."

"Carl—"

"Oh, I know it. And Marlitta knows. Willis doesn't. He thinks he is great. At any rate, he tells himself he is, so he doesn't have to think. Darlin', our mother told him he was great. Would our mother lie?"

His long face got longer, and his tired eyes got tireder. "Yes, little Ellie, one of us killed Dorothy. The only odd thing is that it hadn't happened years ago."

"Stop calling me that. I'm twenty-three years old."

"Sorry. I've got a bit of a hangover, if you must know, and I'd appreciate it if you wouldn't yell."

"The cops are going to find out that Dorothy had all the money."

"That they are, little—sorry—Ellie. And they're going to look at us very closely. And they aren't stupid."

No, Ellen thought. The idea of that lieutenant, Parkhurst, looking at them closely made her hair stand on end. Even Chief Wren with her soft voice. She could have walked right out of an ad for some classy couture place: dark hair, high cheekbones, blue eyes. One look at those eyes and you knew the soft voice was a sham. "What will happen about the money?"

"Unless Dorothy did something tricky, and I don't see how she could have, we'll all get our share."

"And Daddy's paintings?"

"Now, there I don't know." We'll have to talk to old what's his name. The attorney. Hawkins. Maybe we divide them, maybe they all have to be sold and then we divide the proceeds."

"Who needs money that bad?"

"All of us, every damn one. And I think you should drop this whole thing."

"Don't you want to know who killed her?"

He thought. "Depends."

"On what?"

"Who did it. And whether he—or she—will get caught."

Caught. Oh, my God. A trial. Maybe a conviction. Did Kansas have the death penalty? She didn't even know. She didn't think so. She hadn't thought beyond *who,* never considered that was only the beginning.

"If it has to be one of us," Carl said, "I vote for Taylor."

Ellen gave that some thought and decided she'd vote that way too. "Why?"

"Because he's an ass. He married her for the money. Didn't find out until too late it's all tied up. At least I hope it is. Wouldn't that be a pisser? Somebody killed her for the money, and it turned out Taylor got everything." He laughed, a short, bitter sound. "No, little Ellie, I believe it might be better all around if we never know."

"You act like you're glad she's dead."

Carl shook his head. "No, I'm not. Then again, I am. We all are." He drained his mug and got up to refill it. "However, I doubt it's going to be all we expect. It was easy to blame Dorothy for everything. There she was, standing in the way of important goals, self-fulfillment, ultimate happiness, all that crap.'' He laughed again, the same short, bitter sound. ''Somewhere along the way we're going to figure out she wasn't the cause of everything wrong in our lives.''

Ellen shifted in her chair. He was right. Even she blamed Dorothy for everything. Absolutely, she did. Not having enough money, not getting help when she started the gourd business. Even what happened with Adam. And probably lots of other things she didn't want to think about right now.

''We're all going to have to take responsibility for our own lives. That's going to be a shock. And we're going to turn out just as miserable. That's going to be a severe shock.'' Tilting the chair back on two legs, he gazed at the ceiling. ''Maybe I'll cash it all in and buy a farm.''

Ellen looked at him in surprise. ''Farm?''

''Lifelong dream,'' he said wryly. ''Don't look so startled. That's what you're doing.''

''No. Not like that. Banks are built on the bones of farmers who couldn't make it.''

''Maybe it's in the genes. Daddy's family were farmers. None of us wanted to go into medicine, you know. Except maybe Willis. He had this desire to please Mother. Never could, of course, but he didn't know that. She never cared what we did, as long as we did what we were told. Dorothy wanted to be a pianist.''

Dorothy? Wanted to play the piano? Ellen couldn't grasp the idea that Dorothy ever wanted to do anything except just what she did.

''That's why we've all been jealous of you, little Ellie.''

She felt her mouth hanging open and closed it with a snap. ''Nobody's ever paid any attention to me. Half the time, I think you forget I exist.''

"You were the only one, the only one, who dug in her little heels and refused to fall in line."

More credit than she was due. She'd wanted somebody to look at her, tell her she *was* just as smart, and *would* go to medical school. By then Daddy was dead and Mother was dead. And maybe Dorothy was tired of making siblings do what they were told.

"What about the gun? Should I tell the cops?"

Carl rubbed his bloodshot eyes. "Now, there's a hard one. You can be sure Vicky will tell. She'll have a few drinks and blab whatever's in her tiny mind."

He looked at her with an expression she couldn't read. "And I do mean everything. It's going to get real sticky. She'll pass on the juicy bit about your argument, threatening Dorothy about Daddy's painting."

"It was mine."

"Just prepare yourself for a lot of nastiness. And stop this sitting around wondering who did it. That can be dangerous."

The tears she'd been holding back ever since Dorothy's death suddenly overflowed and spilled down her cheeks. Everything just felt so sad.

NINE

MAKING MORNING ROUNDS, Adam Sheffield steeled himself for what he might find in ICU. Sawed-open and stitched-up organic matter that used to be a little girl? He hesitated at the nurses' station.

"Doctor?" A nurse looked at him as though expecting him to ask for something. Being a doctor was great: people standing by to scurry around at the snap of a finger. The downside was the tendency to play God. Especially in ER.

Death was the enemy, and it seldom happened in ER. A DOA was different. The enemy got there first. But if there was even a spark of life, the team went into battle with frenzied determination. Most often they won the skirmish, fanned the spark, and kept it burning long enough to get the patient into surgery. Surgery was where the patient died, or later in ICU.

Miracles were performed in ER. A death made it hard for the team to continue belief in miracles. The doctors, nurses, and technicians weren't used to defeat, and they didn't accept it philosophically. Depending on individual character, they got mad or snappish, or grew very quiet, or took themselves off somewhere to sulk. Nobody, least of all the team physician, ever gave less then a heroic performance. Life was what they were fighting for. They couldn't pause over musings about a life that was no life.

That the Bryant girl had survived the night was a good sign. Still running a fever. Not so good.

He nodded at the uniformed officer by the cubicle; unless the cop knew by sight every member of the hospital personnel, his vigil was close to useless. Keep out unauthorized people, sure; but what if the guy with the six-shooter worked at the hospital? A physician, for instance.

Monitors blipped and flickered, respirator hissed and pumped. He looked at the little girl.

"She's been moving her arms a little," the nurse said proudly, as though a child of her own had done something brilliant. "And once, just five minutes ago, she moved her right leg."

Another good sign. It meant the girl might be regaining consciousness. He didn't like that spiked temp. He wrote orders for more blood work and a throat culture.

"Let me know immediately if there's any change," he told the nurse, and on his way out nodded again at the police officer. He wondered what little Jenifer could tell them. If she was ever able to talk.

The news of Dorothy Barrington's murder had spread rapidly through the hospital, leading to unfunny jokes and wagers thrown around about who might have shot her.

Adam pushed through the door to the stairway and trotted down steps to the next floor. In the doctors' lounge, he pulled the stethoscope from around his neck, struck it in the pocket of his lab coat, and hung the coat in a locker. He was checking for car keys when Dr. Bates breezed in. Mid-forties, round face, ever-present smile.

"Well, well," Bates boomed, "if it isn't the miracle worker."

Adam's smile felt a little strained. "We aim to please." Bates was a pain in the butt, and besides that he was an ass.

Bates opened a locker, shrugged off his suit coat, and reached for a hanger. "Taking it on the lam while the going's good?"

"Even a poor schnook like me—translate dedicated physician—gets a day off now and then."

"Sure." Bates winked. "A talent like you wouldn't sneak out just before the cops nabbed you."

"You know something I don't?"

Bates waved a pudgy hand. "Inside information, my boy, inside information. I happen to be in a position to know that our good Dr. Dorothy didn't approve of your working here. And when she didn't approve of what went on in this hospital, she got changes. Sounds like a motive to me."

He slipped on a white coat. "But then you probably have to wait your turn. Ha, ha."

Adam bared his teeth in a tight smile. "What is this, Bates? You suggesting I killed her? If you are, I might have to do something." He loomed menacingly.

Bates banged the locker shut. "A brilliant doctor like you? Naw. You'd have found a better way."

His smile made him look like a round happy-face drawing. Then the corners of his mouth turned down, somberness set oddly on his jovial face. "She might have had her flaws, but—" He shook his head. "It's probably the sister. The youngest one. Ellen. Always been strange. Probably did it for the money."

Bates bounced out while Adam was still wondering whether to slam him against the wall and squeeze his fat neck.

Better do something, Adam thought, and wished he knew just what the hell to do.

IN THE BASEMENT of the hospital, Susan watched Dr. Owen Fisher's deft, long-fingered hands delicately slice up Dorothy Barrington's body. Death due to a severed aorta. Nothing unexpected about that.

Upstairs, Jen was holding her own. She didn't look any better, but each hour she lived made her odds better.

When he finished, he leaned against a stainless-steel cabinet and peeled off the latex gloves. "Everything else seems normal for a woman of her age. I'll have preliminary results ready probably by this afternoon."

Susan thanked him, headed for the elevator, and left the

hospital through the emergency entrance. Church bells rang in the distance. As she headed for the department, she saw Adam Sheffield take off in a battered Toyota with a determined set to his pugnacious jaw.

Detective Osey Pickett was ambling toward the door when she walked into the police department.

"Where you off to?" she asked.

"Thought I might mosey over to Haskel's Electric."

"Why?"

"Well, I got this nephew. Jimmy?"

She nodded. Osey had four older brothers who owned and operated Pickett's Garage—they all looked alike—and a slew of nieces and nephews.

"Jimmy's in the Boy Scouts. Hank just called—"

Hank was one of the brothers, the eldest, she thought, but wasn't certain. After more than a year in Hampstead, she still couldn't tell them apart.

"—and he said the troop was at Broken Arrow Park on Saturday."

"And?"

"Well, that's the park right near the Barrington clinic. Where the receptionist told us Dorothy sometimes ate lunch. It occurred to me she might have gone there yesterday, and I had Hank ask Jimmy about it. Hank just called to say Jimmy said she was."

"And Haskel's Electric?"

Osey smiled his slow smile. "Bob Haskel's the troop leader."

"Where is this place?" She made a note of the address. "Open on Sunday?"

"Should be."

"I'll check it out. You keep hitting the neighbors. See if you can find anybody who saw her come or go yesterday around noon. Try to pin down times. That goes for the husband too."

"I'll do it." Osey ambled on his way, the most amiable individual she'd ever known.

Haskel's Electric was on Fourteenth Street between a beauty-supply shop and a record store. The sign on the door read, "Wiring, Air Conditioning, Heating Repairs. Twenty-four-hour Service. No Job Too Small."

A bell jangled when she pushed open the door. It was dim inside, a long, narrow place, floor-to-ceiling shelves stacked with supplies and equipment. A large young man, brown hair, no neck, and massive shoulders bulging beneath a blue T-shirt with the snarling Emerson wildcat, came into the shop from a back room.

"Hi." He shoved his hands into the pockets of his jeans and propped a haunch against the counter.

"Bob Haskel?"

"That's me."

"Chief Wren." She held out her ID. "I'd like to ask you some questions?"

"Me? How come?"

"It's about Dorothy Barrington. Did you know her?"

"Sure. Nadine works for Ellen. Anybody who works for Ellen hears about Dorothy." He grinned and then, apparently remembering the circumstances, wiped off the grin.

"Nadine?"

"My wife."

"Did you take a group of Boy Scouts to a park yesterday?"

"Oh. No. You want my dad." He turned his head and bellowed, "Dad! Somebody here for you."

She was relieved everything wasn't shaken off the shelves.

An older, slightly smaller version—gray hair, weathered face, work pants, deliberate tread to his walk—came from the rear carrying a coil of wire. He set the wire on the counter. "What can I do for you?"

"It's about the Boy Scouts," Bob Jr. said, and looked

at his watch. "I gotta go. Catch you later." With a jangle of the bell, he was gone.

"That one." Bob Sr. shook his head. "Always in a hurry."

Not so much hurry as implacable force. "I understand you took a troop of Boy Scouts to Broken Arrow Park," she said.

"Right. Adopt-a-park program. You know about that? Well, acourse you do."

She nodded. All kinds of community groups would choose a site and several times a year pick up trash, take care of needed maintenance, and generally keep the place spruced up. "Did you notice Dorothy Barrington when you were there?"

"Well, I did. Now, wasn't that an awful thing. Nice place like this, something like that happens." He shook his head again. "I just don't know."

"Did you speak to her?"

"No more than to say hello like. Being neighborly. I was keeping an eye on the boys. Good boys, all of them. Need a little directing now and then. My own boy—well, you met Bob—little past the Boy Scout age. Found out I missed it. Had to do something."

"Yes. Did Dorothy say anything?"

"Don't recall she did. Spoke, of course. Pleasant. Real pleasant lady."

"Yes. Did anyone else talk to her? Did she meet anyone?"

"No. No. I don't believe—"

"What did she do?"

He thought a moment. "Just came into the park. Said hello to me and the boys around, what a good job we were doing. Then she just sat on the bench by the duck pond. It's real nice there. Shady, like. Still pretty hot, though. Unusual to be so hot this early. And looking to build up to rain."

"Yes, Dorothy just sat on the bench awhile?"

"She did. Had a sandwich with her and a newspaper. Read the paper, you know, while she ate."

Dorothy went to the park and ate lunch. Getting even that much information had been hard slogging.

She had opened her mouth to thank him and leave, when he said, "Seems like something upset her somehow."

"What do you mean?"

"Just sort of going through the paper like you do. Then all of a sudden she jerked up real straight, looked at something real hard on the page. Then folded up that sucker and left in a hurry."

Susan asked if Dorothy had been on foot or whether she'd driven. He wasn't real certain but thought she must have walked.

Back at the department, Susan tracked down the newspaper that had been in Dorothy's office—the *Kansas City Star*—in the evidence room, cleared a space on her desk, and sat down to read about the latest political scandals, unrest in the Mideast, people starving in Africa, traffic fatalities on the interstate, sports events. There didn't have to be anything in it that upset Dorothy. She'd probably had a thought, realized she'd forgotten to unplug the coffeepot or something equally unrelated.

The second time through, Susan noticed the filler on page twenty-seven: "First in Thirteen Years." A painting by August Barrington purchased for a hundred thousand dollars. No names mentioned, either buyer or seller.

August Barrington?

HAMPSTEAD'S NEW LIBRARY, on the corner of Sixth and Maple, was all brick and spacious in comparison to the old one, with wide windows that actually let in light and a community room bigger than the entire square footage of the old library. It also had added attractions like a juvenile section, magazine racks, and tables and chairs scattered about for leisurely reading. And bathrooms, something the old one didn't have.

The money had come from Fancy French, a longtime resident, who bequeathed several hundred thousand dollars for a new library. The move had taken place over a Saturday, Sunday, and Monday and was all done by volunteers who formed a human chain. The grand opening came complete with flag-raising ceremony and bugler.

The inside smelled of fresh paint and floor polish. Beth Nooley, middle-aged, with frizzy brown hair, looked up with a proud smile. "Isn't this just the greatest place?" She swiveled around to encompass it all. "Wouldn't Helen just love it? What do you hear from her?"

"A card a couple weeks ago." Helen, Daniel's sister, had presided for years over the old library. After selling the family farm, she'd embarked on a round of travel, and sent the odd postcard every now and then. Even that much surprised Susan. Helen had been sorely displeased when she met the wife Daniel had brought home. The last card came from Mira Vista, California, north of San Francisco, and made Susan think longingly of fog and cool ocean breezes.

She told Beth she wanted to find out about August Barrington.

"Oh. Right. One of our own. Just think, a famous painter who lived right here in Hampstead. Have you ever seen any of his paintings?"

Susan admitted she hadn't, didn't admit she'd never heard of him.

"There isn't much. Just newspaper articles. Years back, somebody was around wanting to write a biography, but Dorothy wouldn't stand for it. A shame about her death."

Beth scurried off and returned a few minutes later with microfilm. Susan took it, sat at one of the shiny, new wooden tables, and slipped it into the machine: "Longtime Local Artist Dead at Seventy-three." The accompanying photo was a grainy head-and-shoulders shot that didn't show much: high forehead, deepset eyes, thin, lined face.

August Willis Barrington had died in his home after a lengthy illness. He'd attended the University of Kansas, graduated with honors, married local resident Lydia Weissenburg.

Born in 1903 in Kyane, Kansas, a town with a population of one hundred, August was the son of Julius Barrington, a news photographer. August was in his thirties when he took up art. He had his first one-man show at the Hampstead public library and later went on to have exhibits all over Kansas and then in Arkansas, Nebraska, Missouri, Oklahoma, and later still throughout the country, including New York City and Washington, D.C.

Services were to be held at 1 p.m. at the Emmanuel Lutheran Church. He was survived by his wife, Lydia, and their five children, Dorothy, Willis, Marlitta, Carl, and Ellen.

Articles about August appeared in what she assumed must be every newspaper in Kansas, plus a few other places. She was surprised at the amount of media attention and the gush of praise for his work. A critic for *New York* magazine called him a genius. Other people bandied about words like fascinating, mesmerizing, stunning, bewitching, and psychologically spellbinding.

She turned off the machine and leaned back. Fascinating and bewitching as all this was, she wondered what it had to do with Dorothy's murder. August had died thirteen years ago.

TEN

BY THE TIME Susan left the library it was one o'clock. Instead of heading back to the department, she turned the pickup toward home. On the way, she stopped at Erle's Market. It was so blessedly cool inside she lingered over the heap of apples, finally picked out four, then added two bananas. Jen's favorite. She grabbed a block of cheddar cheese, paid for her purchases, and went out into the heat.

At home, she rinsed an apple under the tap and cut it into quarters, tore the sturdy plastic from the cheese, and rummaged through a drawer for the slicer. Even with Daniel dead over a year, the house still seemed empty. Quiet. Jen had done a lot to change that. With an eleven-year-old girl around, whispers from the past stayed further in the past.

Stacking a cheese deck on a plate with the apple quarters, she sat down at the table to peruse the *Hampstead Herald*. The lead story was about the murder. They must have hustled to get that in, even had a picture of Dorothy's body being wheeled out. Her death shared front-page space with the weather. "Storm Careens Across County." "Funnel Clouds Spotted." Photo of a stalled car on Sixteenth Street getting pushed by a motorist. Heavy rain and marble-sized hail created driving hazards. Street flooding pushed mounds of hailstones onto the curb. "Rain-Delayed Corn Planting Causes Concern." The forecast said, "If you think the rain is never going to stop, you're right."

Perissa had silently materialized on the far end of the table. Susan frowned at her. "Cats are not allowed on tables."

Perissa crouched demurely, simply making her presence

known so if any tasty bits were left over, she'd be handy. Susan crumbled a slice of cheese into the cat bowl. Perissa looked at it dubiously, jabbed at a chunk. When it didn't fight back, she snatched it and played hockey until the chunk disappeared under the refrigerator. Crouching, she peered into the dusty depths, spoke a philosophical word, and trotted back to her bowl for a replacement.

"Right on the forecast," Susan grumbled as she got in the pickup and tossed her raincoat on the passenger's seat. The sky was building up clouds.

The Meer Gallery, on Eighth Street a block east of Main, was essentially one room with partial walls along its length, creating alcoves.

Comach Meer, the owner, sat at a Victorian desk just inside the door. He rose and came toward her, a stocky man in his late thirties, wearing tan pants, tan shirt, and a dark-brown tie, with brown and brown, strong features, and a neatly trimmed mustache.

"I've been expecting you," he said.

Really. Well, then. Gift horses were not to be sneezed at. "You know about Dorothy Barrington's death?"

He smiled, a slight rise of his upper lip. "Doesn't everybody?"

She agreed everybody did. Even before the article appeared in the newspaper, everybody knew. The speed of news-travel in a small town was astounding. "You were a friend?"

"Well, I knew her. You can't live in Hampstead without knowing the Barringtons, and she was first and foremost. I've known Carl for a long time. We're good friends. Had dinner last night, as a matter of fact. He's knocked out by all this."

Damn. The reason Meer thought she'd turn up had, no doubt, been discussed with Carl. "You were expecting me. You want to tell me about that?"

"Dorothy was in here yesterday."

"What time?"

"A little past noon. Twelve-thirty, around there."

"Why was she here?"

He rubbed a forefinger lengthwise back and forth across his mustache. "I'm not real sure, actually. She had a hair up her ass about something. Marched in and demanded to know whether I'd sold the Barrington."

"August Barrington? You have some of his paintings?"

"One. And it's not actually mine."

"Whose is it?"

He smiled again, minute lift of his upper lip. "That's arguable, you might say. Carl claims it belongs to him. Dorothy didn't feel that way."

"Had you sold it?"

"No. Dorothy didn't take my word for it. She trooped right back to see for herself."

"What are you doing with it?"

"It's sort of on permanent loan."

'Permanent loan?"

"There was a time, shortly after I opened, a very dicey period, when it looked like I was going under. Carl brought the painting to hang. For good luck, he said. Maybe it would bring people in."

"Did it?"

"Oh, yes." He paused a moment. "Carl's a good friend. Nice of him to do that. Of course, there was more to it."

"What more?"

Meer shrugged. "Carl struggling against Dorothy's rule. She didn't want the painting out of her control. He prevailed."

"You want to elaborate on that a little?" Susan said when he didn't seem inclined to add anything further.

He rubbed his mustache. "Well, they had their conflicts, Carl and Dorothy."

"Conflicts."

"You'll have to ask Carl. I don't know the ins and outs.

Only that she said one thing, and he said another. They were that way all the time."

It was obvious he wasn't going to give her anything without direct questions. Okay. She'd let him get away with it until she had prompting material.

"May I see the painting?"

"Sure." He led her to an alcove in the rear.

Only one framed picture hung there. Meer nodded at it and crossed his arms. She took a step closer. Something about it made her catch her breath. It was large, maybe thirty inches by forty, the figure of an old man alone in a black room. On one foot was a boot shaped like a rabbit; the other foot was bare. His face had a stricken expression, his hands were gesturing as though asking for help. In one hand dangled a broken bootlace. A rabbit was escaping toward a tiny point of light with a dazzle of rainbows.

The surface impression was humorous, but the second, more powerful, was of pain.

"Effective, isn't it?" Meer said.

"That it is. Is all his work like this?"

"Yes. Everything he did was extremely personal and at the same time universal. All his work had this essentially warm-hearted quality, yet it's devastating. He could show anxiety, despair, isolation, fear in this simple style, and the emotion reaches out and grabs you by the throat."

She could agree with that. After a last look, she turned her back on the painting—it would be disturbing to live with, she thought—and walked toward the front of the gallery. "This one valuable?"

"Very."

"How valuable?"

"Any work of art is worth only what the buyer is willing to pay."

"That doesn't tell me a whole lot."

"Somewhere around a hundred thousand."

"All his paintings that valuable?"

"Some are worth more than others. Size, when in his career he did it, that sort of thing."

"What makes them so valuable?"

"How much time do you have?" Another smile, actual glimpse of teeth. "I could talk for several hours and still not explain it. Simple but strong lines. Exaggerated but quintessential shapes. Simple yet sophisticated compositions. Have I explained it yet?"

"Right." Meer was being cute, and she was beginning to get irritated.

"All his work was about life. His own, really. But it touches everybody's. People respond to it. You familiar with Marc Chagall?"

She decided to ignore the note of condescension and nodded.

"Barrington's paintings have that same quality of child-like wonder. They have the rhythmic contours of van Gogh. The emotional power of Edvard Munch."

"I see," she said before he got even more carried away. "What else did Dorothy say when she was here?"

" 'Is the painting still here?' was about it. She was highly exercised about something. She asked if I knew anything about a Barrington being sold."

"Did you?"

"Not a thing."

"I assume Dorothy had other paintings. How many?"

"Uh—" Meer let out a long breath. "Quite a lot, but I can't give you a number. She won't let anybody really look at them."

"She didn't want to sell them? Why not?"

"I could hazard a guess."

"Hazard away."

"A lot of it is this family-control thing and keeping the valuables under her thumb to keep the family under her thumb. But also, I think, she wouldn't sell them because of the content. The Barringtons have always pretended to the world that everything was rosy. These paintings are intensely personal and reveal a lot of intimate stuff. They show it like it was."

The bell over the door tinkled softly, and two women came in. Susan thanked him and left.

In the pickup, she lifted the radio mike and checked in with Hazel. "Anything going on?"

"Negative."

"Has the preliminary autopsy report came through yet?"

"Not yet."

Susan thought a moment. "I'm on the way to Debra Cole's place. Tell George I need to see him when I get in." George Halpern, her resident expert on the locals, had been with the department for over forty years, had lived in Hampstead all his life, and knew its history front and back.

The first fat drops of rain splotched on the windshield as she started the pickup. The Riverside Trailer Park, on the edge of town, actually was at the river's side, or at least the marshy area nearby. Near enough to guarantee hordes of mosquitos and other voracious insects like gnats and flies. And with the humidity high in general, this low-lying area had it in spades.

The Cole trailer turned out to be one of the smaller, older models that looked in need of maintenance. Uncut grass flourished, encroaching on the walkway.

Grabbing her raincoat, she draped it over her arm and walked up the path. She heard a radio blaring a country-and-western song, a man wailed his puzzlement over why love has to hurt so much.

When she knocked, Debra opened the door, dressed in yellow cotton pants and a long-sleeved yellow shirt.

"Oh," she said. The one word, the body language, and the manner all said she wasn't pleased to see Susan. Not a rare occurrence. Cops investigating a homicide weren't high on everybody's list.

"Hello, Debra. I need to ask you some more questions. May I come in?"

"But I've already told you everything."

"It won't take long."

Reluctantly, Debra opened the door wider and stepped aside. She quickly glanced around as though checking the condition of her home in the wake of an unexpected visitor.

"I was just fixing to have some lemonade. Would you like some?"

"That would be nice."

Debra darted off to the kitchen. Susan dropped her coat on the maroon couch and sat beside it. The plush fabric clung to her linen skirt. The music suddenly died, and in the ensuing quiet, Susan was aware of the hum of the window unit as it struggled mightily to throw out cool air.

The living room area, just large enough to accommodate an easy chair and a lamp table, couch, coffee table, and bookcases of the brick-and-board variety, had a window that let in grayish light and looked out on a neighboring trailer. Hot-pink curtains were the only cheery note to dispel the general air of despondency. Everything was very clean and neat; the tables were shining with polish, the threadbare carpet had recently been vacuumed, even the books were dusted.

Debra returned with two tall glasses beaded with moisture. "Eighty-two on the thermometer by the back door. Would you believe? It never gets this hot this early."

When she stretched an arm across the coffee table to offer the lemonade, her sleeve slid back. Her exposed wrist had a large purple bruise, just the right size for a hand to have squeezed. She sat in the easy chair and rubbed a thumb through condensation on the glass before taking a sip from it. Her face looked drawn, and she had dark circles under her soft brown eyes.

"Do you know yet who—" she took another sip. "Dr. Dorothy, who killed her?"

"I'm going to need your help."

"Mine?" Debra's face tightened. "I don't know anything."

"You worked for her about three years? I'd think she wouldn't have been an easy person to work for."

"She was," Debra said quickly. "She was always so busy, and sometimes she could get a little short, but she would always listen if you had something important. I guess she could get impatient, you know, but she—" She broke off, shot Susan a glance, and looked down at her glass, twisting it back and forth in her hands.

She was nervous, frightened. Understandable in a timid young woman whose boss had been killed almost before her eyes, but experienced cops developed sensors as receptive as seismographs, and Susan's were hitting jagged peaks.

"Did anything unusual occur lately at the medical office?"

"I don't know what you mean by unusual. In a doctor's office, there's always something," Debra said. "But nothing I can think of like you mean."

"How did they all get along? Willis and Marlitta and Carl? Arguments with Dorothy? Differences of opinion?"

"Well, you know, sometimes, but— I mean, nobody gets along all the time, do they?"

Right, Susan thought. Debra was a type who had to be asked specific questions. A general tell-me-all-about-it only caused perplexity; it tied in with her desire to please. You can't please if you don't know what's wanted. "Did you like Dorothy?"

"Of course."

"You'd like to see her killer caught?"

Debra nodded with slight apprehension, as though wary of being led where she didn't want to go.

"My job is to find the killer," Susan said. "And to do

that I need to find out what was happening in Dorothy's life.''

Debra plucked at a cuff, pulling it lower over her wrist. "Willis got along with her the best. They seemed closest, you know? And he mostly agreed with her on things." She looked up.

Susan nodded encouragingly. "Marlitta and Carl had conflicts with Dorothy?"

Debra hesitated. "Well, Dr. Carl sometimes. He just argued about things. Like he wanted to take the opposite side. Just because it was opposite, you know? He kind of like threatened her one time."

"What did he say?"

"I think he wants to quit. Not be a doctor anymore? And Dr. Dorothy wouldn't let him."

"How could she stop him?"

"It wasn't like that. It was more like he wanted to do something else, and he needed money to do it. And Dr. Dorothy just kept saying things like 'stupid' and 'immature.'"

"What did he say to that?"

"It wasn't what he said exactly. More like the way he said it. That she wasn't always going to be around."

"I see. And Marlitta? She have any disagreements with Dorothy?"

"Not that I know of." Debra took a thoughtful sip of lemonade. "But she has been kind of different lately. Sort of quiet. And seems like she's unhappy or worried about something."

"What might that be?"

"I don't know. Maybe nothing. Maybe just work and everything." Debra gave her a little smile. "Ed always says I just imagine things."

"Your husband?"

"Yes." Debra glanced around as though he might have slipped in when she wasn't looking.

Susan's instincts snapped to attention. She kept her voice low. "What does he do?"

"Oh, well, he's a student. You now, at Emerson."

That explained the bricks and boards and the general air of not enough money. Students the world over lived in housing of this ilk. "Did he know Dorothy?"

"Not really. Just who she was. My boss and all."

"How did he feel about your working there?"

Debra shifted uneasily. She didn't say, what the hell business it is of yours? "Oh, fine."

"He didn't want you to stop working?"

Debra shook her head, quickly.

Bingo, Susan thought. Nervousness centered around husband Ed. He didn't like her working. Was Debra afraid he had killed Dorothy?

"We need the money," Debra said.

A little girl toddled from the bedroom, clutched Debra's knee, popped a thumb in her mouth, and stared sleepy-eyed at Susan.

"Who takes care of her when you're working?" Susan asked.

"Ed's mother." Debra put an arm around the child and hugged her close.

The little girl began patting Debra's leg and babbled words Susan didn't understand.

"She wants apple juice," Debra explained.

Susan left them to it and drove through drizzle to the hospital.

In the intensive care unit, she looked at Jen, still and small in the railed bed. Her face was no longer gray but a rosy red. She looked much more alive. Susan's heart lifted. A nurse, by the bed, was flushing Jen's IV line; then she ran a knowing eye over the tangle of lines and tubes, equipment and monitors. Watching a monitor tracing, she fiddled with an EKG lead, studied the respirator dials, and aspirated water from the tubes. She snapped wrinkles from the sheets, looked up at Susan, and smiled.

Round face, short blond hair, she looked entirely too young to know what she was doing, but her movements had been sure and competent. "Just making certain she's comfortable." She peered critically at Susan. "You look tired. Are you getting enough sleep?"

No. Whenever she thought of Jen, motionless in that bed, she wanted to yell and scream and kick somebody. Or collapse on the floor and sob. "Why is her face so red?"

"We thought at first it might be an allergic reaction to the antibiotics. I probably shouldn't be telling you this—"

"What?"

"She has measles."

Susan's heart plummeted: instead of a good sign, the rosy face meant Jen was more at risk.

"Try not to worry," the nurse said.

Sure. Easy. No problem.

"She's in good hands." The nurse gave Susan a motherly pat on the shoulder and scurried out.

Susan curled Jen's limp fingers in her own hand. "You have measles," she murmured. "But everything's okay. You came through the surgery like a champ. You're going to get well and go home. Soon as the doctor says all right, we're getting tickets for a ballet. That's a promise."

Jen's chest rose and fell with the hiss of the respirator.

"See you later, kiddo," Susan whispered.

ELEVEN

"WET ENOUGH, for you?" George Halpern said when Susan came dragging into his office. His gray suit coat hung over the back of his chair; his white shirt sleeves were rolled up. In his early sixties, he had gray hair with a bald spot in back. He was a compassionate man who still believed in the innate goodness of mankind despite over forty years in law enforcement, maybe because his professional life had been spent dealing with small-town crime.

"That asinine remark is one I'm tired of hearing." She nudged the chair a little closer to his desk and collapsed into it.

"Weather like this has everybody worried. Funnel clouds have touched down all around us. We're all wondering if we're going to be next."

"Don't even think it." Oh, Christ, that would really test her mettle as chief. In her year and a half in Kansas, she'd yet to see a tornado, but she'd seen the devastation they left in their wake in nearby areas, and experienced top-notch anxiety what with tornado watch, tornado warning, and tornado alert, which was when the sirens went off. One thing about earthquakes, there wasn't all that buildup. "Tell me about August Barrington."

"August," he said thoughtfully. George Halpern was invaluable; she'd never have survived as police chief without him. Invariably polite, invariably kind, with a large capacity for acceptance, he was what parents had in mind when they told their children, "If you're in trouble, go to a policeman."

Dropping his pen on the desk, he took off his wire-rimmed glasses and polished them with a handkerchief.

"August was a very nice man." He put his glasses back on, folded his hands across his comfortable mid-section, and regarded Susan with mild blue eyes. "Let me think. I know he was born in Kyane. That little town doesn't even exist anymore. It had about a hundred souls, and then people started moving away, dying of old age. The final blow was losing the post office. When that closed they weren't, anymore, listed on maps."

"George, you think we might move along a little here?"

"Now, Susan, you have to learn not to be always so much in a hurry. A good small-town cop needs to know all this local history."

"Right. Another time. Let's get along to August, successful painter."

"There are those who say painting saved his life. He was one of them. It was right sad. Highly intelligent man. Studied architecture. Won all sorts of recognition as a student. Long about that time was when he married Lydia. You know about her? Doctor. Greatly loved by the community."

A clap of thunder rattled the building. She jumped.

"Five children," George said. "But August's troubles, I believe, started early. Very shameful back then. Mental illness, poor soul. Depression. Serious depression to the point where he couldn't even move. Give her credit; Lydia hung in there with him. It couldn't have been easy. She was a proud woman. Always kept her head high and pretended to the world everything was fine. In and out of mental hospitals, August was. That was back in the days of shock treatments. Several attempts at suicide. Heavy doses of medicine. The whole thing. All very grim."

Rain lashed against the window, sounding like rifle fire.

George leaned forward, rested his elbows on the desk, and spoke louder to be heard over the noise. "That the sort of thing you want to know? He died thirteen, fourteen years ago, as I recall. Does this have anything to do with Dorothy's murder?''

"I don't know. I'm just filling in background. Being a good small-town cop.''

"We need to get cracking on this, Susan. The Barringtons are important people here. Especially Dorothy. Head of a prominent family. Already the mayor's been on the phone demanding an immediate arrest.''

"Tell me about it.'' She grimaced.

"Uh oh.'' He jumped up and dashed out.

Susan turned around to see what the problem was. Water poured in under the closed window, spilled over the sill, and ran down to soak into the carpet, an icky brown color.

George came back with a bucket, a mop, a roll of paper towels, and an armful of rags. He handed her a rag. She knelt to soak up water.

"Genetics is a funny thing.'' He stuffed rags along the sill. "Every one of those Barrington children looked like their mother: blond hair, blue eyes, fair skin. The family resemblance is strong. Then along comes the youngest. Way past the time, I expect, when Lydia thought she was done with all that. And here's Ellen looking just like her father. Dark hair, dark eyes, kind of intense. It worried Lydia something fierce. She was always watching that one with a hawk eye, checking for signs of her father's mental illness.''

"And did Ellen ever display any?'' Susan grabbed sopping rags one at a time from the sill, wrung them out over the bucket, and replaced them.

"Not that I ever heard. Poor kid. But then the Barringtons would have kept that real far under wraps. She did give them trouble, but not that kind.''

"What kind?'' Jesus, this rain wasn't falling, it was horizontal.

"Not our kind either. She was always just a defiant little thing. Never loud or rowdy or scrappy, just obstinate and

planted like a rock when she didn't want to move.'' He
plied the mop against the indoor-outdoor type carpeting and
squeezed it over the bucket.

"Dorothy never had any children of her own."

"That she didn't. Maybe didn't want any. After her
mother died, she was left in charge. Strong woman, Lydia,
and Dorothy was just like her. Took care of the four
younger siblings, saw they got educated. Even after they
all grew up, she thought they still needed looking after. And
like her mother, she worried about that youngest. Ellen just
didn't fit in with the rest of them. Never did what she was
told. Carl was a little bit that way too.''

"He went to medical school, ended up working at the
clinic." The rain was winning; the puddle on the carpet
kept growing.

"He did that, finally came through like he was supposed
to, but there were times when she would tear her hair about
him. One time when he was in high school, he and a friend
set off to join the Marines.''

"What happened?"

"Dorothy sent somebody after them and brought them
home. I don't really believe he meant to do it. I think Carl
just wanted to rattle her. She kept too firm a hand on him.
He was a wild driver, speeding and reckless. Parties when
he was at school. He was too smart, was his problem. Never
had to work to learn anything. Graduated high school at
fifteen and college at eighteen. Sailed right through medical
school with honors. Not like Willis. Willis always had to
bend his mind and labor away.'' George left to empty the
bucket.

"What about Marlitta?" she asked when he returned.

"No trouble with her. She did what she was told, no
argument, never got out of line.''

Maybe there were advantages to being an only child,
Susan thought, although as a kid she'd felt deprived and
longed for an older sister. Her best friend in first grade was

always talking about "my sister, Sybil." Susan, intensely jealous, had made up a sister just so she could say "my sister, Jacqueline." She'd thought Jacqueline a much prettier name than Sybil.

When the rain slacked off, at least started coming down instead of coming in, she went back to her own office. She turned on the desk lamp, edged aside the three piles of messages—first stack, important; center, not important but better get to right away; third, no importance at all but get around to when time permitted—and found what she was searching for.

Ballistics had come through on the slugs. A match. No surprise. The bullet from Jen's heart and the one that had killed Dorothy had been fired from the same weapon.

She picked up the phone and asked Osey to come to her office.

A moment later, he ambled in. "Ma'am?"

"Any luck with Dorothy's neighbors?"

He folded himself into the armchair with a series of uncoordinated jerks. "Found out a little. Doesn't amount to much. Dorothy went over to the Coffee Cup Café, walked over, appears like. They were real busy at noon. People nodded hello and not much else. She got a chicken sandwich and took it with her, stopped by the door outside, and got a newspaper from the box."

Osey raked straw-colored hair off his forehead. "There was a gardener working across the street from the house. He saw her drive in sometime midday. He couldn't give me any time closer than that. Said Dorothy was in the house maybe twenty-five, thirty minutes and then drove away again."

So. Dorothy took her sandwich and paper into the park, sat on a bench, read as she ate. Found the bit about the painting and scooted off home. Why home? Talk to her husband? Then she stalked into Meer's gallery and demanded to see her father's painting. Went back to the medical office and made phone calls to all her siblings. Why did she call them?''

Mentally, Susan heard her former boss in San Francisco accuse her of speculating ahead of the evidence.

"What about Taylor?" she asked. "Anybody see him yesterday?"

"Two car dealers. Haven't found anybody so far who saw him at home around the right time. Pretty much run out of people to ask."

She opened Dorothy's newspaper out on the desk, turned it around, and tapped the filler about the painting with an index finger. Osey unfolded himself and bent over to read it. He looked up at her.

"Get onto the *Kansas City Star*," she said. "Find out who wrote this and where the information came from. Get names, who sold and who bought."

"I'll do it." He straightened up and waited with an inquiring look.

"That's all."

He nodded and ambled out. The phone rang and she picked it up.

"Brookvale Hospital just called," Hazel said.

NOT BOTHERING with the elevator, Susan raced up the stairs to ICU. The very air seemed bubbly with jubilation. Dr. Sheffield, wearing scrub greens, stood at the nurses' station making a notation on a chart. He caught sight of her, slid the chart back into place, and gave her a dazzling smile.

"We are all walking around three inches off the floor," he said. He seemed set to leap in the air and click his heels.

"What happened?"

He looked at his watch. "Forty-three minutes ago that incredible little girl opened her eyes and looked around."

Susan felt like she'd been kicked in the stomach; she couldn't get air in her lungs.

"By God, let's hear it for modern medicine. The system

worked. Everybody knew his job and did it without fumbling. They were right there. They came through." In dry medical terms, he laid out physiological details of why everything had worked.

He shook his head. "Oh, Jesus. This is sweet. A miracle." He grinned at her. "The truth is probably closer to a whole lot of luck. And timing. And aggressive paramedics. Minor evidence like no heartbeat and no respiration didn't slow them down."

Susan's heart was beating so loudly she almost couldn't hear him. "Jen's going to be all right?"

"Oh, well," his voice dropped into professional caution. "She is still a very sick little girl. And she's got a long way to go."

The grin broke out again. "Oh, sweet Jesus." He made a wide half-circle with his thumb and middle finger and gazed at them. "I had my fingers plugging holes in her heart." He looked at Susan, shook his head. "A goddamn miracle."

She felt a grin stretch across her own face. "I have to see her."

Abruptly, he gathered up the shreds of professional demeanor. "Oh, hey, you can't subject her to any kind of questioning. I meant it when I said she's still critical."

"Yes."

He crossed his arms and looked at her. "I'll give you two minutes."

She nodded.

"I will be there, and when I say no more, that's it."

"Yes."

Jen looked pretty much as she had when Susan last saw her: face splotchy-red, lying perfectly still, eyes closed, tubes and wires snaking around her, monitor bleeping and flickering. Except her thin chest rose and fell on its own. No hiss of the respirator.

Susan crept slowly to the railed bed, lump in her throat the size of a melon. "Jen?" she said softly.

Jen's eyes opened, those unusual yellow-green eyes, sleepy and unfocused.

Suddenly realizing her chest was aching for air, Susan took a breath. "Hi, kiddo."

"...Susan...?" Jen's voice was hoarse and so faint Susan had to lean close to hear her.

She picked up Jen's hand and closed both of hers around it. "You are some fantastic kid. You know that?"

Jen moved her head, eyes drifting to Dr. Sheffield over Susan's shoulder.

"You're lots better."

The monitor bleeped and spiked. Dr. Sheffield watched it closely.

"...don't..."

"I'm proud of you."

"...was?" Jen's eyelids fluttered closed.

"We're going to the ballet. Soon."

"...black...black...can't...remember..."

Dr. Sheffield touched Susan's elbow and shook his head. He jerked a thumb over his shoulder.

Susan nodded. "You're doing just great," she murmured to Jen, and gently squeezed her hand. "I'm going to leave now. You get lots of rest. I'll be back later."

She followed Adam Sheffield out to the corridor.

"The memory loss isn't unusual," he said. "It often occurs after a severe trauma."

"Yes."

"It may all come back, or bits and pieces, or she may never remember."

"Yes."

She managed to hold it together until she got to the parking lot, then she lost it. Her legs felt rubbery; tears welled up and she couldn't see. After all the rain, the sun was dazzling. She found the pickup through a watery blur and bent her head against the side window. It felt hot.

The door handle burned her fingers when she opened it. She slid inside, found a tissue in her bag, and mopped her face. On the way back to the department, she had to stop twice; tears leaked all over, and she couldn't see where she was going.

She edged into a parking space and just sat there. Come on. Pull yourself together. Stiff upper lip. The show must go on. Halellujah. Hallelujah. Oh, dear God.

She slid from the pickup, blouse sticking to her back.

"Susan?"

Her head snapped up; she turned and almost stumbled into Parkhurst. He put a hand on her elbow to steady her.

"You okay?"

"Yes. Oh, yes. The world may not be such a bad place after all. The birds will sing. The sun will shine." That seemed pretty funny, since the birds were already singing, the sun already shining, so bright his white shirt made her squint. Joy fizzed in her throat. "She is alive."

His dark eyes lit up, a smile flashed across his face, and he caught her in a hug. She wrapped her arms around him, and snatches of an old song zinged through her mind— "Oh, what a beautiful morning, oh, what a beautiful day."

Her forehead rested against his throat. His skin felt warm, smelled faintly of soap and sunshine. She was aware of traffic sounds, the faraway scream of a jet, his heartbeat. On the street a car horn honked. She started, stepped back.

A guarded look closed over his face. "Did you talk to the girl?" His voice sounded husky.

"Briefly." She sounded breathless. She started toward the door, Parkhurst in step beside her. "She wasn't about to tell me anything." She related what Sheffield had said about Jen's memory loss.

Parkhurst reached for the door and held it open for her. Cool air rushed at her. She wondered if her face looked as flushed as it felt. She headed straight for her office; he veered off toward the corridor with the soft drink machine, and she heard the clink of coins and the thunk of cans rolling down. She hung her bag over the coat tree and sat behind the desk.

A moment later, he came in with a can in each hand and held one toward her. She took it. Moisture beaded on the outside, and she wanted to rub it across her forehead.

He stood a moment with his back toward her, looking out the window, then turned, took three paces, and slouched in the armchair in front of the desk, legs stretched out in front of him. He took a long sip of cola. "I've been poking around some, trying to get a better handle on the money picture. I've convinced the Barrington attorney to grant us an appointment tomorrow morning."

"Good." She thought she'd get herself out of here, before the mayor called again. Head home. Some sleep would help too. Suddenly, she was aware that the silence seemed to have gotten heavy. She looked at Parkhurst and found him watching her. Her pulse picked up.

"Susan—"

She stood up. "What?"

He waited a beat, then also rose. He started to say something, then changed his mind and said matter-of-factly, "See you in the morning."

She nodded curtly and waited until he left before she moved, greatly relieved he hadn't said whatever it was he was going to say. With Dorothy's murder and Jen's precarious hold on life, her defenses weren't as impenetrable as they should be. If she wasn't careful, she was apt to do something she would, without a doubt, regret.

TWELVE

THE AIR in Parkhurst's Bronco was thick with ignored tension as he drove them to the attorney's office on Monday morning. He looked darkly handsome in a blue suit Susan had never seen before.

He glanced at her with a thin-lipped smile. "Thug in disguise."

My thoughts must be showing.

The Barrington attorney had offices in a Victorian house that had started out as someone's family home. The grounds had well-trimmed grass, neat shrubs, and well-disciplined flowers in flower beds. Anything so mundane as parking space was delegated to the rear, where it wouldn't be seen.

A secretary ushered them into the presence. Leland Hawkins sat behind a desk large enough to be rented out to a small family. He might glory in the past, but his tailor didn't. The pinstriped suit was strictly today and fitted beautifully. Hawkins must be at least eighty. He was thin, with sparse white hair, patrician features, and gnarled fingers that suggested arthritis. He unhurriedly finished what he was writing before he looked up to acknowledge them. The office was weighty with dark wood paneling, substantial armchairs around a table, a dark-red carpet and drapes. It looked like something out of Dickens. She halfway expected to be offered a glass of sherry. Hawkins obviously didn't deal with anything as messy as criminals.

He frowned his displeasure at this disruption of his orderly routine, then rose, walked around his desk, and offered a hand for Parkhurst to shake. To her, he offered a nod and a murmured "Mrs. Wren." He fairly oozed with legal importance.

She decided wisdom lay in letting Parkhurst do the talking, and gave him a barely perceptible nod. Hawkins wasn't a man who would take kindly to being asked questions by a mere female.

"As I informed you on the phone, there is nothing I can tell you."

"Good of you to give us your time," Parkhurst said. "We understand the sensitivity of the situation and would be only too appreciative of anything you might be able to tell us."

My, my. She didn't know Parkhurst had it in him.

"There is the matter of confidentiality."

"We understand that, sir, and are fully aware of your concern. Perhaps you might allow us to ask a few questions?"

A laugh tickled her throat. She covered it with a cough. Hawkins glanced at her reprovingly, as though she'd done something unseemly.

"As long as you understand, we may as well sit down." Hawkins gestured toward the armchairs and waited until Susan was seated, then pinched the crease in his trousers and lowered his bony rear to the waiting leather.

"As I informed you on the telephone—" Hawkins spoke directly to Parkhurst, what he had to say was beyond her understanding "—there is nothing I am at liberty to tell you."

"As you, no doubt, are aware, there has been a—" Parkhurst paused.

She wondered whether he was considering sticking in an adjective like "dastardly."

"—murder. We need to discover all we can about Dr. Barrington's financial affairs."

Hawkins frowned with the regret of a teacher at a pupil he'd thought was coming along nicely, but had just made a glaring error. "That's precisely what I cannot talk about."

Parkhurst nodded. "Perhaps you can explain a few things for us. Have you always been the Barrington attorney?"

"Yes, I guess I could say that. Lydia Barrington and I—" With the ponderous dignity of a turtle, Hawkins rotated his head to explain to Susan. "Lydia was Dorothy's mother." Slowly, his head turned back to Parkhurst. "We had known each other for a long time. I took care of all her legal matters."

"And you knew August Barrington?"

"I did."

"Did he have a will?"

"Since that is a matter of public record, I believe I can answer that. I drew up wills for both August and Lydia. This was when August first started having so much difficulty with his illness. The wills were drawn up leaving all they possessed to the surviving spouse. At that time they didn't have much in the way of monetary assets. It was quite the acceptable thing to do. Later on, of course, the situation changed."

"Changed how?"

"There were oil rights, which came to August through his family. And then August began to make a name through his art. I suggested at one point they might want to make changes in the wills, since so much more monies were involved, but Lydia felt no need."

"Everything went to Lydia when August died. She must have made a new will after his death."

"Certainly." Hawkins bestowed on Parkhurst a peevish glance, as though remission of duties had been implied. "With the exception of certain bequests to charities of special interest to her, the bulk of her estate went to Dorothy, to be hers for her lifetime. At Dorothy's death, it was to be divided equally among the siblings."

Susan recrossed her legs. Talk about motive. It's a wonder Dorothy survived as long as she did.

"Did none of them ever contest the will?"

Hawkins shook his head. "I did suggest to Lydia that this might be a possibility she might like to think about carefully. She wouldn't hear of doing it any other way, and so, of course, I did exactly what my client wanted. There is one thing you must understand about the Barringtons. They are a proud family. They wouldn't want that kind of squabble revealed to the public."

Rather a murder than a squabble, Susan supposed.

"Even the best of the families have been brought to contentiousness by an unfavorable will."

Contentiousness?

Hawkins' mouth twitched in a slim smile. "Lydia's will has a forfeiture provision."

Of course it does, Susan thought, eyeing Hawkins with new respect. Any beneficiary foolish enough to contest the will risked losing everything he or she would have received.

"The law, you see," Hawkins droned on, "creates a presumption that the testator was competent and the will is valid. A rebuttable presumption, to be sure, but an extraordinary degree of evidence is required to overcome the presumption of validity and thus allow the will to be discredited."

"In regard to Dorothy's will," Parkhurst said. "She could not legally leave any money to anyone she chose outside the family?"

"Not the estate monies, no. Her own personal monies, of course, are entirely different. With those she was free to act as she saw fit."

"Can we assume there is nothing untoward about her will? The bulk of her estate goes to her husband?"

Hawkins tightened his thin lips. "All I can tell you is that Dorothy Barrington was a very conventional lady."

Parkhurst thanked him for the generosity of his time, Susan gave him what she hoped was a ladylike smile, and the secretary ushered them out.

The sky was a uniform gray, with ominous dark masses in one corner. The air was what you'd expect in a sauna.

Parkhurst loosened his tie and shrugged off his suit coat. He opened the door of the Bronco for her, then went around to the other side, tossed his suit coat in back, and slid under the wheel. He stuck the key in the ignition, then rolled up his shirt sleeves.

"Motive aplenty there." He twisted to look out the rear window and backed the Bronco from the slot.

"Right," she said dryly. "All we have to figure out is which one got greedy. Or which ones teamed up. That ridiculous will was just asking for trouble. You know about August?"

"Outside of his being a genius?"

She told him what she'd learned from George. "Lydia must have been a strong woman. Had to be, with five kids and a husband in the loony bin more often than not. I wonder what he was like."

"Dorothy was a relatively young woman. She could have lived another forty years. What good is money if you can't get your hands on it for forty years?" He cut over to Ninth Street, then went south on Iowa toward the campus.

"We can't rule out her husband. Taylor's probably going to inherit whatever she had. Not peanuts. What have you found out about the financial situations?"

"Odds and ends," Parkhurst said. "Some of it interesting. Taylor's a trust officer at the bank. They seem to think highly of him. No complaints."

"No hint of dipping his hand in?"

"Not that I've been able to find. Banks get very nervous when you start asking those kinds of questions. His salary, which might seem more than adequate to the ordinary working drudge, wasn't enough to keep him in Mercedeses.

For that, he had to rely on Dorothy. Maybe he got tired of asking, or maybe she got tired of giving.''

"What about the rest of them?''

He took Crescent Road to get across campus, passing old stone buildings: the Romanesque hall that housed the natural-history collection, the damaged Gothic-style auditorium, struck by lightning a year ago; fire had virtually destroyed the interior.

"With the exception of Ellen,'' he said, "they all make a lot, and they all could use more. Ellen's struggling along, barely keeping her gourd business alive—falling behind, letting the bills pile up, then just getting her nose above water again. I checked on her story about collapsed plumbing. It's true, and it's going to cost her. She doesn't have the money.''

"Carl?''

Parkhurst pulled the Bronco into the parking lot, and they set off uphill for Karr Hall, where Marlitta's husband was giving a lecture. Brent the Beautiful, as Parkhurst snidely referred to him.

"Carl is definitely not a happy man. Indications of friction between him and Dorothy. One interesting thing; he's been going around looking at land.''

"What kind of land?''

"Large acreages of farmland. With all the farmers going under, there's a lot of it out there. This has been going on for over a year, near as I can figure. I can't see why anybody in his right mind wants to farm. Maybe he wants to start a commune, retreat from the world. Drinking a little more than Dorothy approved of.''

"Anything on Willis?'' They took a path along Pauffer Lake. Two white ducks paddled serenely on the slate-gray water, rippling through the reflection of the campanile.

"Ah, the heir apparent.'' Parkhurst touched her elbow to guide her up the left fork, overhung by tall trees bright green with new leaves. "Likes being looked up to. Pillar of the community. Likes playing golf. Not too swift. Lives well.''

"Needs money?"

"No more than the others. Might have gotten tired of being second fiddle and snuffed her so he could take his rightful place. As eldest son, he felt he should have been the one left in charge, gotten all the money so he could dole it out to the sibs as he felt inclined. Resentment toward his mother, and Dorothy, who didn't always use the money the way he would have. You reckon this means money doesn't buy happiness?''

Karr Hall, the stone weathered to a creamy color, was four-story, ivy creeping up its face, air conditioners incongruously jutting out from the odd window.

In addition to his clinical practice, Brent Wakeley gave a lecture series of human development. Busy man. Or so he claimed. Maybe he compensated for being the only doctor in the medical group whose last name wasn't Barrington by getting adulation from students. They clamored to attend his lectures, fluttered around him in flocks.

Parkhurst held the door for her, and they trucked up to the second floor.

Brent was still lecturing when they found Room 220. They eased in and stood against the back wall. Every desk was occupied, and the students, predominantly female, gazed entranced. Like an actor, he spoke clearly, paused at crucial moments, and altered the shade of his voice for emphasis.

He had to be aware of two cops standing in the rear, but he didn't so much as flicker a glance. "…abandonment. Physical desertion. Left all alone. It takes no great effort of imagination to realize the consequences in a child. Ah, but what about physical presence and emotional abandonment? To be abandoned by the physically present creates even more far-reaching results.''

His voice, rich and resonant, was used expertly. As he

spoke, he paced back and forth in front of the class and along one side, occasionally brushing a hand through dark hair that fell appealingly over his forehead. The dramatic effect was enhanced by his clothing: black pants, turtleneck, and jacket.

The stage setting was perfect: gray sky outside two tall, narrow windows, shadowy room. He ought to be pacing around emoting to be or not to be, she thought.

"We give of our time to that which we love, be it activities or people. The impact of not having the parents' time and attention engenders feelings of worthlessness in a child. There is something wrong with me, or else my mother or my father would want to be with me."

He paused to let his words be absorbed and let the notetakers catch up. "The child's identity comes from the mirroring eyes of the parent or caretaker. Children can't learn who they are without these reflective mirrors. In the nonverbal early stages emotional interaction is crucial. Emotionally damaged parents are unable to affirm the child's emotions. Without this affirmation he cannot thrive.

"As this child grows, he is loved for his achievements, she is loved for her performance. He or she develops in such a way as to reveal only what is expected. The result?" He paused and lowered his voice. "Disconnection with feelings."

Susan looked at Parkhurst. He raised an eyebrow, crossed his arms, and propped a shoulder against the wall.

"This child develops a sense of emptiness, loneliness, and futility." Wakeley strode to the front of the room, leaned back against the desk, and gripped the edges with his hands.

Susan felt like applauding. The class sat perfectly still, as enthralled as an audience when the curtain falls on Act One.

"Next class," Wakeley said into the silence. "Denial,

idealization, repression, disassociation. Survival mechanisms."

Conversation rose as the students gathered their books and notebooks and drifted toward the door. One young woman, an armload of books clutched to her chest, went up to speak to him. He stopped popping books and notes into a briefcase and listened to her, actually listened, looked at her while she spoke, gave her his undivided attention: intoxicating to young female students. A charismatic, flamboyant man, the stuff of which romantic fantasies are made.

"Slaying dragons for the fair maiden, you think?" Parkhurst said softly. "Born too late. He'd look great with tights and a sword."

Wakeley asked the student something. She nodded, tossed blond hair over her shoulder, and responded earnestly. Wakeley smiled, and patted her shoulder, and she tripped out, pretty young face flushed, eyes shining. Wakeley picked up his briefcase and strode toward the door, putting on a great act of being unaware of them.

"Dr. Wakeley?" Parkhurst held out his ID. "A few questions."

Brent Wakeley sighed, switched the briefcase to his other hand, and shoved the free hand through his forelock. "More about Dorothy, I assume." Without waiting for a response, he said, "My office. This way." He turned right and strode down the corridor, not bothering to check if they were following.

"The take-charge type," Parkhurst muttered.

"Without a doubt."

Several paces in the rear, they followed him down the corridor and down the stairs and caught up with him as he pulled keys from his pocket and unlocked a door.

"I have an appointment at the clinic in forty-five minutes," he told them.

Susan smiled pleasantly. "I certainly hope we'll be finished by then."

Wakeley moved behind the gray metal desk, stood looking at them for a moment, and then sat down. The window at his back framed a large maple tree; beyond were hills crisscrossed with footpaths and buildings obscured by trees. A ray of sunshine poking through the clouds made his hair gleam blue-black like the iridescent feathers of a crow. He wasn't as young as he liked to pretend—mid-forties, most likely, with tiny lines around the eyes and a slight softening to the chiseled jaw.

A laptop computer sat on the desk, surrounded by stacks of books and papers. File cabinet, two shabby chairs covered with a worn fabric, prints on the wall. Bookcase crammed with books, center shelf sagging under the weight.

"Please have a seat." He gestured to the two chairs, as though the interview being conducted on his turf would be dictated by his terms.

She'd been a cop enough years to recognize bravado when she saw it. She wondered what he was trying to prove. Or hide.

"I don't know why you're wasting your time here," he said. "There's not a thing I can tell you."

"Background information is always useful," she murmured. She stood in front of his desk, forcing him to look up at her. He wasn't intimidated, regarded her openly, a polite look of skepticism on his handsome face.

"How long have you been a cop?" he asked.

She was aware that Parkhurst made a slight shift in his stance behind her, irritated by Wakeley's stage-managing. "Long enough to recognize evasion when I hear it."

Wakeley studied her with the same intent interest he'd given the student. "I was just wondering about your background. Why people become police officers is often quite revealing."

"My background has no relevance."

He switched his gaze to Parkhurst. "How about yours, Lieutenant?"

Parkhurst, standing in the doorway, was at his most wooden.

"Did you know that a great many cops come from alcoholic families?"

"That right?"

Wakeley turned the full blast of his charm back onto her. "What did you want to ask me?"

She shifted books and papers unceremoniously from a chair to the floor, sat down, and took out her notebook. "Where were you at one-thirty on Saturday afternoon?"

"I believe I've already answered that. More than once, I may add. So if that's all—"

"If you'd just answer the question, sir."

His good humor started to slip. He grabbed a pen and tapped it against the desk. "I was right here. In this office. At this desk."

"We've not been able to corroborate that statement. How do you explain that?"

He tossed down the pen. "I don't have to explain it. But if I did, I'd say it's not that surprising. Not everybody works on Saturday."

"Why were you working on Saturday?"

"I was preparing this week's lecture."

"Here and not at home?"

"That is correct."

"Who in the family has reason to want Dorothy dead?"

"You might benefit from my next lecture, Ms. Wren."

He'd deliberately omitted her title. Reducing her stature. "Yes?"

"Denial, idealization, repression, disassociation."

"All this applies to the Barringtons?"

"Young children make themselves responsible for the abuse they suffer."

"The Barringtons were abused?"

"Not all abuse is physical." Wakeley leaned back in his chair. "The family is the scene of the most intimate and powerful of human experiences. Family situations are bloodier and more passionate than any others, and the costs are greater."

"You suggesting a member of Dorothy's family killed her?"

"The family line is a drug addict killed her simply because she happened to be there." His voice shifted from lecture mode to banter.

"You toeing the family line?"

"Yes, ma'am." He smiled.

Beautiful Brent had a beautiful smile. "You don't want Dorothy's killer found?"

The smile decayed a tad. "I certainly want to see justice prevail."

Not exactly an answer. "Anything you can tell me to gain that end?"

He shook his head. "Family pathology is part and parcel of its secrets."

Right. Sounding profound and meaning nothing. She could feel Parkhurst, even though he hadn't moved a muscle, getting steamed. "Did the Barringtons have secrets?"

"All families have secrets. There's more than one kind of secret. The secret nobody knows, and the secret everybody knows but nobody talks about. You'd be amazed at how many families harbor this type. It is often the case with alcoholism, for instance. Everybody knows Daddy's a drunk. They tiptoe around it, never mention it. The hippopotamus in the living room. You've heard of that? Nobody looks directly at it. Mama crochets a tablecloth and covers it. Everybody carefully steps around it. Nobody mentions it."

"You sound very sincere. Personal experience?"

"Quite sharp, Ms. Wren. It was something that puzzled me greatly as a child. My father had a debilitating illness."

Alcoholism, she wondered.

"How long have you been lecturing here?" Parkhurst asked.

"This will be my third year."

Parkhurst took a step closer. "Enjoy it?"

"Certainly."

"Like being looked up to?"

Wakeley lost a little of his composure. "What are you trying, in your heavy-handed way, to imply?"

"Admiration. Not getting a whole lot from these Barrington doctors down there at the clinic?"

That dart hit home, she could see.

"Room full of eager young women all looking at you with adoring eyes. Must be pretty heady stuff. Ever take advantage of all that adoration?"

Wakeley leaned back in his chair, an attitude of nonchalance that didn't come off. "You have any evidence for throwing around accusations of this sort?"

"Not an accusation, a question. Would you care to answer?"

"Give me some credit, Lieutenant," Wakeley said with exasperation. "Do I look like a stupid man? Would I risk my career, my reputation, for some eager young body?"

"I don't know. Would you?"

Wakeley shot forward in his chair, glared at him, then turned to Susan. "Don't you people have to have some evidence before you can harass the innocent? You spread this kind of thing around, and I'll slap a lawsuit on you so fast you won't even see it coming."

He leaned slightly back again and got his breathing under control. "What does any of this have to do with Dorothy?"

The man had a temper; that much was clear. "Who would want to kill her?" she asked.

"Isn't that your job?"

"Yes, Dr. Wakeley, it is my job, and it entails asking a

lot of questions, annoying questions sometimes. Dorothy's death means your wife will be coming into some money."

"Are you accusing me of killing Dorothy so Marlitta will inherit money?"

"We're not accusing you of anything, Dr. Wakeley. We're trying to find out what happened."

Suddenly, he smiled, Brent the Beautiful with a beautiful smile.

"If we're getting down to truth here, Ms. Wren, I won't deny that money is a nice thing to have. But I can tell you, in truth, that I didn't kill her."

"Who did, Dr. Wakeley? Who wanted her dead?"

"I really can't help you there. Shouldn't you be searching for the weapon? I hesitate to tell you how to do your job, but I'd think that would be your top priority."

"Do you own a gun?"

"I do not."

"Your wife?"

"Marlitta knows nothing about guns."

"I see. Does she have one?"

"No."

"Anybody else in the family? Have you ever seen any of them with a revolver?"

"No."

"Has any member of the family been acting differently lately? Anyone who has seemed more troubled?"

"Ellen. She's trying hard to be independent, self-supporting. It's a struggle in a lot of ways. Money is a part of it."

"Anyone else?"

"Taylor. He's always wanted to be a big financial success. He may have made some risky investments that he's worried about."

So the good doctor wasn't above tossing out a little spite where he could. "What kind of investments?"

"I wouldn't know. Something with the possibility of a great payoff."

"Stock market? That kind of thing?"

"Something like that, perhaps. Speculation in high-risk ventures; that would be the kind of thing he might try." Wakeley glanced at Parkhurst. "It's somewhat uncomfortable for him to be a member of the Barrington family and not have some outstanding achievement of his own."

"You think that's what he's trying to do? Gain outstanding achievement?"

"I think it's a possibility." Wakeley looked at his watch. "Now, if that's all, I have patients waiting."

"Certainly, Dr. Wakeley." Susan got to her feet. "We may need to talk with you again."

She and Parkhurst went back along the hallway and outside. The clouds were darker and larger; rain was imminent. Again.

"Talks rather well around questions, doesn't he?" Susan said.

"My daddy used to maintain, if you have to use ten-dollar words, what you're trying to say isn't worth a dime."

THIRTEEN

IF SHE HAD any sense, Marlitta thought, she'd skip dinner and go straight to bed. She dragged the chicken out of the refrigerator. No sleep last night. She barely got through the day by putting one foot in front of the other. Dorothy's patients had to be shared out to the rest of them. She got the Ackerbaugh baby. Problems there. But maybe not. Ackerbaugh was very angry. More work. So tired. Brent saying he'd be late. How could he, when he knew she needed him?

She thunked the chicken on the cabinet. Cooking was something she never really cared for. She was a Barrington; they took care of the sick. She collected potatoes from the bin and tumbled them in the sink. In the living room, the clock chimed six. Rubbing her aching head, she wondered if she was up to peeling potatoes. She hated peeling potatoes. Dirt and starchy white stuff all over her hands. She could still smell it even after she washed it off. Maybe baked potatoes.

With the point of the knife, she stabbed the plastic around the chicken and ripped it off. Blood trickled over her hand and puddled on the cabinet. Her stomach clenched. Blood. Oh, God.

Dorothy lying in a pool of blood.

For God's sake, you'd think you'd never seen blood before. When she was tired, her mind did odd things. Odd things. Dorothy dying. Odd. Something she'd thought about. Now, instead of thinking what that meant, she could only think Dorothy was gone. The police asking question after question. The family sitting around talking, pretending—

She really didn't expect they'd do anything different, but she had thought she'd be more in control of herself. Instead, she'd been awkward and apprehensive. Just like when she and Carl were young and had done something Dorothy didn't like and they waited for her to chew them out.

Last night they had all looked at each other and thought about Dorothy. Dead on the office floor. Dead and bloody. Today that piece of carpet was missing. Cut out and gone. Like Dorothy. Gone.

And they still all looked at each other and waited, as if Dorothy would walk in at any moment.

Marlitta stared at the chicken—slimy, white, dimpled skin, legs sticking out, bloody paper packet of neck and gizzard—and felt she might be sick.

Last night she'd been so tired she thought she'd drop before she'd even gotten herself to bed. She never even went to sleep. She lay there, Brent asleep next to her, and stared at the ceiling. And she'd been so cold. So cold. Even with the heat wave and Brent's warm body right beside her.

Abruptly, Marlitta turned on the tap and rinsed the clammy chicken. The doorbell rang. She started and dropped the chicken, splattering water all over herself. She leaned over the sink, holding on with all her strength.

When the bell rang again, she turned off the water, grabbed a towel, and wiped her hands as she went to the door.

"Carl," she said. Baggy jeans wearing thin at the knees, loose cotton shirt, he looked like a bum. Ragged. He really ought to dress better. "What are you doing here?"

"Thought I'd see how you were holding up. You were a little shaky today."

"Why wouldn't I be shaky?" She turned around and plodded back to the kitchen.

He closed the door and followed. "Brent not home?"

"No." With her back to him, she stared at the chicken

in the sink. A corpse with its head chopped off. "He had a meeting."

"Right."

She wheeled around. "What's that supposed to mean?"

"Nothing." He looked as tired as she felt. "Calm down."

"I can't calm down. I just can't. I think I may opt for a nervous breakdown. So peaceful. Nothing but lying in bed. No sick people to take care of. No disgusting chicken to cook." She had the urge to pick it up and throw it against the wall.

"Here. Let me do that. Sit down." He pulled out a chair and nudged her into it. "You got any tea?"

"Top left-hand cabinet."

He ran water in the tea kettle and put it on the stove, opened the cabinet, and rummaged through boxes. When the kettle shrieked, he poured hot water in a cup and dipped in a tea bag. He plunked it in front of her and turned back for the sugar bowl. "Put some sugar in it and drink it."

"I don't like hot tea." She sniffed the spicy orange flavor and felt like weeping.

He rattled around finding a roasting pan and banged it on the cabinet. "You like baked chicken?"

She nodded. Nobody would eat it anyway. She certainly couldn't eat, and God knew when Brent would get home. It just seemed important to carry on with all the usual rituals.

Carl busied himself, patting dry the chicken, sorting out spices, and peeling potatoes. "Carrots?"

"In the refrigerator."

"Where are the onions?"

She pointed.

He selected one from the bag in the pantry and reached for the chopping board. "We have to do some talking."

She took a cautious sip of tea and burned her lip. "No. I don't want to talk about it. I won't."

"Marlitta—"

"No. Willis is right. An addict looking for drugs."

"Maybe."

"Of course."

"There's no 'of course' about it. It's a possibility, but a remote one, and you better prepare yourself for a lot of nastiness."

"I don't see why. The police will look into all that. They might even find the person. They won't want to investigate us. We have standing in the community."

"You're right about one thing. They won't want to investigate us."

"There you are, then."

"But they will. They'll have to." He scraped chopped onions into a bowl.

"I don't see why."

"Oh, for Christ's sake. Because we have *standing,* as you say, they will have to solve this murder. They'll mess around with addicts and hassle a few people, but they'll keep coming back to us."

She wrapped both hands around the cup.

"Ellen's been talking to me." He put the chicken in the pan and surrounded it with potatoes and carrots.

"What about?"

"She's worried about Daddy's gun."

"What about it?"

"It's missing."

"I don't see what that matters."

"Use your head, Marlitta. The cops will find the gun. It will turn out to be the one that killed Dorothy. Then we're all up shit creek."

The room seemed to spin around. "No," she said. "Don't say it. Don't say one of us killed her."

He opened the oven door, slid the pan inside and banged the door shut, then turned to face her, leaned back against the cabinet, and crossed his arms. "It's not going to do any good to bury your head in the sand."

"I don't want to hear it."

"You never did like to look anything straight in the face." He opened the refrigerator door and selected a bottle of beer. "Imported. Going fancy." He twisted off the cap and sat down across from her.

She stared into her tea.

He took a long swallow. "Marlitta, did Dorothy ever mention Daddy's paintings to you?"

She couldn't make sense of what he was saying. Nothing made sense anymore. She squeezed the cup so tightly her fingers turned white. "Why would she? What do they have to do with—"

"I don't know. She dashed over to Comach's gallery on Saturday to find out if he'd sold the one he has."

Sold Daddy's painting? Why was she so slow and thick? Thick like blood. Thicker than water. "Had he?"

"No. Did she talk to you about them?"

Marlitta rubbed her face—it felt numb—and shook her head. "She never talked about them. Nothing's ever been said, except when Ellen wanted to take one. Right after she bought that place. She said the painting was hers and she wanted it. They fought about it, but Dorothy wouldn't let her have it."

Marlitta took a sip of tea. "Nobody ever got away with one of Daddy's paintings." She raised her eyes and looked at Carl. He looked older. When had he gotten older? "Except you."

He grinned, and suddenly looked like Carl again, the Carl she had always known, about to suggest something that would get them both into trouble. "Daddy gave it to me. I always liked it the best of all his stuff."

"I don't see how you could. It's so—"

"Marlitta, you never were one to look very far under the

surface. I got that one away before Dorothy knew what was happening, and she never could figure how to get it back.''

"I never wanted one. I don't think Dorothy liked them much either. I don't think she ever even looked at them. They were always just there. In that room.''

"When was the last time you looked at them?''

"I don't—'' She squeezed her eyes shut tight. They stung, felt dry and scratchy. "Years. I—''

"Are you sure they're all still there?''

AFTER THE RAINSTORM, the sun came out to blaze fiercely, making the most of the short time left before it had to go down. Trees dripped; water rushed along the gutters and flooded over the curbs. As Susan drove by the Tudor-style house on Kentucky Street, a car backed out of the driveway and took off in the other direction. The driver was Carl Barrington. She U-turned at the end of the block and parked in front.

With a finger against the bell, she heard the ding-dong, ding-dong, ding inside. Nobody answered. She pressed again. Just as she was about to give up, the door opened.

"Good evening, Dr. Barrington. I wonder if I could speak with you a few minutes.''

Marlitta looked at her blankly, then seemed to focus, realize who she was, and stepped back with a sigh.

The wide entry had slate tiles, and Marlitta's flat-heeled shoes made a weary thumping sound as she showed Susan into the living room.

The rich smell of roasting chicken permeated the house, making Susan hungry. Pick up something on the way home and actually cook it? Nah. It was a lot quicker to pick up something already cooked. And that way, no cleanup.

"Can I get you anything?'' Marlitta asked. "A cold drink, or some tea?'' She looked tired to the point of dropping, still dressed in working clothes: a gray skirt, a white blouse, and hose.

"No thank you. I have only a few questions."

Susan was struck by how much Marlitta resembled her older sister, but a blurred, softer version; her hair, slightly longer but still short, was lighter, her face less defined. A plain woman, not unattractive, but next to her startlingly handsome husband, she must look drab. She blended in with the muted colors of the room. Two chairs in a soft peach color, and a couch in a still paler peach, two watercolors above the couch: a bride being driven in a horse-drawn wagon to a church in the distance, and a row of ducks in tall grass by the edge of a stream.

Marlitta dropped into the wing chair as though she couldn't take another step. "I'm sorry I seem so slow-witted, but I really don't think there's anything else I can tell you."

Susan settled on the couch. "Is your husband home?"

"I'm sorry," Marlitta said again. A smile flickered thinly across her face. "I seem to be saying that a lot lately. Brent isn't home yet. He has some kind of meeting."

Susan wondered whether Brent's meeting was with a female.

"There's really nothing he can tell you. He knows nothing about Dorothy's—about what happened. He was on campus Saturday afternoon."

So he claimed. "We have to keep going over things. I know it's difficult, but it is important. What happened the week before Dorothy's death?"

"Nothing happened," Marlitta said with a bewildered shake of her head. "It was an ordinary week."

"Nothing at all unusual or different?"

"No."

"You must have talked with her."

"Of course. We talked about patients, other things. I don't know. There wasn't anything. I'm truly sorry—" She stopped and sighed. "There I go again. I've tried to think, but really there was nothing."

This family didn't seem to go in much for cozy chats with each other. If Dorothy'd had anything on her mind, she might not have mentioned it to any of them. But unless the perp had indeed skulked into the medical building and shot Dorothy for no other reason than because she'd caught him, something had led up to her death. "What did Dorothy like to do when she wasn't working?"

A facsimile of a smile. "Dorothy was always working." Marlitta laced her fingers, held her hands palm up in her lap, and talked to them. "She liked to play the piano. We all played together. Used to. We haven't done that much lately."

"You all play the piano?"

"Only Dorothy. She said it relaxed her. Carl and I— Oh, how we hated to practice." Marlitta separated her hands and smoothed the skirt over her knees.

"She'd been—" Marlitta paused. "Oh, I don't know, remembering things."

"What things?"

"I don't know if that's the right way to say it. I don't mean depressed or anything like that. Feeling nostalgic perhaps. Actually, I believe she was quite liking it."

"Liking what?"

"Gathering up all the old photographs. Going through them."

"Did she do that often?"

"None of us had looked at those old pictures for years. They were just packed away someplace in the house. You can't imagine what-all is packed away in that house. She found it kind of fun, I think, going through them. Albums and boxes."

"Why was she doing this?"

"The Historical Society—well, it's really Holly Dietz— wants to do a photo book of the early history of Hampstead. She asked Dorothy to bring her old pictures. Oh—" Marlitta rubbed her eyes. "Friday, I think, she meant to do that."

"Dorothy did some work at the battered women's shelter. Did that pose any difficulties for her?"

Marlitta took in a slow breath; otherwise she simply sat like a lump. Susan couldn't tell if she was avoiding an answer or if the switch in subject had come too fast for her.

"It made her mad. She got very angry that the men would do such a thing. And even angrier when the women wouldn't even get themselves out of the situation."

"It's not always—"

"I know. It's not as simple as all that."

"Did anyone ever threaten her?"

"I don't—" Something shifted in her eyes. Susan had no idea where to go with it. "Maybe."

"Who?"

"I don't know. She got a phone call at the office."

"When?"

"One day last week. I don't even know what was said. Only that Dorothy said she wasn't intimidated by threats."

"What else did she say?"

Marlitta shook her head.

"What might the threat have been?"

"I don't— Dorothy is—was—very strong. She'd never let anything stop her from doing what she felt was right."

Marlitta's fatigue and air of confusion seemed real, but something about this threatening phone call smelled like a false scent to lead the dogs astray.

"What can you tell me about Debra Cole?"

"I don't understand what you want to know. She's worked for us for several years. Her work's always been satisfactory. She's—" Marlitta closed her eyes and shivered. "I'm really very tired. Could we do this another time?"

"Of course." Susan stood up. "I'm sorry to bother you. Do you know Ed Cole?"

"Debra's husband? Yes. Well, only who he is." Marlitta put the heels of her hands against her face and rubbed them down her temples and over her cheeks. "I don't think there's anything I can tell you about him."

Susan left carrying her own brand of fatigue, the fatigue and irritation she always got when an investigation was still bits and pieces and she didn't yet know which pieces were useful and which should be thrown away. She climbed into the pickup and pointed its nose toward Brookvale Hospital.

Jen's mother was standing by the elevator when the doors opened. "Oh," she said. Makeup perfect, brown hair in tumbling curls, Terry wore a full skirt, red with white swirls, and a white blouse with ruffles down the front. She snapped open a straw handbag and made sharp little jabs into it.

"You're going to talk to her again, aren't you?" Ordinarily a bubbly woman, all smiles and dimples, Terry had no fizz around Susan. "You're just going to bring it all back. She needs to forget. Remembering makes her sicker. How can she get better if you keep on at her about it?"

Jen would not be safe until the killer was caught, even with word spread around that she hadn't seen her attacker, knew nothing. "I'll try not to upset her."

"Why can't you leave her alone? You're giving her bad dreams."

What Terry really wanted to say, Susan thought, was stay away from my daughter.

Terry stepped into the elevator, and the doors closed on a face of unguarded dislike.

With a sigh, Susan trekked into ICU. Terry's attitude made difficulties. The last thing Susan wanted was to cause conflicts for Jen.

Jen had her eyes closed, face splotchy-red with measles.

The monitors bleeped and flickered; an IV tube dripped fluid into one arm.

"Hi," Susan said softly.

Jen's eyes opened sleepily. "Mom?" focused, then blurred. "...worries." Her voice was faint, the words squishy.

"Moms worry. They're programmed that way."

"...yeah."

"Everybody's been doing some worrying."

A faded grin. "...you?"

"Especially me." Susan nudged the chair closer and plopped down. "You're really something. A hero."

Jen shifted her shoulders, embarrassed. "...didn't...do anything."

"You survived. Feel like talking?"

"...I guess." Her eyes closed. "...can't...remember..."

"You remember going to the doctor's office?"

"Yeah." She opened her eyes. "Sad...sorta mad...the ballet."

"When the doctor says okay, and your mom says okay—" that part might be hard come by "—we're going."

"...promise?"

"Absolutely."

"...okay."

"Is it scary to talk about what happened?"

"Sort of..." Words breathy, soft. "Like a dream... like...didn't really happen."

"Your mom said you're having dreams. What about?"

"...dumb."

"Dreams aren't dumb. They're just dreams. You ever hear of anybody who had smart dreams?"

"Don't...make sense."

"Is it a scary dream?"

"...kinda." Jen pinched a crease in the sheet; eyelids drooped shut. "I'm in...some place...dark. A monk."

"What does he do?"

"Black robe...hood...can't see..."

"Then what?"

Jen's words came even more slowly as she drifted toward the dream. "Belt...rope thing...like in pictures...medieval times..."

"Right. What then?"

"Hood turns...looks at me..." Her eyes opened, gazed unseeing. "No face...just black and...a skull...like a pin." She touched her shoulder just below the collarbone. "The arm raises...the sleeve, and he...points...at me...a finger...long, bony finger."

She blinked, looked at Susan. "Dumb."

"Sounds pretty scary."

"...yeah."

"What happens after that?"

"Nothing." Jen moved her head slightly back and forth on the pillow as though checking the reality of it. "Who...shot...?"

"I'm working on it. What do you remember about being in the doctor's office?"

"Kinda not...anything."

Susan patted her wrist. "You probably remember more than you think. You remember being in the waiting room?"

"I guess so."

"The doctor came, and you went with her."

"...open mouth...stick out tongue..."

"Yes. Close your eyes and think for a minute. You're sitting on the examining table. Dr. Barrington asks you to stick out your tongue."

Her eyelids were so heavy that Jen didn't have any trouble closing them. "Throat culture." Surprise at remembering. "She went...to get...a Q-Tip thing...stuck it down my throat."

"You're doing great. Now what happens?"

"She left...pretty soon...bang. I went...to see...and..."

"What?"

"On the floor...and blood...all this blood."

"Yes," Susan murmured. "A lot of blood. What else did you see?"

"...nothing."

"Did you hear anything?"

Jen moved her head. "I remember...thinking, 'Wow... so much blood'...and then...I don't...remember anything..."

Susan hesitated about pushing too much. Narrative questions—the tell-me-what-happened variety—generally produced the most accurate information. Interrogatory stuff—did you see this, did you hear that—brought out more details. The problem was the details weren't necessarily correct. More errors occurred when subjects were urged to answer specific questions than when they were allowed to choose their own specifics.

Picking words carefully so she didn't plant a suggested response, she said, "When you saw Dr. Barrington on the floor, what else did you see?"

"...only...black...a shadow." Her eyes opened.

The killer must have been in the hallway. Dorothy came from the examining room, angled across the hall toward her office, and went in. Got what she came for, started to leave, and was shot. A second or two must have passed before Jen came running out. She focused on the body—all that blood, a riveting sight for an eleven-year-old.

Then Jen herself was shot.

"You've been great. You don't have to think about it anymore. If you remember something else later, just tell me. You know Officer White?"

Jen nodded, weary.

"He's just outside there. If you want me, he'll get me right away."

"...okay." The eyelids drooped again.

Susan stood up, put her hand over Jen's, and squeezed. "I'll be back later."

Damn. She jabbed the button for the elevator. She'd hoped for something on the shooter. Size, shape, sex. Anything to work with. Jen had given her the grim reaper.

FOURTEEN

ELLEN PADDED QUIETLY into the kitchen in search of breakfast. Carl was right. There were lots of guns in this world. Just because Dorothy had been shot, it didn't mean she was shot with Daddy's gun. "Oh, yes?" a little voice way back in her mind said. "Then why is it missing?"

Opening the cabinet door, she peered at the shelf, pulled down a box of cornflakes, and shook some in a bowl. From the refrigerator she took a carton of milk, sloshed a dollop over the cereal, and picked up her spoon.

Taylor came into the kitchen and, with little more than a glance at her, got a glass and filled it with orange juice. "I heard you up early."

"Trouble sleeping."

He looked at the orange juice, tipped the glass, and sipped. "I'm having the same problem."

She believed him. Even freshly shaved, neatly brushed, and properly dressed in conservative suit, white shirt, and subdued tie, he looked like he hadn't had any sleep. His face was sallow, with deep lines from nose to mouth and a haunted, worried look in his eyes.

She tried to see him objectively. Attractive, in a quiet sort of way. Dark hair with silver at the temples, neatly trimmed, but there was something slick about him, polished, as though he put on a facade when he put on the suit. He fit the picture of staid banker, if you didn't look too closely.

He hadn't said a word about her staying here. Would he like to boot her out? This house was so much a Barrington monument, maybe he was the one who felt like a guest.

She sure didn't. She felt like home. And there was something wrong with that.

She wished she knew what he was so worried about, then felt tons of shame. His wife had been brutally murdered. Wasn't that enough? She was more of a Barrington than she admitted. How neat and tidy if Taylor were guilty.

"Taylor, why did Dorothy want us all here Saturday night?"

Something slipped very fast across his face and slid under—simulated?—pain and grief.

Superflash: he knew why.

"I told you, all of you, I don't know. I wasn't even aware she'd asked you."

"That doesn't sound like Dorothy."

He sipped orange juice. "I'm sure she meant to tell me, but before she could, she was—" He pinched the bridge of his nose.

Ellen felt a gush of sympathy. Sorrow? They should be sharing this. They were all knocked out, all isolated in their own space, and couldn't reach for each other.

"It might be—" he said hesitantly.

"What?"

"It may have had something to do with Carl."

"Carl? What about him?"

"She was worried about him."

"Why?"

Taylor took a slow breath, placed the orange juice glass carefully in the sink, and said evenly. "She thought he was drinking too much. She was afraid it was affecting his work."

"Dorothy told you this?" Fat chance. Barringtons never told anybody anything. Especially each other.

"I guess there was something going on in Carl's life. He wanted money."

Taylor was deliberately tossing suspicion on Carl. Any

sympathy she'd felt just went right out the window. This stuff pointed the finger away from himself.

"Sorry to disappoint you," he said as though he knew what she was thinking. "I know how much you'd all like it to be me, but I didn't kill her." He fished car keys from his pocket. "You Barringtons always think you're better than everybody else."

Not me. I'm the one not good enough nohow.

"I'm not going to let you, any of you pin it on me," he said.

From the kitchen window, she watched him back his shiny maroon Mercedes from the garage and drive away. He was nervous; he was scared; he was worried. She planted that firmly in mind to overshadow the nonsense about Carl.

She dumped her soggy cereal and put the bowl, along with Taylor's glass, in the dishwasher. She wished she knew where he was going, or, more to her purpose, how long he'd be gone.

She wasn't exactly sure why she felt the urgent need to search the house: the gun, of course, and some indication of why Dorothy had told them all to come here Saturday night. Whatever the reason it must have something to do with her murder. The cops had already searched, but they didn't know the place like she did.

When Ellen found herself tiptoeing along the ten-foot-wide hallway with its crystal chandelier, she made herself walk normally. It didn't help. She still felt like a guilty, sneaky snot. The empty bedrooms were easy: a quick look through closets, under beds, and in dresser drawers. There were seven of them, and even before she finished the last one, she realized how impossible the whole idea was. The house was too big. Originally built as Hampstead's first hospital, in addition to eight bedrooms, six bathrooms, ten fireplaces, living room and dining room, it had a sunroom, music room, library, kitchen and pantry, and two small office rooms, one used by Dorothy and one by Taylor.

Too many possible hiding places. The gun could be squirreled away in some small niche easily overlooked. It would take weeks to search thoroughly, and even then she couldn't be sure. This was stupid, and she was already hot and sweaty. Give it up.

The door to the room with Daddy's painting was closed. It always was. She didn't open it. She didn't feel up to seeing the paintings. They were sort of humorous, but mostly sad. They made her cry. Always a man in some kind of overwhelming isolation.

None of them had really known Daddy. The ever-ready tears popped out. Silly to get so emotional. She'd never really known her mother either. And she certainly didn't know her siblings.

She paused in the doorway of Dorothy's bedroom. First her parents, now Dorothy and Taylor's. It was much the same as it had always been: antique mahogany four-poster bed with carved headboard, heavy mahogany dresser, rocker with curved armrests. Windows on two sides let in bright light filtered through crisp lace curtains.

Ellen felt edgy even standing in the doorway. She'd never make a detective, too many restricting inhibitions. She went downstairs and along to the offices tucked away toward the rear.

The hell with principles, she told herself firmly, and went into Dorothy's office. I'm doing this for a reason, not just to snoop. She sat at Dorothy's desk and looked at the stack of medical books on one corner with bookmarks sticking out. She opened drawers. Neat, as she'd known they would be. Stationery, envelopes, prescription pads, pens, correspondence. She quickly flipped through letters; none seemed relevant. Canceled checks, filed in boxes. This was ridiculous. She wouldn't know anything important even if she found it.

She went through the connecting door into Taylor's office. Originally, these two small rooms had been one, used to store linens in the hospital days. A small desk, a recliner, and a file cabinet. She continued to ignore the voice in her head nagging that she had no business being here. Just hurry before he comes back.

She started going through desk drawers. They weren't neat like Dorothy's, but neither were they any more interesting. The bottom right-hand drawer was locked. Well, well. What might be in here? The desk had belonged to her father. She had no idea what he might have kept in it, if anything, but she did know where there used to be a key.

She trotted upstairs and nipped into the sunroom. The window ledges had storage places beneath that were used for music. Kneeling at the south window, she raised the hinged top and removed books—Wagner, Bach, Telemann, Scarlatti—and loose sheet music, then ran her fingers along the edges at the bottom.

The key was there, along with some dust. If Dorothy had known about the dust, she'd have seen to it immediately. Back in Taylor's office, Ellen slipped the small key into the lock and turned it. The lock made the tiniest click. Heart kicking up a beat, she slid open the drawer. Inside were file folders, two of them. One held bank statements and canceled checks; the other was full of correspondence.

She opened it out on the desk and read the note on top: *It's all going to work out fine. Just come up with the money.* It was signed with the initial H. Below the note was a sheet of paper filled with figures.

Feeling that any moment someone was going to demand to know what she was doing, she flipped through bank statements. They meant nothing to her. Money deposited, checks written. Receipt for safe deposit rental.

There must be a reason Taylor kept this in a locked drawer, but if there was anything incriminating here, she wasn't smart enough to spot it. Wait a minute. At the back, photographs. Aerial photographs. Four of them. And one of them— She squinted closely. A section of her land? Couldn't be. From the air, hills and trees all looked alike. She laid them out side by side on the desk.

A car came up the driveway. He's back!

Heart ticking away in her throat, she shuffled papers together, stacked the photos, shoved the file back in the drawer, and twisted the lock. She slipped the key in her pocket and scurried out.

The front door opened. "Hello?"

Not Taylor, Marlitta. "Up here." Ellen hurried to the stairs and trotted down.

"Where's Taylor?"

"I don't know. He left a couple hours ago."

Marlitta seemed as haggard as Taylor had. Ellen thought they probably all had that same pinched, worried expression. Marlitta, in working attire—a dark skirt, a tailored white blouse, and sensible shoes—was put together with less care than usual. There was a smudge on the skirt, and the blouse was unevenly tucked in. Ellen was looking— really looking—at all her siblings, and had the bizarre thought that none of them looked like she'd thought. "Shouldn't you be at the clinic?"

"Yes. I'm on the way. I stopped by to see how you were. Are you all right? You look a little flushed."

"I'm fine." Stopped by to see how she was? Ellen couldn't ever remember that happening before.

"Also, I need some papers Dorothy has."

Oh. That made more sense.

"All the stuff about the offices. The deed and everything."

"Wouldn't that be at the clinic?"

"I can't find it. That's why I thought she might have it here. Probably in her office." Marlitta started up the stairs.

Ellen trailed along behind.

"Could you bring me a cup of coffee?" Marlitta sat

down at the desk. "I'm feeling a little dragged out. Caffeine would be welcome."

Obediently, Ellen trudged back down the stairs. In the kitchen, a little bell went off in her head. Marlitta had just gotten her out of the way. She poured a cup and dashed back with it.

Marlitta was simply sitting at the desk with such sadness on her face that Ellen was ashamed of herself.

"Here." She placed the cup near Marlitta's elbow. "Did you find what you wanted?"

"No." Tears glistened in Marlitta's eyes, and she blinked. "Maybe it is at the clinic. Everything's all topsy-turvy." She took a sip from the cup and then rubbed her forehead. "Ellen—"

Ellen waited.

"Listen—it's good that you're staying here." Marlitta hesitated. "You can keep an eye on Taylor."

Ellen got a queasy feeling. She was beginning to feel a little sorry for Taylor.

"Who knows what he might do?"

Like steal the family silver?

"It would be better if he didn't—search through Dorothy's papers and things."

And just how am I supposed to stop him? Come to think of it, he probably has more legal right than any of the rest of us.

Marlitta got wearily to her feet and tucked in her blouse more snugly. "I'll have to take some things back with me."

"Marlitta, you can't. That would be like stealing or something. I don't think you should—"

"I'm not taking anything personal. Only records that belong at the clinic." Marlitta stuffed folders and papers in her briefcase. She peered around as though concerned she was missing something, or wanted to include something she dare not.

"Marlitta—" Ellen had the uneasy feeling Marlitta

shouldn't be doing this; and besides, Ellen really wanted to know what was in those files. Why hadn't she thought to look through them while she had the chance?

Marlitta put the medical books back on the bookshelf. "I have to get back." She picked up her briefcase.

At the front door, she turned. "Ellen, be careful what you say to the police."

"What do you mean?"

"There's no need to mention the little disagreement that Willis had with her."

"Little disagreement? You mean the new office building?"

"It was only a misunderstanding."

Right. The little misunderstanding had made Willis furious. Ellen really didn't know the whole of it, only that Willis thought the offices were too crowded and they needed more space. He had a new building all picked out. Dorothy had squashed the whole idea.

"There's no reason the police need to know about things that should be kept in the family," Marlitta said.

Of course. United front. No need to let a little thing like murder change anything.

"You do understand, don't you, Ellen?" Marlitta shifted the briefcase to her other hand. She seemed to be pleading with Ellen, but for what, Ellen didn't understand.

"We have our differences sometimes," Marlitta said. "But we're a family. We stick together."

"Yes."

Marlitta opened the door, waited as though she wanted to say something more, and then rushed off.

As Ellen closed the door, she remembered the time Marlitta had needed money from Dorothy to pay off some debts for Brent. Was that really what she was asking her not to spill to the cops?

How did everything get to be such a mess? And with Dorothy gone, how were they going to get out of it?

She ripped a paper towel from the roll in the kitchen, blew her nose, and told herself it was time to grow up. She'd just have to figure out for herself what to do. And one thing she ought to do was drive out to her own place and see if the plumbing was being worked on.

A VAN SAT in her driveway, along with a battered Toyota and a pickup. Two men, stripped to the waist and sweating in the heat, were digging up pipes. Mounds of dirt were heaped in a row along the trench.

"Morning," Ackerbaugh the plumber said. He rubbed a forearm across his forehead, drove the spade in the dirt, and rested a foot on it. His red hair gleamed like fire in the sun.

"How's it going?"

"With all this rain, haven't been able to do much. Might take longer than I thought."

Of course. With everything else, what did a little longer matter? She had a theory, anyway, that everything took twice as long as the estimate. "How much longer?" she asked.

"Might be as long as two weeks. That's if the rain lets up and we can get to it."

No, no, no. Tears threatened again. Any little thing, seemed like, made her cry. Damn it, where's your backbone? "Do your best," she said, and tramped toward the house, rummaging through her purse for the key.

"Well, Ellen, looks like you got yourself a problem here."

She turned and faced Harlen Dietz. "Nothing that can't be fixed."

"That so?" He had his feet, in cowboy boots, planted wide on her gravel driveway, big fat cigar in one hand. Late forties, jeans, and western-style shirt, dark hair going gray around the ears, flat gray eyes. "Looks like it might be an expensive problem." He stuck the cigar in his mouth and smirked around it.

"I'm busy, Harlen. What do you want?"

"Just came by to offer my condolences." His voice rasped with the ravages of tobacco.

"Thanks. Anything else?"

"You're mighty snippy to a neighbor who's trying to be friendly." He studied the lit end of the cigar, then flicked his gray eyes over her. They had the color and chill of a winter dawn.

She stiffened her spine, glad of the plumbers' presence.

"Thought any more about my offer?" he asked softly.

"I never thought about it in the first place. I'm not selling." He owned farmland adjoining her property and wanted her land. She didn't know why; it was only twenty-five acres, much of it wooded and unsuitable for farming.

"Think it over," he said. "I'll give you a good price. Young lady like you, not a good place for you to be all alone. Anything could happen way out here. I'll be checking with you." He crunched away down the driveway.

No way would she sell, not after she'd worked this hard. For sure, not now. She wouldn't have to. Unless Dorothy had done something none of them knew about and fixed it so the money was tied up some way.

Head down, she dug through her purse for keys as she scuffed to the house.

"Who's your friend?"

Her head snapped up. Adam stood in the open doorway. Her throat went dry, her heart went crazy. She stomped to the house, swept past him, and banged the door shut behind her. She leaned against it. "What are you doing here?"

"Trapping you."

He looked good. The same, no change. Heavy jaw in need of a shave, thick, dark, curly hair in need of a haircut. Amusement in the hazel eyes. Maybe a line or two that wasn't there before.

"You hang up when I call. Tear off when I get near. If at first you don't succeed, leap in with both feet."

"How'd you get in?"

"Door was unlocked."

"It was not."

He grinned. Confident, full of himself. Dr. Adam Sheffield, presumptuous prick.

"How'd you know I'd be here?"

"You live here. I drove out. You didn't answer. The door was unlocked. I stuck my head in, called hello. I phoned Nadine. She said you were at Dorothy's. I started to leave. You drove in." He looked at her, steady and long. No doubts. Sure. Arrogant.

She shook her head to stop the thoughts spinning around. "What do you want?"

"You."

A giant fist grabbed her somewhere in the region of her mid-section. "Listen, it didn't work. We split. Let's just leave it at that."

"Is that what you want, Ellie?"

"Yes!" She studied the way his black hair curled toward his collar, remembered the feel of his body beneath her hands.

He folded his arms, shook his head slowly, smiled. "It's not what I want."

"Just go, Adam. Leave me alone. I can't handle this. Not on top of Dorothy and—everything." The words clogged in her throat.

"Ellie—" He reached toward her.

She scuttled aside.

He dropped his arms and ran a hand through his hair, making the curls stand up. "Ellie—" His voice was soft and sweet. "I know it's hard. Dorothy's death. Let me help."

"Would you just go, please? Just get out of here."

The way he looked at her made her face hot. Until this

moment, she'd thought she never wanted to see him again. Too much pain. She couldn't go through it again. Just seeing him made the scabs start bleeding. To her horror, she felt tears spilling down her face.

"Ellie—" He put his arms around her.

She'd forgotten how good that felt. Memories tumbled around like wind-blown leaves: the two of them hanging out at the student union, late nights studying for exams, picnics by the river, sweaty romps in bed. For a moment, she leaned into him, then she stiffened and pulled away.

"Look, Adam, everything is just awful right now. I can't handle—"

With a thumb, he rubbed tears from her cheek. "Whatever I can do, Ellie. Just ask me."

"Go." She shoved against his chest. "I can't think. Just go."

"I'm going." He held up both hands, palms out. "Right now. But just listen, if you need anything call me. Anything?" He brushed a light kiss on her forehead and murmured, "I'll be back."

The arrogant prick. Did he think he could just waltz in here and she'd say all was forgiven? She'd fantasized this moment a million times. Part of her wanted to hang onto him and sob, "Just don't leave me again."

She tramped to the kitchen and yanked a paper towel from the holder. The entire roll unraveled. "Damn it!" She rerolled it raggedly and with care tore off one piece, blew her nose, and threw the towel in the trash under the sink.

In the bedroom, she pulled open a drawer, grabbed clean underwear, and slammed the drawer shut. She slid the next one open and rummaged around for shirts. Her hand touched something cold and hard.

She froze, pulse fluttering in her throat. Reluctantly, she lifted out cotton shirts and stared at the gun. Daddy's gun. Oh, shit.

FIFTEEN

ELLEN STARED at Daddy's gun and tried to breathe. Oh, God. Her hand, seemingly of its own accord, reached toward it. Don't touch it! Why not? It probably already has my fingerprints all over it. And probably nobody else's. Otherwise it wouldn't be here. And just because it is here doesn't mean it was used to kill Dorothy.

Oh, yes. Yes, it was. You can be damn sure of that. Otherwise, it wouldn't have disappeared and then come back.

I don't know what to do. She rubbed a hand hard over her face. Why is it here? Somebody wants me blamed for Dorothy's murder?

Oh, God. She rocked back on her heels, sat on her rear, and slumped against the wall. One of her siblings hated her that much? She felt hard pain all through her body, folded her arms across her stomach, and leaned forward.

Her eyes strayed back to the gun. She'd never realized before how ugly it was, black and lethal. Adam was here when she got here. He could have shoved it in the drawer. Adam Sheffield killed Dorothy? Of course he didn't. He had no reason. He wanted her out of the way so we could get married and live happily ever after with the money? That's just stupid.

With both hands, she grabbed her hair and pulled hard. I'm only thinking about Adam to stop myself from wondering which one of my family is a murderer. Or keep me from thinking what to do.

She knew what she should do. Immediately call the police. They'd want to know why she hadn't told them about the gun in the first place. Why hadn't she?

There she went, wandering down side trails again. She had to decide what to do. Talk to Carl. Ask him what to do. What if he put it here?

He didn't. Not Carl. It wasn't Carl. Then why not tell him about it?

The gun. Daddy's gun. He bought it to kill himself. It ended up killing his oldest child.

She pictured him in his wheelchair in the sunroom. She would stay with him sometimes. Why in the sunroom? That's where he'd painted before his stroke. When he was home, when he wasn't in the hospital.

He was so closed in, so isolated. Mother always kept her away from him. Don't bother your father. He's not feeling well. As though what he had was catching. He was so sad, so lost. Even when he was painting. But there was a difference when he was painting, something different. Not happiness, or even contentment, but sort of a way of making his presence known. Like a lonely wolf baying at the moon.

He painted fast and sure, as if that was the only thing he had control of. And after his stroke, he was wheeled into the sunroom, the only place where he had found some release from pain. And he could do nothing.

Now she thought that must have been a very cruel thing. She would slip in and stay with him, talk to him. She felt his pain, felt so useless, longed for the ability to do something for him. Near the end, his speech was almost gone. She believed he had thoughts, but he could no longer connect them with words.

He would sit and stare at the unfinished painting on the easel. She was twelve years old.

"I could help, Daddy," she had told him. She got out his brushes and paints and studied the canvas. It had a black funnel whirling down. Inside the funnel, a man laboriously climbing up with a cuckoo clock clutched in one arm had stumbled. The other arm reached out for a yellow bird that had its mouth open and a rainbow of butterflies swarming out.

Very industriously, she painted a butterfly that had turned into a flower at the rim of the funnel. She meant to paint flowers all around the rim.

Daddy's gnarled fingers plucked at her arm. She turned to look at him.

"In as much as," he said, "heretofore within the above forementioned in lieu of notwithstanding therefore prior to unless hereby." Tears were sliding down his face and dripping off his chin.

Rubbing a hand over her face, she discovered her own face was wet with tears. I can't just sit here and cry. I have to do something about Daddy's gun. Get rid of it somehow? How? Drop it into the river? Bury it?

And get caught doing it. Oh, yeah, that would really help.

How could she get rid of something that might point to the killer?

She heard the front door open downstairs and stopped breathing.

"Ellen?"

She let out a long breath. Nadine. "In here." She shoved the drawer shut and got to her feet on rather shaky legs. Grabbing up a T-shirt, she rubbed it across her face and dropped it on the bed. She brushed off the seat of her blue jeans, pulled her shirt straight, and went into the living room.

"Hi." Nadine, in jeans and a white blouse with damp spots on the shoulders where the baby had drooled, had a diaper bag over one shoulder and a squalling Bobby in a carry cot. "I saw your car and— Ellen, are you all right? You're white as a sheet."

"Yeah, I'm okay."

"Come on in here and sit down. You look like you're going to fall over." She shepherded Ellen into the kitchen, set the carry cot on a chair, and nudged Ellen into the adjacent one.

"You need a glass of water." Nadine took a glass from the cabinet and turned on the tap. No water came out. "Oh, damn, I forgot." She unzipped the diaper bag, pulled out a baby bottle, and poured the water from it into the glass. She set the glass in front of Ellen.

"How did you know I was here?"

"I didn't. Bob's studying for an exam, and this guy—" Nadine nodded at Bobby, waving pudgy fists and squawking "—has been yelling all morning. I thought I'd stay here awhile, where his fussing wouldn't bother anybody." She plugged a pacifier in the baby's mouth and sat down. "What happened?"

Ellen picked up the glass and took a sip. "Oh, God, Nadine, I wish I could tell you."

"Just tell me."

She wanted to, there was nothing she wanted more than to tell somebody what was upstairs in her dresser drawer. She was afraid. She didn't want to get Nadine in trouble. Her knowledge of anything legal was hazy, but she didn't want to make Nadine an accessory to anything. "Adam was here," she said.

"Here? What was he doing here?"

"He said he came to see me."

Nadine smiled softly. "Well, you knew it would happen. What other reason would he have to come back to Hampstead except to see you?"

Ellen rubbed angrily at her face. "I don't know. I don't know that I believe anything anymore. Not even that airplanes can fly."

The baby squirmed and made small, mewling noises. Nadine gathered him in her arms and cooed at him. "What was it like to see Adam?"

"Damn it," Ellen said angrily. She took a breath. "Good. He looked good. I wanted to hurl myself at him and tickle my fingers through his curls. Incidentally, he needs a haircut.''

"So why don't you? Hurl yourself.''

"Oh, hell, Nadine. Because I hate him.''

"Doesn't sound like hate to me.''

"Well, it is. How could it be anything else after what happened?''

"What did happen? You never really explained.''

Ellen slouched back in the chair and took another slug of Bobby's water. "Oh, it all just got too much. Seemed like we fought all the time. Mostly because we didn't have any money. And seemed like no matter how much we tried, we couldn't pay school expenses and rent and be able to eat.'' She shrugged. "We tried, we really did try. I worked, and Adam worked, and we both tried to find time to study.''

She looked at Bobby nuzzling Nadine's shoulder. "We just couldn't do it. Dorothy didn't like him, and after we started living together, she would no longer pay my school expenses.''

"I know that,'' Nadine said.

"Then Adam just up and left.''

"Why?''

"The fights and no money.''

"Yes, but there must have been some final straw.''

"I guess so.'' Ellen ran a shoe tip up and down the table leg. "Dorothy paid him to leave.''

"What? How do you know?''

"Well, it was pretty obvious. He was gone.''

"Yes, but—''

"Dorothy told me,'' Ellen said flatly.

"Oh.'' Nadine resettled Bobby. "Well, maybe—''

"Don't even try to think up excuses. You're entirely too nice, Nadine. You know that? You always believe there's two sides. I don't want any shilly-shallying in loyalty here. Anybody who would do that is a slime, and I don't want anything to do with him.''

Bobby fussed, and Nadine moved him from her shoulder, cradled him in her arms, and gently jostled him. "Maybe you should at least hear his side."

"I shouldn't listen to a word he says. I shouldn't be within a hundred miles of him."

With little whimpering sighs, Bobby drifted off to sleep, and Nadine placed him tenderly in the carry cot. "Are you trying to stay here without any water?"

"No. I just came to see if Ackerbaugh was on the plumbing job and pick up some clothes. I'm staying at home." Home. Still, after all my attempts to get away. Damn it, this is my home.

"It's really weird, Nadine. I keep expecting Dorothy to be there. Or come trotting in and ask me why I'm not practicing my flute."

"Why don't you go someplace else?"

Ellen laughed with no humor. "I don't think it will matter. The trap is closing."

OSEY KNEW a runaround when he heard one. He'd been on the phone for over an hour trying to pry loose the name of whoever had put the piece in the paper about the painting being sold. Hundred thousand dollars? Must be nice to have that kind of money to hang on your walls.

He was getting tired of trying to get hold of people who weren't in, or were busy and would call back and never did. Shit. He might as well have gone to Kansas City in the first place. Get him out of the department. Air-conditioning wasn't working too well. On top of what you might call the general tension of the place, getting out began to sound like a right good idea.

He picked up the receiver again and punched in the number of the *Kansas City Star,* a number he was beginning to remember quite well. He wondered if maybe he wouldn't save time by making a record and just playing it every time he punched in the number.

"Detective Osey Pickett," he said when the call was picked up. "Police Department." This time he left out Hampstead. Maybe he'd get further faster if the other end thought he was dealing with the Kansas City police. "I need to speak with Jim Barnes."

After clicks and buzzes, Barnes came on the line sounding harried and irritated.

Osey identified himself again and went into his story.

"Filler on page twenty-seven? Oh, for God's sake."

"It's important," Osey inserted.

Muttering came over the line, then Barnes said, "You working on a theft?"

"No, sir. I just need this information."

More muttering and then more clicks. This time the phone was answered by a female voice. He didn't catch the name. He went into his spiel again. "I'm sorry, ma'am, I didn't get your name."

"Lisa Mona," she said, real slow and drawn out, like she was speaking to an idiot. "And don't bother with the jokes. I've heard them all."

"Excuse me?"

"Yeah, right. Why do you want to know this?"

"I'm afraid I can't give out that information, ma'am." He knew better than to mention homicide to anybody in the newspaper business. After some more palaver back and forth, she finally came across with the name of the gallery that had sold the painting.

Osey felt like whooping when he hung up, and took off for Kansas City in pouring rain.

An hour and a half later, he was at KCPD, letting them now he was on their turf and asking what they knew about the Jennings Gallery.

"Not a damn thing," Sergeant Barker said. "Far as I can tell you, they're lily clean. No smell of fraud or handling stolen merchandise, no complaints. Matter of fact, this is the first I've heard of them. You want some assist?"

"Not necessary."

"Good. I got enough with our own crime."

Osey thanked him, asking for directions, and found the place with no problem. Parking, on the other hand, was a mite problematical. He circled the block and was about to widen his field when a car backed out ahead of him. He swung in and thumbed coins in the meter.

He got soaked sprinting from the squad car to the door. He wiped his forehead and went inside. Uh-huh. Not the type of place he generally spent a lot of time in. Soft classical music. Pictures all over the walls. Sculpture and glass stuff displayed here and there. Elderly male seated behind a counter, intent on perusing a catalogue.

Osey, careful not to bump anything—if he broke it, it would probably cost ten years' salary—made his way to the counter.

The old guy shut the catalogue, lined it up true on the edge of the counter, and stood up. "Good afternoon. Anything I can help you with?" Standing, he didn't seem much taller than sitting down. Fluffy hair the color of rain clouds, face as netted with wrinkles as a ripe cantaloupe. Dark suit, white shirt, dark tie with gold tiepin, and gold cufflinks.

"I'm looking for Claude Jennings."

"I am he."

Osey hauled out his ID and laid it on the counter.

Jennings took a pair of gold-rimmed glasses from his inside coat pocket—how had he read the catalogue?—and slowly unfolded the ear pieces, hooked them over his ears, adjusted the fit over the bridge of his nose, picked up the ID, and moved it back and forth as though to catch the light better.

Not a man to go off half-cocked, Osey thought, waiting patiently while Jennings compared the photo with the real thing.

"And what might it be that the police would like to

question me about?" He removed the glasses and tucked them away.

"It might be about a painting."

"I see."

Osey thought he saw a twinkle in the small gray eyes and wondered if Jennings might not be having a little fun here. He explained what he was after.

"Ah, yes, the Barrington. I believe I did read about the death of his daughter." Jennings made a *tsk tsk* sound and shook his head. "Such a tragedy. I didn't know the lady myself. A family that has had more than its share of tragedy." He tipped back his head and peered up at Osey. "You think the death has something to do with the painting? I find it hard to believe that is a possibility."

"You did have the painting? You sold it?"

Jennings nodded slowly. "It has been many years since I've handled a Barrington. I must say, it was a pleasure just to hold one in my hands again."

"Where did it come from?"

"Young man, that is not a very specific question. Are you asking me how it came about that I had one to sell?"

Osey grinned. "Well, you can tap dance some better than me, but that's about it, yeah."

The wrinkles rearranged themselves into a smile. "I used to know him. August. Many, many years ago. Before his death."

"I figured."

The wrinkles slid around again. "I sold many of his paintings. Most. Perhaps even all. You may have noticed, young man, that I'm getting along in years. I thought I'd never have one pass through my hands again."

"How'd you get this one?"

"It didn't take long to sell, I can tell you that."

"Where'd it come from?"

"Why, the family, of course."

"The Barrington family."

"That is correct. It was quite an honor and a pleasure that they chose me after all these years."

"Which member of the family are we talking about?"

"The youngest one. Ellen Barrington."

SIXTEEN

"YOU WERE RIGHT about Ed Cole. He's a piece of shit." Parkhurst stood with his back toward the window. Rain was falling like a warning to Noah. He took three paces to the armchair in front of her desk, nudged it with his toe, and sat, resting low on his spine.

Susan shoved aside the stack of urgent messages she was working through, twisted sideways in the chair, and crossed her legs.

"I've been doing some digging," Parkhurst said. "Little chats with the neighbors, visit to the emergency room. They know Debra well there. Her story is she's clumsy. Accident prone." He paged through his notebook. "Hell of a klutz. Broken wrist, cracked ribs, battered face. Those are just the highlights."

"We ever get a domestic disturbance on them?"

"So far they've kept all their disturbing to themselves. But—" He leaned forward, opened his suit coat to tuck the notebook in the inside pocket, and leaned back again. "And you might find this interesting. The check on license plates turned up Ed's car in the area at the time of the shooting."

"Did it indeed." Battering husbands spread their violence around on anybody who tried to help their wives. Friends, family; the wives weren't safe anywhere. "If Dorothy was telling Debra to leave, get herself and baby into a shelter— Dorothy gave her a job. That got her away from him for some of the time. He wouldn't be thrilled by that, and—"

Her phone rang, and she picked up the receiver. "Yes, Hazel."

"Mayor on the line again. You want to talk to him?"

No, she did not. The last thing she wanted to do was talk to Mayor Bakeover. Or listen to him talk. "Put him through." She aimed a thumb at the door. Parkhurst nodded and left.

"Miz Wren," the mayor's voice boomed in her ear. "I have left several messages."

She spread out the pile of urgent messages on her desk, and there they were, four slips with the times noted.

"Are you on the point of making an arrest?"

"We are making progress," she said.

He cleared his throat in a dismissing sound. "That sort of nonsense is what you hand out to the paper. I want to know what's going on."

She looked at the stack of reports on her desk: suspects questioned, area canvassed, preliminary autopsy report. "We're in the process of gathering information," she said. "Checking alibis, tracking down leads."

"You cannot let this drag on. Dorothy Barrington was a valuable member of this community. Her assailant has to be found immediately. It's not good for the town to have an unsolved murder. It makes us look bad, and it makes people nervous."

One day, she thought with her teeth clamped, I'm going to say screw it, I've had it, I don't work here anymore.

She unclamped her teeth enough to say, "Yes, Mr. Mayor, I understand."

"Do you have enough people on it?"

"We're covering all angles."

"I hope so. Don't limit yourself by concentrating on the family. Look outward."

"Yes, sir." Ah. Did this mean one or more of the Barringtons was grousing to the mayor?

"Keep me informed."

There was a click. She took the receiver from her ear and grimaced at it. Barringtons were all valuable members of the community. The mayor didn't like to upset anybody valuable.

She replaced the receiver and retrieved her raincoat from the coat tree in the corner. To keep the mayor from having apoplexy, she'd go and harass some non-valuable members of the community. Starting with the shelter for battered women. Now, there were people about as non-valuable as you could get. She didn't ask Parkhurst to accompany her. Generally speaking, these people didn't care for males.

SUSAN PICKED UP a cheeseburger at one of the fast-food places—she'd been doing that a lot lately and could feel Hazel's disapproval just over her shoulder—and ate it on the way to Victory House. She slurped the last of the cola just as she pulled up in front, stuffed the wrappings and paper napkins inside the empty cup, and dropped it in the passenger seat.

The battered women's shelter had started life as some family's proud home and gone through several incarnations—apartment building, corner grocery, paint store—before getting to its present state: faded white paint, blistered and peeling, over a clapboard structure, wooden steps that made sagging creaks as she trotted up on the porch, weedy grass beaten down by rain. She poked the door bell.

Several seconds elapsed before a female voice called from inside, "Who is it?"

"Chief Wren."

"What is it you want?"

"I need to talk with Joyce Norvell."

"Just a minute."

Susan waited. Standard procedure; nobody opened that door without permission from a staff member, usually Joyce herself. Sure enough, moments later Joyce Norvell unlocked, unbolted, and opened the door.

"Is this really necessary?" Joyce said in a tart voice so in contrast to her grandmotherly appearance: sweet, round face, prim smile, short white hair, and plump figure. In contrast, that is, until you looked at her sharp, penetrating eyes. "It upsets the women to have police hammering on the door."

"Better me than someone of the male persuasion."

"*Humph.* That were the case, this door wouldn't have opened." She stepped back. "Come on it, if you must."

Susan heard women chatting in another room and children's voices as she followed Joyce into the kitchen. The floor had faded, mud-colored, cracked linoleum and a long wooden table stacked with what looked like breakfast dishes. A coffee maker sat on a counter along with a collection of mugs.

Without asking, Joyce filled two of the mugs, placed them on the table, and before she sat down, transferred stacks of dirty dishes to the sink.

"I need to talk to you about Dorothy Barrington," Susan said.

"I assumed as much." Joyce added sugar and powdered cream to her coffee.

"Debra Cole, Dorothy's receptionist. Has she ever stayed here?"

"What has that got to do with anything?"

"Maybe nothing." Maybe something, if Dorothy was trying to convince Debra to get some help and her husband didn't like it.

"I wouldn't tell you if she had," Joyce said.

"Why not? Aren't we on the same side?"

"I don't have sides. I do everything in my power to help these women, and that does not include passing out their names to everyone who asks. They have enough to contend with. They've already been horribly victimized, and they don't need any more."

"Tell me about Dorothy's work for you."

"It was good of her to do it. She donated her time, and

her skill. Money is always a problem.'' Joyce looked around the shabby kitchen. "There's never enough.''

"How was it that Dorothy came to do this?''

Joyce grinned. "I asked her to. I got my way with a little coercion, a little sprinkling of guilt. I can work wonders when I really get going.''

Susan believed it.

A toddler staggered to the door, tried to hold on, then flopped onto his padded bottom. He waited with frustration. A thin woman with stringy blond hair picked him up and cuddled him as she took him away.

Joyce suddenly looked tired. "Now I guess I'll have to start knocking on doors. Find somebody else. Start polishing up on the guilt.'' She sighed.

"How did that work? Did Dorothy come here to see the women?''

"Sometimes. It depended on the injuries. We have children here too. If it was minor, she would come here and take care of it. If it was more serious, she'd tend to it in her office. Sometimes after hours, so nobody would see them. Or if it was really serious, at the hospital.''

"Did anybody ever threaten her? One of the husbands?''

"The husbands always threaten. Anybody who works here is in danger. They're not cops, they don't carry guns, they're just ordinary people. The husbands are all violent. That's why the women are here in the first place. Because they got the crap beaten out of them.''

Susan had heard Joyce use such language before, but it always surprised her, coming from this sweet-looking lady.

"The bastards have to control everything their wives do,'' Joyce said. "And they get enraged when the wives slip out of their reach. I don't know of anybody who threatened Dorothy, but that doesn't mean it didn't happen.''

"I'd like to talk with the women staying here.''

"No. You'd need a lot more than a vague possibility before I'd let that happen. They have enough trauma. I won't have you adding to it. I'd have to see something legally forcing me before I'd let you talk to anybody here, and even then I might not allow it.''

Susan didn't push it. "How was Dorothy at taking care of these women? Sympathetic? Did they like her?''

Joyce lifted the mug to her mouth and sipped thoughtfully. "Dorothy was an odd mixture of helpful and unsympathetic.''

Susan raised an eyebrow.

"Since she was such a strong woman herself, I don't think she fully understood the dynamics of these situations. I don't mean she was unaware. Intellectually, I'm sure she was. But there was always that slight hint of impatience. As though deep down, she couldn't accept that the wives wouldn't leave the bastards. And no, the women didn't really like her.''

"When did you last see her?''

"Friday night. One of the children fell and cut his head. She brought us a few things, first-aid things. Hydrogen peroxide, Q-Tips, Band-Aids, Ace bandages. A few things like that. That may not sound like much to you, but all these things cost money.'' Joyce looked down at her mug, then up at Susan. "I'm going to miss her. She was always available when we needed her. No matter what time of day. The women were uncomfortable around her. She wasn't— warm-hearted, there was always this hint of disapproval. But she certainly couldn't be faulted for her medical skill. And that's what she was here for.''

"Is there anything at all you can tell me?''

Joyce took a breath. "Oh, Susan, I really wish I could help. I want you to catch the bastard, but there's really nothing.'' With the edge of one hand, Joyce scraped together a little pile of crumbs. "Friday night, she did seem— preoccupied. I commented that she looked tired. She shook her head and said she knew something she didn't want to know.''

"And what was that?"

"That's all she would say."

Susan left Joyce washing breakfast dishes and made a mental note to see whether there wasn't some way to get them a dishwasher. Joyce had done a guilt trip on her, and she wasn't even aware of it. Locks and bolts clicked shut behind her.

Rain sluiced down the windshield as she pulled away from Victory House. Joyce was too wily a lady to give any impression of whether or not Debra had ever been in residence. *Dorothy knew something she didn't want to know.* That had a fine sinister ring to it. Might even be helpful, if Susan knew what the hell it was about.

She glanced at her watch: five minutes to noon. Making a right, she took the cross street to the Barrington clinic hoping to catch Debra before she took off for lunch.

The waiting room was empty. Debra, behind the reception counter, looked up as Susan walked in and froze like a deer at approaching headlights.

"Just a question or two."

"I don't know anything. I already told you."

"Just filling in, trying to get everything clear. How did you get to work on Saturday? Did you drive?"

"Not on Saturday. Sometimes I do. But mostly Ed drives me. He did on Saturday."

"Where was he in the afternoon?"

"Ed? He was— I don't know exactly—"

The door opened, and a stocky man with red hair came in. Beefy shoulders strained the seams of a blue work shirt, "Winslow" stitched on the pocket, "Ackerbaugh Plumbing" on a patch on the sleeve. He snapped a piece of paper onto the counter. "Where's Dr. Marlitta?"

"I'm sorry, Mr. Ackerbaugh. She's busy right now."

"Where is she? I want to see her."

"Is there a problem?" Susan asked.

"Who're you?"

"Chief Wren." She shoved her ID at him.

He glanced at it, his eyes flicked over her, his brain registered cop, and he pulled back on his anger.

"You have a complaint?"

"Got a right. Doctor didn't know what she was doing. Kid is still sick."

"What kid?"

"My boy."

"You think Dorothy made your child sick?"

"Got two others. Nothing wrong with them."

"Would you care to explain?"

"All they do is explain. Kid's not any better. I told Dorothy, he didn't get better, I was gonna sue. Tests!" His anger got away from him again, and he slapped a hand against the paper on the counter. "Always more tests. Trying to cover up."

"Cover up what?"

"Negligence, incompetence."

The door leading into the inner offices opened. "What is it?" Marlitta caught sight of Ackerbaugh, and emotions—fatigue, anxiety, maybe irritation—chased across her face before she collected herself. "Mr. Ackerbaugh, is something wrong?"

"Yeah, something's wrong." He crumpled the paper in his fist and shook it. "More tests. I'm damn sick and tired of tests."

Marlitta glanced at Susan, then back at Ackerbaugh. "Why don't you come into my office and we'll talk about it?"

"No more talk. No more tests." He flung the paper at her and turned on his heel.

Marlitta closed her eyes and exhaled a long sigh. Moving slowly, she went along the hallway to her office. Susan followed.

Marlitta slumped in the chair, elbows on the desk, hands on her cheeks.

"What was that all about?" Susan asked.

Marlitta stood up immediately, resting a hand on the desk to steady herself. "Oh, dear," she said with a long-suffering smile. "Some people simply expect a doctor to know with a look what the problem is. They can't seem to understand that doctors aren't magicians. We need to find out the symptoms and sometimes run tests."

"What's wrong with his baby?"

"That's what the tests are for."

"Necessary tests?"

With the condescension of the overworked physician, she said, "If we're going to know how to treat the child, yes."

"Was it Ackerbaugh who threatened Dorothy?"

Startled, Marlitta drew her head back. "Of course not."

"How can you be sure?"

Marlitta's mind seemed to tick over slowly. Either she'd forgotten she'd mentioned the threatening call, or there never was a call in the first place.

"It wasn't Winslow Ackerbaugh."

"Why are you so sure?"

"I cannot discuss a patient."

Doctors and lawyers. Whenever they didn't want to answer, they claimed confidentiality.

Debra was collecting her purse to leave for lunch when Susan got back to her.

"Before you go," Susan said. "Where can I find your husband?"

Debra pressed the purse to her chest as she turned around. "Why do you want him?"

"I need to talk with him."

Horror washed across her face. "He didn't," she whispered. "No. He wouldn't."

"Where was he on Saturday?"

"I don't know. He said he was going to Emerson to study."

"What time did he come home?"

"I don't remember. Maybe around four o'clock." Debra's fingers made tiny scratching movements on the leather bag. "He didn't do it. He would never do anything like that."

"Doesn't he have a temper? Yell at you? Hit you?"

"Of course not!"

"Never?"

"Sometimes he gets upset. Everybody does sometimes."

"What makes him upset?"

Debra shook her head. "He has a lot on his mind. Studying and classes. Worry about money. Sometimes I forget. If I'd be more understanding—"

Like all battered wives. "Where can I find him?"

"At Emerson. He has classes."

SEVENTEEN

SUSAN CRUISED along Learned Street checking house numbers. According to the phone book, the Ackerbaughs lived at 829. She spotted it and pulled up in front: a neat white frame house with a wide porch, a picket fence, roses climbing up a trellis on the side.

A young woman opened the door, with two little boys, maybe four and five, clinging to each side of her flowered skirt and a baby less than a year old in her arms.

"Mrs. Ackerbaugh?" Susan flipped open her ID.

Linette Ackerbaugh stood silent and motionless in her doorway, and stared.

The little boys grinned and started dancing around like friendly puppies, looked up expectantly at their mother, and tugged at her skirt. "Mommy, mommy. A pretty lady. Let her in."

The baby, clutching at her faded blue T-shirt, was barefoot, and a tiny pair of sneakers dangled from her hand. He was a beautiful child with lots of dark, curly hair and large, dark eyes. Compared with the two older boys, he was pale and seemed listless, the eyes not alight with interest and mischief.

"I'm Chief Wren."

The woman's lips rounded as if she was about to say, "Oh," but she didn't. She didn't move, didn't glance at the ID, simply stared.

"Mrs. Ackerbaugh?" Susan stuck her ID in her bag. The rain dripped dismally over the eaves, and the damp air held the sweet scent of roses. Linette Ackerbaugh didn't seem to want to look at Susan's face; instead she seemed fascinated by her gray linen pants. They were creased and wrinkled as linen will do once you sit down, but when a cop turned up on your doorstep, the attention-grabber wasn't generally the cop's apparel.

"Mom-mee!"

"You are Linette Ackerbaugh?"

She blinked, shaking off her fugue, and her eyes softened. "Yes, of course, I'm Linette." She made hesitant steps around the boys, dropped a sneaker, and smiled with embarrassment. Holding the baby tight, she stooped to grab the sneaker, overbalanced, and did an awkward shuffle to recoup. She tenderly cupped a hand behind the baby's head.

There was a sweetness about her, and she moved with the leggy, awkward charm of a colt. Her hair, honey and satin, was pulled back in a ribbon. She was all delicate and light. Hard to picture her married to lumbering, heavy-handed Winslow and his practical world of sewer pipes. She was staring again. Her eyes were blue-green, the color of the ocean on a sunny day; their expression said, "Oh, no, why have you come?"

"Mrs. Ackerbaugh?"

"Linette, please." She smiled, suddenly friendly, easy.

"You know about Dr. Barrington, Dorothy Barrington?"

"Oh." The smile vanished; her eyebrows, which slanted slightly up like a bird's wings, got furrows between them. "I couldn't believe it."

Susan had been a cop for a long time, and she'd heard that line over and over when dealing with the bereaved, the angry, the bewildered, but there was something not right about Linette Ackerbaugh. It wasn't the usual dazed, trying to comprehend terrible reality, but a sort of searching for the correct reaction. Instead of a routine interview, just covering all the bases, Susan went on full alert. Something was going on here.

"Mom-mee!" Little hands yanked at Linette's skirt.

"Oh. Yes. Would you like to come in?"

The boys scampered ahead, and Susan followed Linette

through a living room with toys scattered across the carpet to a spacious kitchen. She accepted an offer of iced tea, partly because she hoped saying yes would encourage Linette to relax and talk, and partly to give herself an opportunity to get a fix on the woman.

With one hand, Linette cleared toys and plates and glasses from the table. The little boys stuck close to Susan, asking her name and where she lived and whether she liked to swim. They had a friend who had a swimming pool. They patted her hands, patted her arms, patted her knees, patted her shoulder bag.

Linette got ice-cream bars from the freezer, gave one to each boy, and shooed them off to a screened porch. They raced out with shrieks of joy.

Susan sat back and waited to see what Linette would reveal. Still holding the baby, who hadn't made one peep, Linette got down glasses, took a full pitcher from the refrigerator, poured tea, and handed a glass across the table.

"I'm sorry you missed Win. He just left."

Susan had counted on it. Linette sat down and settled the baby in her lap.

"Your husband is angry about the medical treatment the baby's been receiving," Susan said.

"He's worried. They keep doing tests and not finding out what's wrong."

"He made some threats to Dorothy Barrington."

"It's only his way." Linette got stopped by a memory; her eyes narrowed in an attempt to prevent tears. She curled a wisp of the baby's hair around one finger. "He doesn't think a whole lot of doctors, and he feels if we'd just stop coddling him he'd be all right."

The pronouns got a little mixed, but Susan followed along with no problem. "You feel that way too?"

The softness in Linette's eyes turned fierce. "If I did, I wouldn't be taking him there, would I?"

"Can you tell me where you were Saturday afternoon?"

Linette smiled, all softness and sunshine again. "Three children and pouring-down rain? Where do you think? Right here."

"And your husband?"

"At work."

Squabbles broke out on the porch. Linette stood up. Susan stepped in front of her. "Mrs. Ackerbaugh, what are you hiding?"

"Why would I hide anything? I don't know what you mean."

"Yes. You do. And you need to tell me what it is. Because I need to know—and I intend to find out."

"No. The boys. I need to— Excuse me."

"Mrs. Ackerbaugh—"

"There's nothing." Linette dashed out to the screened porch.

Susan went back to the department and picked up Parkhurst. The rain had stopped; the sun shone fiercely, causing steam to rise from the rooftops, and the Bronco simmered in the heat. Parkhurst cranked the window down and shrugged off his jacket, started up the motor, and headed for campus.

As they were rolling along Iowa, a heavyset woman in orange pants rushed out, waving her arms. Parkhurst stopped, and she darted to the window.

"You've got to help me."

"What's the problem, ma'am?"

"Snake. In my car. This long." She sketched out three and a half feet.

"Where's your car?"

She gestured at a white Ford in the driveway. "I just came out of my house to get in, and I saw this snake. It crawled straight up the wheel. The left one, the rear. Oh, my God, do you think it got inside?" She patted her chest as an aid in catching her breath.

"No, ma'am. There's no way it could have gotten inside."

"You have to get it out."

Parkhurst looked at Susan. She just turned in her feminist badge, all of a sudden struck by the conviction there were some things a man ought to do. He pulled to the curb and cut the motor. Susan got out when he did and trudged at his heels.

"Would you release the hood, ma'am?"

She handed him the keys. "I'm not getting in that car."

He unlocked the Ford, popped the latch, then went around and raised the hood. The woman stood well back, jittering from one foot to the other. Susan understood the impulse. She stuck to Parkhurst's side while he looked, moving back and forth, bending and peering. She wondered whether she should draw her weapon. She'd never shot a snake before, never dealt with snakebite either. How fast could she get the Bronco to the emergency room?

"I don't see it, ma'am."

Susan didn't either, nothing but a jumble of hoses.

"It must have gotten out."

"No. I would have seen it. It's there."

Parkhurst peered around some more, went to the Bronco, and came back with a burlap bag.

"See it?" Susan asked.

He gave her the bag. "Tucked above the fuel lines, snug against them. Hold the bag open."

Oh, Lord, give her an armed and dangerous anytime. She rolled down the top of the bag and held it wide. He leaned in, shot her a look, and made a snatch. He pulled. Long, rusty-black snake. Jesus, at least three and a half feet. He'd grabbed it just behind the head. It whipped and lashed. He dropped it in the bag. Lightning quick, she knotted the top.

The woman trotted up, gushing thanks. He yanked on the knot, just making sure, and gingerly lowered it into the Bronco. They drove to the river. Little beads of sweat dotted his hairline. When he opened the bag and dumped the snake, it slithered away through tall weeds.

"Poisonous?" she asked.

"Oh, hell, no. Rat snake." A sickly grin touched his mouth. "Unless it was a copperhead."

A RECEPTIONIST in the administration building directed them to Parker Hall; Ed Cole was in the biology lab. They meandered along wet pathways and located Parker Hall just as classes broke. Students poured from the building.

"You know him?" Susan asked.

"Over there." Parkhurst nodded at a slender young man in khaki pants and an open-collared white shirt chatting with a group of classmates at the foot of the stairs.

Like any good partners, they worked with much reliance on instinct, not needing verbal cues. That's what happened here. Parkhurst spoke; she hung around with her mouth shut. "Ed Cole?"

"Yeah?"

Parkhurst held out his ID. "Talk to you a minute?"

Ed's eyes slid from Parkhurst to Susan and back to Parkhurst. The classmates drifted away with murmurs of "Catch you later."

"What's this about?" Cole squinted at them. Blond, clean-cut, wholesome. Every inch the college student. Not a kid to make a mother's heart quaver if her daughter went out with him.

"You want to tell us where you were on Saturday at one o'clock?" Parkhurst said.

"Any reason I should?"

"Any reason you shouldn't?"

Cole backed up onto the bottom step, either to gain distance or allow himself to look down at them. "This is Tuesday; that was three days ago."

"Anywhere near the Barrington clinic?"

"You asking me about the murder, man? Hey, I had nothing to do with that."

Parkhurst gave him a look of top-grade disbelief. "Your wife works there."

"So?"

"You were there when the doctor was shot."

Cole didn't respond. He knew the sound of a trap being set.

Students slipped by in clumps or pairs, clutching books or toting backpacks, chattering. Out on the grass, a young man stood by a tree with a peanut in his palm trying to coax a squirrel to come down and take it. The squirrel skittered around to the other side of the trunk.

"Okay, so I was there."

"Why?"

"I thought I'd surprise Deb. Take her out to lunch."

"She'd already been to lunch."

The kid with the peanut scooted around the tree and held up his palm hopefully. The squirrel flicked his tail and, upside down, inched toward the offering.

"Well, I didn't know that. I mean, I probably got there later than I meant to."

"Did you go inside?"

"No. There was all that commotion going on, and I—I just didn't," Cole added.

"Have you ever been inside the office?"

A blue jay zoomed in out of nowhere and snatched the peanut in a fast hit-and-fly. Both the kid and the squirrel looked nonplussed.

"Maybe once or twice. If I needed to see Deb."

"Ever been inside when they were closed?"

Cole's jaw tightened. Susan got one of those instant "by God" flashes.

"No. Why would I?"

"Checking up on your wife." Parkhurst said. "Late getting home. Trying to find out where she was."

"I don't know what you're talking about."

Yes indeed, you do, Susan thought.

"Ever get a little steamed at her? Show her what's what?"

"I don't know what your problem is, man, but I got a class I'm already late for." Cole swept up irritation and indignation, and edged around Parkhurst as he stepped down off the step. After a skinny second, he moved off.

"You look like you have a thought," Parkhurst said.

"No. Just a hunch."

"Want to share it with me?"

"Cole was the intruder the janitor mentioned. He had to know where his wife was; maybe she'd gone somewhere without his permission. He had to find out whether she was there, probably knock her around when he caught her."

"What do you want to do about it?"

"I don't know." Which was exactly the problem with hunches.

"His type ferrets out the helpless. Dorothy wasn't helpless."

"He'd be mad, though, if Dorothy convinced Debra to leave him."

"So where does that leave us?" he asked.

"Moving right along. Not only did we not eliminate a suspect, but we've added another one." She told him about Ackerbaugh boiling up in anger because Dorothy hadn't helped his child despite a lot of medical tests.

EIGHTEEN

ONE END SUSAN could tie up was at the Dietzes'. Marlitta Barrington had said Dorothy meant to see Holly Dietz on Friday. Outside of town, the landscape ambled along in dips and rises. The endless sky constantly changed in a roiling mass of gray and white clouds. Some low-lying fields held standing water; in high areas white, yellow, and pink wildflowers covered the hills. White-tailed deer, half-hidden by trees, raised their heads and watched warily as she drove past.

She found the place without too much trouble. As a working farm, it had all the earmarks of imminent decline: weeds in the gravel drive, fence with the top rail listing to the ground, barn door propped against the side instead of in its rightful place.

The house was a pleasant Queen Anne style but the white paint looked too old to keep the rain out. She went to the rear, having learned that was the polite custom in the country. The door stood open, and she knocked on a screen with jagged holes. Dogs weaved around inside—a collie, a Lab, and a small black mutt, all hair—and greeted her with barks and whipping tails.

"Come in," a voice called.

Hesitantly, she opened the screen, but the dogs only pranced and sniffed and licked. "Mrs. Dietz?"

"Would you mind coming in here? I'm kind of in the middle of it."

Susan followed the dogs into a living room, where too much furniture sat on a patterned rug long since faded to a mottled brown. The Oriental rug, silk curtains drawn back with tasseled ties, and Tiffany lamps suggested money somewhere in the past, but arms worn through on the chintz chairs and holes in the couch cushions indicated leaner times now.

Photos and snapshots covered every flat surface—tables, couch, chairs—and there was an uneven pile on the floor by the chair where Holly was sitting. Her feet bare, she wore a tent-like shift with red poppies and held a stack in her lap. In her late thirties, she had brown hair down to her shoulders with loose curls around a thin face.

She looked at Susan, said, "Oh," and transferred the photos from her lap to the floor.

"Don't get up," Susan said quickly, but Holly was already on her feet. "I'm Chief Wren. I'd like to ask you a few questions."

"I'm sorry the place is such a mess." Holly scooped up an armful of pictures from one end of the couch and added it, precariously, to the heap on the opposite end. "Can I get you something to drink? Iced tea? Coffee?"

"No thank you." Susan sat in the cleared spot. "I can see you're busy."

"Bitten off more than I can chew, is what it is." Holly settled back in the chair, brought her knees up sideways, and tucked the shift around her bare feet. "Everybody's been so generous. I had no idea."

"You're putting together a book?"

"Just pictures. Early Hampstead. Look at all this." She waved her hand around.

It looked, indeed, a formidable task. "Dorothy Barrington brought you some pictures?"

"Yes."

"When was that?"

"Friday. It's just awful what happened."

"Dorothy came here? What time?"

Holly tucked a strand of hair behind one ear. "It was about twelve-thirty, I guess. I told her I could sure come and pick them up, she didn't have to drive all the way out here, but she said she wanted to, it was nice to get away, even for just a little while. She couldn't stay. Didn't have time for a cup of coffee or a bite to eat, or even a minute to chat. She had to get right back.''

''What did she say when she was here?''

''Not anything, really. We mentioned the rain. Seems like everybody's talking about that.''

Susan looked around at the piles of photos and thought she might as well get back to whatever was piling up on her desk. ''May I see the pictures Dorothy brought?''

''Uh.'' Holly looked with some dismay at the litter. ''Sure.''

It took her a while to find the right ones, but she gathered a stack and handed them to Susan.

Old buildings on Main Street, old cars, people wearing the styles of bygone times. The Barrington house when it was a hospital: an old-time surgery room, a nursery with a row of four babies, graduating nurses with pointed caps and long capes, an old-fashioned doctor's office.

''That was her mother's office,'' Holly said.

''This is her mother?'' Susan looked closer. A thin woman with deep-set eyes, an angular face, and light hair, wearing a long, dark dress. Dorothy had resembled her mother a great deal.

''This is her too.'' Holly tapped a finger on a snapshot.

A hospital room, a man in the bed. Dorothy's mother stood by his side. The man looked familiar. ''Who's the patient? Do you know?''

Holly bent nearer and nodded. ''That's Brent Wakeley's father. He had some serious illness.''

The next picture showed a teenage Dorothy in a party dress with a young man in a tuxedo; both were grinning at the camera, standing in front of a brick school building.

''Do you know who he is?''

''I sure do,'' Holly said with a tight smile. ''That's Harlen.''

"Your husband?"

"They went together in high school. He figured they'd get married. She wouldn't have him." There was a bitter note of triumph in Holly's voice.

"He married you instead."

"Sure did. Took over the farm when my father died. This land belonged to my family, you know. Since my great, great, great grandfather." It was said with pride. "That's the old high school they're standing in front of. It was torn down right after."

Harlen Dietz harboring resentment? She done him wrong. Right. After all these years, he picks up a gun and does her in.

If that's the best she could come up with, she might as well get back to the office.

RAIN FELL RELENTLESSLY, rippling down the office window, while she read, initialed, and moved paper across her desk. At five-thirty, just as she was thinking she'd had enough and should get out of here, Osey ambled in. He sketched a salute, crossed his arms, and propped his lanky body against the door frame. "I found out something maybe a mite interesting."

She tossed down her pen, leaned back, and gestured toward the armchair by the desk. He lowered himself in a series of uncoordinated jerks and related what he'd learned from Claude Jennings.

"He must be near a hundred," Osey said. "Sharp as a tack, but I don't know about his eyesight. Doubt if he can see a blame thing."

"You suggesting the painting was a fake?"

"The thought did cross my mind. Can he see well enough to tell forgery from the real thing? Spotless reputation. I got no smell of dishonesty. Not nervous talking to me. Matter of fact, he likes to talk. Even to a cop."

Osey leaned back, bent a leg, and rested the ankle on his

knee. "Mostly done by telephone. All the arrangements. Only at the last did she come in with the painting."

Susan told him to take off and headed out herself. On the way, she poked her head into Parkhurst's office. He looked up from his desk.

"Why are you still here?" she asked.

"I love this place. Can't get enough of it."

"In that case, care to come with me to talk with Ms. Ellen Barrington about a painting?"

He rose, rolled down his shirt sleeves, and grabbed his jacket.

TAYLOR TALMIDGE, still wearing a suit and tie as though he'd just come in from work, looked at them dripping on his doorstep. "Have you found out something about Dorothy's death?"

"We'd like to speak with Ellen," Susan said. "Is she here?"

He relaxed slightly, betraying an inner tension that until then she hadn't noticed. "Come in. I'll see if I can find her. I just got in myself, but her car is here, so she must be around." He collected their wet coats and left them standing in the entryway.

"I don't think Mr. Talmidge was thrilled to see us," Parkhurst said, as they moved into the dim living room.

She went to the tall windows with rain rushing down the glass and looked out at the garden: grass under an inch of water and flowers tossed by the wind.

"You wanted to see me?" Ellen, in jeans and a white cotton shirt, was wound up tighter than guitar strings, voice clipped and breathless.

What have we here? Ellen was just this side of flying apart, hands clenched into fists, dark eyes fixed on Susan with the look of a rabbit seeing the dogs close in.

Play my cards right, and maybe we'll get some answers. "Do you mind if we sit down?"

"Sit down," Ellen repeated as though the words were foreign.

Susan sat on the couch, Ellen, elbows tucked tight against her sides, backed into a wing chair, ankles pressed together, shoes flat on the floor. Parkhurst remained standing, just enough behind her so she couldn't see him without turning her head, which she obviously didn't like.

"We want to ask about your father's painting," Susan said.

"Daddy's paintings?" Ellen's set little face went slack with relief. Her fists slowly uncurled. "What about them?"

Lost her. What the hell? "Tell us about the one you sold."

"I haven't sold any of Daddy's paintings."

"Do you own any?"

Ellen ran a hand through her short, dark hair, making it stand on end. "I suppose I kinda do, in a weird sort of way. After he died, Mother said we could each choose one that would be our very own. She wouldn't let us have them, you understand. They just belonged to us, but they stayed right here."

"After your mother died, you took the painting?"

"Are you kidding? I tried one time. Is that what you're talking about? If you know about that, then you must know about the fight I had with Dorothy. Carl said somebody would tell you. Was it Vicky? She must have said Dorothy won. I lost."

"Your brother Carl took one."

Ellen grinned. Whatever she was so uptight about, it had nothing to do with paintings. "Carl just took one. It was all over before Dorothy knew about it."

"She let it go?"

"She didn't want to. But Carl has a lot more clout than I do. There was much discussion. Not shouting arguments. My family has never gone in much for loud. Carl just kept saying he would make trouble."

"What kind of trouble?"

"He never said specifically. Just hinted. Like the will."

"He threatened to contest the will?"

"No. Just mentioned that he could. Or talk to reporters. Writers. There was one around about that time, wanting to write a biography of Daddy. Dorothy backed down. She agreed the painting could stay at the gallery, but it couldn't be sold."

"Has Dorothy sold a painting lately?"

Ellen shook her head. "I don't think so. I suppose she could have."

"Any of your siblings have a painting to sell?"

"I don't see how they could. Why are you asking all these questions about Daddy's paintings?"

"One was sold recently."

"There were some sold before he died. Anybody who owned one could have sold it."

"This one was sold by someone in the family."

"I don't believe it. Who?"

"There is a man at a gallery in Kansas City who says you sold it."

"What?" Her face went white; her dark eyes got a hunted look. "That's impossible."

"Tell me why it's impossible."

"Because I didn't do it."

"Where are the paintings stored?"

Ellen vaguely waved a hand toward the ceiling. She looked numb, face even paler, hands in her lap twisted together.

"If you'll show me where they are," Susan said as she rose, "I'd like to take a look at them."

Like a dutiful child, Ellen stood and trudged toward the stairway.

"I don't think that's a terribly good idea, Ellen." Taylor put a hand on her arm to get her attention.

She pulled away and looked up at him. "Why?"

"Don't be stupid, Ellen. At least get a lawyer before you do anything." He turned to Susan. "Have you got a search warrant?"

She did not. The warrant they'd used in searching for the murder weapon wouldn't apply. She wasn't sure she could get one.

"Are you going to arrest me?" Ellen asked.

"Right now, I'm simply trying to gather information. One of your father's paintings was recently sold for quite a lot of money. I need to know if it came from here."

Without a word, Ellen turned and headed for the stairway.

"Ellen—" Taylor said in warning.

"I have to know," Ellen said without stopping.

Susan and Taylor followed her up the stairs; Parkhurst trailed in the rear. The hallway went on long enough to resemble a hotel. It was dim, but Ellen didn't bother to turn on the chandeliers.

The dark, angry sky could be seen through a window at the end. Ellen stopped in front of a door, seemed to steel herself for a difficult ordeal, then took a breath and turned the knob.

Susan wasn't quite sure what the legal position was here. One of the paintings had been taken before Dorothy's death. Dorothy'd had ownership, at least until her death. Now that she was deceased, Ellen had some claim on them. A charge of theft by one of the other heirs would be required before any kind of arrest could be made.

Ellen stiffened her back, stepped into the room, and turned on lights. Two cut-glass chandeliers cast a sparkling rainbow pattern on the polished oak floor. The room was about fifteen by twenty, with no furniture except for three straight-backed Victorian chairs. The walls were covered with paintings. Susan made a quick estimate and came up with forty.

No obvious gap. If one were missing, she had no way

of telling. But Ellen obviously could. She stood in the center of the room and looked intently at the north wall, then turned and looked just as intently at the east, and the same with south and west. Her face was set, carefully blank, but Susan could see the effort it cost to cover up a jolt.

Taylor, face a mask of worry, said nothing. Hands in his pockets, he stood nervously by the door.

"Ms. Barrington?"

Ellen brought her thoughts back from some far place and focused her dark eyes, angry and afraid, on Susan. "I never sold one of Daddy's paintings."

"One is missing?"

"It looks like they're all here."

She was lying. A painting—at least one—was gone. Ellen had known immediately. Lord knows, Susan had been lied to before and fooled, but she'd bet money this was the first Ellen knew about a missing painting. If Ellen hadn't stolen it, who had?

She turned to Taylor. "Mr. Talmidge, how many are missing?"

"I don't believe any are missing. It's hard to say; there are so many."

Ellen shot him a look, then quickly lowered her eyes. Susan couldn't read it. Were these two in collusion? The impression given was that they didn't even like each other. Though that didn't mean diddly. All they needed was mutual benefit.

She questioned them, Parkhurst questioned them; they got zip. Neither would even admit there was an inventory listing. There was no way to check what was here and what should be here.

"What do you think?" she asked Parkhurst as he started the Bronco.

"I think we're getting nowhere. We've got suspects hanging all over the place. Nothing that points to any one of them. Now we've got another motive on top of just whacking her for the money. And we've got young Ms. Ellen fingered for the theft.''

"You think she did it?"

"On the face of it, I'd say no, but that doesn't mean I'd be right. We could put her in a lineup and have old Claude Jennings in to see if he could pick her out.''

"Not without some charge we couldn't.''

Rain drummed on the roof of the Bronco; water rushed along the gutters and fountained over the curbs.

"Taylor's jumpy,'' Parkhurst said.

"Most people are around cops.''

"I've been looking at his finances. He's strapped pretty tight. Down to nickels and dimes. His salary's nowhere near poverty, so where's all the money going?''

"Investing in the stock market?''

"Could be Beautiful Brent was right about that. How about we grab something to eat before we take on the physicians?''

Best suggestion that had come along all day.

NINETEEN

WOULD THEY EVER LEAVE? Ellen felt as though rubber bands stretched to breaking point were all that held her together. Any second they'd snap, and she'd fly apart. Oh, God, let them get out of here. Cops in the house. Her only thought on first seeing them had been, *They've come to arrest me.* It took up all her mind. She couldn't clear space for Daddy's painting. Stolen?

And Taylor giving advice. Why? Maybe she should be nicer to him.

Questions and questions and questions. She couldn't bend her mind around what they were asking.

Finally they stopped hammering at her, and Taylor opened the door for them. Just when she thought she could take a breath, Chief Wren turned in the doorway and looked at her. Ellen's heart flopped around like a landed fish.

Go! Please just get out of here!

"We'll be back," Chief Wren said softly.

Ellen watched them trot through the rain and get in the Bronco.

When they drove off, she turned to Taylor, standing in the archway to the living room. "Did you know about the painting?"

He tried to paste surprise all over his face. "Are you saying one *is* missing?"

Right. Hot news. Like bat shit. Use it for fertilizer. "Why give me advice?"

A smile, the fond-uncle kind. "You needed it. You should have followed it."

She needed a lot more than that. She needed to find out what was going on, who was trying to frame her, and figure out how to get out of this trap somebody was busily closing over her head.

"I've never had any quarrel with you," he said. "Of all you Barringtons, you've been the least uncordial. I had no desire to stand by and see you let yourself get into trouble."

Least uncordial? He was saying he liked her? Yeah, right. Brain flash. Taylor, painting under arm, furtive look, tippytoeing down the wide staircase. Who easier than Taylor? He lived here. Dorothy. Would she? No. Ellen couldn't see her selling one without saying something. She wasn't underhanded.

Shit. What am I going to do? Somebody stole a painting. Sold it. Somehow used my name. First the gun and now the painting. Why make me look guilty? A sneaky thought lit up like fireworks in her mind. *One of her nearest and dearest hated her.* No, let's not get blown out here. Had to hate her, to do this. She suddenly felt bereft, all alone in a little bitty boat adrift in a storm. Always, she'd felt she really didn't fit in with the rest of them, now and then wondered whether they even liked her. But at least they were there. Family. She was part of it.

No, she told herself. No. No. No. It doesn't have to be Willis or Carl or Marlitta. Not Carl. What about Willis' wife? Vicky always seemed halfway scared of Dorothy, maybe glad she wasn't around anymore. Maybe she'd wanted Willis to do something Dorothy wouldn't let him do. Now Vicky could get Willis to do it. Do what? I don't know what! Anything. But Vicky wasn't all that swift. Was she bright enough to pull off a murder?

Marlitta's husband. Now, there was bright. Brent was a shit, and maybe not as smart as he thought, but clever enough to work out a murder and frame her.

And Taylor, what about him? He might have given her good advice, but maybe there was more to it.

She realized she was still standing by the front door staring at him. Just how bright was she, staying in this house with a man who might be a killer and who might be trying to frame her?

Nuts, going nuts. She grabbed her hair and held on. Taylor gave her a weirded-out look.

She dropped her arms, folded them across her chest, and dropped them to her sides. "I need to call Carl," she said, and headed for the kitchen.

She punched in the number, turned to face Taylor, who had followed her, and leaned back against the counter with her fingers twined through the cord. "Carl," she said when he answered, "I think I know why Dorothy wanted us all here for Saturday night."

That got them. Two hours later, they were in the music room just like they'd been the night of the murder.

All those music sessions, Mozart and Bach and Telemann and Vivaldi. Oh, hell. Ellen was all of a sudden overcome by astuteness. The music let them get together without having to talk to each other. She could do without these visions of clarity. Like a plow horse, she was better off with blinders.

Same as Saturday, they were sliding glances at each other. All here but Dorothy. Ellen looked at the piano gleaming under the chandelier and got weepy. Dorothy had wanted to be a pianist. Ellen hadn't even known. She looked at her siblings one by one.

Carl wanted to be a farmer. She hadn't known that either. Willis. What did he want? To be looked up to, take his rightful place as head of the family? And Marlitta? Only thing she ever wanted—that Ellen knew about, and she was finding out she didn't know anything—was Brent. Well, she had him. Lately, she hadn't seemed really, really happy. Seeing him clearly at last? Not likely. Her face glowed with love and admiration whenever she glanced at him.

Willis seemed like he'd aged ten years and lost part of his soul. Inside his suit and tie, he seemed to be shrinking, as if he were slowly getting hollow. His eyes were sunken, face gray. He poured a soda in a glass, added an ice cube with a plop, then another, and went to sit beside his wife on one of the Victorian sofas. Vicky tucked an arm through his, a gesture of comfort, or a way or reminding him she was there. Whichever, Willis ignored her, didn't even offer her anything to drink.

Carl, in baggy khaki pants and a loose white shirt, face hard and lined, opened a bottle of red wine, poured a glass, and took it to Marlitta, who gave him a murmur of thanks. Ellen couldn't guess what he might be thinking. She never could with Carl. If Marlitta had any expression besides fatigue, Ellen could only think it was bewildered.

Carl asked Vicky if she'd like a glass of wine. Vicky shook her head and asked in her sweet little voice if she could just have some club soda. No alcohol? Vicky didn't want to flap her tongue? That always happened after a drink or two.

Ellen got up and poured her own glass of wine, returned to the wing chair, and tucked her feet up under her. Nobody seemed eager to dive right into conversation. Even for this family, the silence was getting thick, everybody worried what was slithering around underneath.

Taylor dipped at his drink, keeping an eye on them in a chicken-among-hawks sort of way. Brent was watching too, in his usual thoughtful observation pose, giving the impression brilliant cogitation was washing around inside. Probably the truth of it, his mind was on getting out of here and on to his swimming session. Tuesday was one of his swimming nights.

"I'm not terribly surprised," Willis said. "I've been telling Dorothy for years better security arrangements should be made. Anybody could break in and make off with the lot."

"Nobody broke in." Carl filled up his glass again, slouched to a wing chair, and sat, legs stretched out in front of him, crossed at the ankles.

"She wanted us here because of Daddy's paintings?" Marlitta acted like a brain dead.

"There was mention of a sale in the *Kansas City Star*," Carl said. "And for those of you who are uninformed, the seller is $100,000 richer." He raised his glass high in the gesture of a toast and then took a sip.

That must be how the cops knew. How did Carl know? Ellen felt Vicky's eyes on her and looked up. Vicky peered into her soda real fast.

"Carl, I don't understand you," Willis said. "First you imply one of us might have something to do with her death, and now you're saying one of us sold a painting."

"I'm saying," Carl said, "Dorothy knew one of us had stolen it. It pissed her off. She wanted us here to tell us whoever did it was going to get chopped."

"She didn't know who?" Marlitta said dimly.

Marlitta, get a clue. What are we talking about?

"The cops think I did it," Ellen said. Eyes snapped her way, like somebody had clicked a switch.

"Why?" Marlitta asked.

"I didn't. If anybody wants to know."

"Of course you didn't," Willis said. "None of us did. The police have got it wrong. Somebody bought a painting years ago and recently sold it. That's all there is to it."

Vicky slid another glance at Ellen. Why all of a sudden was Vicky looking at her?

"Dorothy believed one of us stole it." Ellen tried to take in them all, head wobbling around like one of those cutesy things on a dashboard. Willis and Vicky on one sofa, Marlitta with Brent on the other, Taylor on one side of the fireplace, Carl on the other side. All of them looked back at her with varying degrees of interest. "That's why she was killed."

Nobody's face lit up in neon, flashing guilt. Stupid to think she could spot the guilty. They just looked like they looked.

"You don't even know a painting has been stolen," Willis said.

"One is gone." The one she'd added a butterfly to, a dreepy attempt to make Daddy feel better after his stroke. Her daubs probably meant the painting wasn't worth a dime. Would the cops tack on fraud to a murder charge? It was her painting, the one she'd chosen when Mother said they could each have one, the one she'd fought with Dorothy about.

Did whoever took it know it was worthless? Carl would, for sure, the only one besides herself who'd ever cared about them. Willis or Vicky? She couldn't even guess. The same for Marlitta and Brent. Taylor might know. She didn't think he had any interest in them, except they were valuable. Dorothy probably never looked at them. If it hadn't been for the bit in the paper, the painting might not have been missed for years.

Willis got up, splashed more soda in his glass, and stood in front of the tall windows. If Dorothy had done that, everybody would have watched her, waiting for a pronouncement. Willis barely got a flicker.

"Taylor." He turned to Dorothy's husband. "You know anything about this?"

Taylor shot to his feet. "What did you do, take a vote and decide on me? Why me? Because I'm only an in-law, not a Barrington?"

They were a lot alike, Willis and Taylor, Ellen thought. Except Willis was fair and Taylor dark. Both in suit and tie, both concerned about the impression they made, both lacking a sense of humor, both slightly stuffy.

"Opportunity," Carl said softly. "You were on site."

Hairs stirred along Ellen's arms. She'd never heard Carl sound like that, didn't know he could.

"Opportunity." Taylor snorted, paced to the fireplace, and stood with his back to it.

Back to the wall, Ellen thought.

"You're all in and out of here all the time. What about Vicky?" Taylor pointed at her. "She's not a Barrington."

"Now, just a minute," Willis sputtered.

"She was here the day before Dorothy was killed."

"I didn't take anything," Vicky whispered.

We're like a pack of wolves, ready to turn on the weak.

"Why were you here?" Taylor demanded.

"I came to see Dorothy."

"She wasn't home."

"I didn't know that, did I?" Vicky stuck out her chin. "I know you all think I'm stupid. I'm not so stupid I don't see things. I know you wear a raincoat when it rains." She changed from scared rabbit to spitting cat. "I know when people meet other people by the side of a country road they aren't picking wildflowers. I've heard of core samples. I know money can buy things."

"Nobody thinks you're stupid." Willis crossed to the sofa, sat down, and picked up Vicky's hand. She didn't look comforted. "I won't have accusations tossed around," he said to Taylor.

"Unless they're tossed at me? What about Brent? Let's toss a few his way."

Marlitta hauled in air with a hiss.

Brent touched her with one finger. "Careful, Taylor, you're about to take on more than you can handle."

Brent had a great voice, Ellen had to admit. Deep, rich, with a sensual undercurrent, a hypnotic hum. Didn't matter what he said, you wanted to listen. Then you wanted to applaud. He probably practiced with a tape recorder.

"You think I can't handle you?" Taylor's glance swept over them. "Any of you?"

"I suggest it would be unwise to try." Brent leaned back and put his fingertips together across his manly chest.

Ellen wondered what script he got his dialogue from.

"You are aware we live in an insular community?"

"What the hell does that mean?"

Brent smiled.

What was he reaching for here? Menace? Irony? Whatever, it came through as the same old bullshitting Brent.

"It means, my dear Taylor, it doesn't take long for word to get around."

Oh, my, Ellen thought. Probably the only person in the world who hears things. Yep. I'll betcha he knows all these things 'cause he's just got so much more brain power than the rest of us folks.

Taylor didn't seem to take it as bullshit; it made him draw in his horns right quick. Though he did try one more jab, he'd lost the note of righteous indignation. "You threatening me?"

"Interpret it any way you wish." Brent stood up to get himself another drink. On the way he winked at Ellen.

What did that mean? She stared stonily back and was aware that Vicky was watching. Uneasily, Ellen wondered if they were wrong about Vicky. Maybe she wasn't as dim as they thought.

Taylor slid a glance at Vicky that seemed to mean something. Wouldn't it be funny if they were having an affair, Taylor and Vicky? No. Not funny. Anyway, Vicky was devoted to Willis. Brent was the one who had affairs. Ellen figured that's what all the swimming was about.

The telephone rang. Both Willis and Marlitta started to get up. Extensions were all over the house, but there was none in the music room.

"Since I live here," Taylor said, "maybe I should be allowed to answer my own phone."

Neither Willis nor Marlitta acknowledged his sarcastic tone. He returned in a moment to say the call was for Willis.

When Willis went out to take it, Vicky got up, went to the cart with the liquor bottles, and poured soda in her glass. There was a deliberateness and defiance in her actions that made Ellen feel she was missing something.

Brent tilted his glass, emptied it, and got up for a refill. He said something to Vicky in a soft voice that Ellen couldn't hear. Vicky turned her back on him and went to sit down on the sofa.

Willis returned, fishing keys from his pocket. "That was the service. A patient fell against a window. A long cut on his leg needs stitching. We weren't accomplishing anything here anyway. I don't like all these suggestions that one of us had anything to do with Dorothy's death. The painting may have been gone for years. I suggest we all get back to our lives as best we can with Dorothy gone and stop making trouble for ourselves."

He gave Vicky a brief kiss on the cheek and took off. Vicky stood up and took a step after him. "Willis—"

She stopped, got a look of irritation on her face, and then shrugged.

"I'll run you home," Carl said.

"I can walk. I like to walk. I do a lot of it."

Hidden meaning in Vicky's words? Stop it, Ellen told herself. Overworked imagination. If Vicky knew anything, she'd come right out and spill it to the cops. Except, she might protect Willis. He wouldn't have killed Dorothy. Of all of them, he was the most devastated.

Ellen felt suddenly boneless-tired. Her world had turned upside down. One member in this family of loved ones was trying to frame her for murder. She knew it, and she didn't want it to be. Not Willis. Not Carl. Not Marlitta. Ellen glanced at Marlitta. She looked lost and bewildered. Maybe that's how I look too. We're all lost and bewildered without Dorothy here to tell us what to do.

"We might as well go home," Carl said. "The gathering of the family is now over."

Marlitta got to her feet and plodded to the door like an old woman. Brent finished his drink and followed. Carl offered again to give Vicky a ride. She hesitated. Vicky afraid of Carl? No. Nobody could be afraid of Carl. Then she smiled prettily and accepted.

After everybody left, Ellen put the liquor away in the cabinet and stashed the cart in the closet. She was gathering up dirty glasses to bring to the kitchen when she heard the back door close.

Dashing to the window, she was just in time to see Taylor drive off. Where was he going? Why hadn't he told her he was leaving? Don't be stupid. No reason he had to tell her anything. And even though it felt like midnight, it was only nine o'clock.

Overly neurotic. Take a nice long shower and get yourself to bed. She stashed glasses in the dishwasher, trudged up to her bedroom, sat on the window seat, looked out at the garden, and listened to the locusts. Hey, could be worse, right? At least it's stopped raining. Was Vicky trying to say something tonight? Bloody hell. I don't know. I don't know anything.

She got in the shower and stood under hot water hoping the steam would boil up a useful thought.

The phone rang. She started to jump out, then decided to ignore it. It rang and rang and rang. Grumbling, she turned off the water, grabbed a towel, and blotted at her legs as she hurried to answer. Whoever it was would probably hang up before she got there. The nearest phone was Dorothy's office.

She snatched the receiver, slightly breathless, slightly irritated, "Hello."

"It's Vicky."

Loud music in the background. Ellen couldn't hear.

"Can you come over?"

"Now? I was just getting ready for bed." A click and the dial tone. Ellen grimaced and started to call back. Whatever it was could wait until tomorrow. She stood there a tick, dripping water on Dorothy's Persian carpet. Some-

thing odd about the phone call, but she couldn't figure
what.

She tugged on a clean pair of jeans and a blue tank top
and peered around for her beige sandals. One was at the
foot of the bed, the other beneath the rocker. She slid her
feet into them and ran the brush through her wet hair. From
her purse, she dug out car keys.

Six blocks away, she pulled into the driveway, then realized the garage door was open and one of the cars was
gone. Willis wasn't home yet. She backed out, so he could
get in the garage when he got here, and parked in front.
Crickets sang in the shrubbery, the air was warm and vel-
vet-soft against her bare arms, billions of stars glittered in
a black sky.

She trotted up the steps and rapped on the door. Music
blared at high volume inside. She rapped harder.

How could anybody hear anything? She slapped down
the steps and around to the rear. Vicky had called. The least
she could do was answer a knock. Light from the kitchen
window spilled a large rectangle on the lawn.

She pounded on the door, waited a few seconds, and tried
the knob. It turned under her hand. She pushed it open and
stepped in. "Vicky?" She squinted in the light.

Jesus, why did she have the music so loud?

"Vicky? Where are you?"

She went through the dining room and peered into the
dim living room. Vicky was slumped on the couch. She
wasn't moving. She didn't look so good.

TWENTY

"VICKY? WHAT'S WRONG? Why are you sitting in the dark?" Beethoven blared in her ears. Bad smell. She groped along the wall for the switch that turned on the recessed ceiling lights.

"Vicky, for heaven's sake, what's so important it couldn't wait till morning?"

She hit the switch and got more light. "Oh, my God." Her heart crashed around in her throat. The light lit up Vicky's face. It was blue. Blue isn't a good color for a face. Clashed horribly with her blue dress. She'd vomited. On the floor. On the couch. All down her dress.

Ellen gagged and clapped a hand to her mouth. Do something. She couldn't make her legs work, couldn't take her eyes from that ugly blue face, eyes half-open, staring. Vicky was beautiful. She couldn't look like this.

Beethoven swelled. Music to die by. A high, keening wail forced its way through her throat. She clamped her teeth and backed away. Abruptly, she turned, moved numbly to the stereo, and snapped it off. The silence was heavy, thick. Then little sounds came creeping in: the hum of the refrigerator, the ponderous tick of the mantel clock, a car driving by. Her ears made tick-tick-tick sounds like cooling metal.

I have to call— Ambulance. Police. Carl. I'll call Carl. He'll know what to do. Phone. In the kitchen. If she concentrated very hard, she could make her feet move. Yes, she could. Oh, God, Vicky. Poor Vicky.

Hauling in quick gulps of air, she made it to the kitchen and reached for the phone. She couldn't dredge up Carl's number. Fingers icy cold, she punched 911.

"Vicky— She's—"

"Can you tell me what the problem is?"

"I'm afraid she's— She doesn't seem to be breathing."

Despite the calm voice telling her to stay on the line, she hung up and called Carl. This time his number came out with no difficulty.

"Carl, Vicky's dead. On the couch. I just came over— and found her—all slumped—and her face—" She slid to the floor, back against the cabinet, and clasped her hands around her legs.

AT ELEVEN-THIRTY at night, the streets were bare of traffic, the houses dark. A soft wind trailed gauzy wisps of clouds across an almost full moon and plucked at Susan's hair through the open window of the pickup. She made a quick left onto Longhorn Drive and pulled up beside a squad car, overheads still flashing. An ambulance was parked next to it, empty and waiting. A handful of neighbors, in pajamas and robes, stood watching from front yards and open doorways.

Susan slid from the pickup, tucked her gray blouse more tightly into her gray pants, and nodded to Officer Yancy, standing at the door. In the entryway, two paramedics lounged against the wall waiting to be summoned. She went through into the living room and paused to take in a sense of the scene.

Dr. Fisher stood by the body while Osey took photographs. They both looked up at her and then went on with their business. Vicky's immaculate living room seemed defiled by the presence of the body and the pools of vomit on the Oriental rug and the pearl-gray couch.

Vicky had slumped over onto her left shoulder, left side of her face resting on the couch, left arm beneath her, right arm dangling to the floor, fingers loosely curled. She wore a simple blue cotton dress with a flared skirt and high-heeled sandals. Her perfect oval face was a cyanotic blue.

Her shiny chestnut hair picked up highlights from the recessed ceiling fixtures. A mug of what looked like hot chocolate sat on the glass-topped table by the couch.

Susan stood out of the way and made a crude sketch of the room. Parkhurst, face impassive, came to stand next to her.

"Anything outside?" she asked.

He shoved his hands into the back pockets of his black denim pants. As good a way as any to keep from touching anything until Osey had done all he could in the way of collecting evidence.

"Not yet. I've got Demarco and White canvassing."

Dr. Fisher straightened and stripped latex gloves from his hands, delicate, long-fingered hands that didn't fit with the rest of him. A stocky, barrel-chested man in brown pants and a white shirt with the sleeves rolled up, he had a thick neck, a shock of white hair, and heavy, dark eyebrows. He looked like a truck driver with the hands of a pianist.

"Well?" she said.

"Overdose of something. Cyanosis, pinpoint pupils. Bite marks in the mouth from convulsive activity."

"Any idea what?" She looked at the mug with a half-inch of thick brown liquid.

"Codeine, I'd say."

She looked at him sharply. He never said anything definite until after he'd sliced, diced, and examined.

With a glint of amusement, he pointed at a small vial that lay partly under the couch. "It's got a label, but that's all I can see of it until Osey gets done printing. You might want to get a sample of whatever's in that mug."

She did not make any snide remark having to do with sucking eggs. "Suicide?"

"That's more your job."

"No sign of a note," Parkhurst said.

That didn't mean a lot. Some suicides left a note, some

didn't. A suicide strongly implied guilt in Dorothy's murder. Was that going to be it? The mayor would jump on it. Get this whole mess cleaned up. "How long has she been dead?"

Fisher put one arm across his chest, propped an elbow on it, and pinched his chin between thumb and forefinger. "Mucous membranes dry. Body temp down two degrees. Lividity just starting. No beginning of rigor yet. I'd hazard a shot at two hours tops, but if you won't hold me to it I'd say an hour is more what you're looking at."

She turned to Parkhurst. "Have you reached her husband?"

"No. He didn't answer a page at the hospital, and he hasn't responded to his beeper."

So where was he?

Off the kitchen and two steps down was a room where Carl Barrington and Ellen waited on a white leather couch with Yancy keeping herd on them. The room was just as spotless and lifeless as the rest of the house: television set, wet bar, sliding glass doors onto a patio.

"Yancy," Susan said, "would you go with Dr. Barrington into the dining room, please?"

Carl shot her a hard look but made no protest as he got up, ruffled Ellen's curls, and let Yancy shepherd him out.

Susan sat in a chair at a right angle to the couch, a deep leather chair that she sank into. Scooting forward a little, she leaned toward Ellen. "Ms. Barrington, are you up to answering a few questions?"

"She called me."

"What time?"

Ellen drew in a breath and closed her eyes. "I don't know," she said as she exhaled. "Nine-thirty, maybe."

"You came immediately?"

Ellen's face went greenish-white. "Would it have— If I'd been here sooner—" Wide-eyed horror.

"No," Susan said calmly. "There was nothing you

could have done.'' Whether this was true or not, she wasn't certain, but she didn't want Ellen prey to the swampy menace of imagination. "How long after she called did you get here?"

Ellen rubbed a hand across her mouth. "I didn't hurry. I was in the shower. I just— I got dressed. Not too long. I could have been faster."

"You came directly here? Did you see anybody?"

Ellen shook her head.

"A car?"

Another head shake.

"What did Vicky say?"

"I couldn't hear very well. She wanted me to come."

"Why couldn't you hear?"

"The music was so loud." Ellen rubbed her face hard with the heels of her palms. "Something was odd, but I don't— I can't think—"

"Odd about the phone call?"

Ellen nodded uncertainly. "Was she calling for help?"

Pop an overdose, start drifting, then have regrets, make a desperate attempt to get help. Why call Ellen? With all the physicians in the family, why not one of them? "Did Vicky say your name?"

She could see Ellen try to remember and not get back through the grim mental picture of the body.

"I don't remember."

"Were you close friends?"

"We didn't really have much in common. We never really talked. She was—she was—so beautiful, so—" Despite a hard effort at control, tears welled up in her eyes.

From her bag, Susan got a tissue and offered it. Ellen blotted her face and blew her nose.

"What else did Vicky say on the phone?"

"Just to come. She was kind of whispery. And the music was so loud. When I got here, the music was—" Ellen got a startled look on her face. "Beethoven," she said with dawning awareness.

"The music? That's what was playing?"

"How could that be? I don't understand. It doesn't make sense. It doesn't make any sense."

"What doesn't make sense?"

"She wouldn't listen to Beethoven. Only if Willis was home. She hated classical music. She never listened to it. She liked country-and-western. Why would she have on Beethoven?"

Because somebody turned it on too loud and made the phone call. Somebody who didn't want to be recognized. "It was still playing when you got here?"

"I turned it off," Ellen said guiltily. "It was so loud."

"Tell me what you were doing this evening before you got the call," Susan said.

In a flat voice, Ellen told her everybody had been at the house, talking about the missing painting—*the* painting, not *a* painting, Susan noted. There was hesitant and reluctant mention of accusations and responses.

Susan took her through it twice. Ellen was saying more than she probably realized, and, with a talent for mimicry, she gave a clear picture of what had gone on.

"How did Vicky seem different?"

Ellen clutched the soggy tissue and dabbed at her nose. "I don't know. She wasn't drinking. Willis wasn't either, but he was on call. And she— Usually she didn't say anything, but this time—" Ellen was seized by hiccups. "It was like she—*hic*—got fed up all of a sudden—*hic*."

Susan went to the kitchen and brought back a glass of water. Ellen took a gulp, hiccuped, took another gulp.

"Was Vicky frightened? Angry?"

"No. I don't know. She just seemed—for just that moment—I guess angry, but—" Ellen shook her head, drew away, and huddled into herself against the arm of the couch.

Officer Ellis came through the kitchen, stepped down the two steps, and cleared his throat. Susan looked at him.

"They're ready to take the—" he glanced at Ellen "—uh, her away now, if that's all right with you."

Susan stood by as the ambulance attendants bundled Vicky Barrington into a body bag, loaded her on a gurney, and wheeled her away. She told Ellis to accompany them to the hospital and take possession of the victim's clothing.

She let Ellen go and had Carl brought in.

"Does Willis know?" he asked.

"Not yet. Please sit down, Dr. Barrington." She gestured toward the couch. "We haven't been able to reach him. Do you know where he is?"

"At the hospital." Carl, in baggy khaki pants and a loose white shirt, resembled a starving peasant. His thin face had the inward, suffering look of a martyr. "Vicky poison herself?"

"Why do you think she was poisoned?"

"It doesn't take a brilliant mind. Cyanosis. Vomiting. Why would she kill herself?"

"You know any reason?"

Carl looked at her with tired mockery. "Only the obvious. She killed Dorothy and was overcome with remorse."

"You think that's a possibility?"

"Thinking is something I try not to do too much of."

She waited, but he was not a person who felt obliged to leap in and fill the silence. "Tell me what happened when you were all together this evening."

He took a breath with a slight *huh* sound. "Clever of you to start with Ellie." In a flat voice, he briefly stated who had said what, with no speculation, elaboration, or emotional overtones.

When he stopped, she let the silence lengthen, with no effect. "Taylor accused Vicky of killing Dorothy," she said.

"No. He felt he was being accused and went on the defensive."

"He pointed at Vicky. She responded by saying she knew something. What could she have known?"

Susan could sense Carl analyzing, weighing alternatives, computing, all the while not missing a word she was saying. "Vicky responded like a frightened kitten, with a hiss."

"What exactly did she say?"

"Ellie must have told you."

"I'd like you to tell me."

"Vicky insisted she wasn't so dumb that she didn't know things."

"Like?"

"Like: You wear a raincoat when it rains. If you meet somebody on a back road, there's a reason."

"What did she mean by that?"

Carl shook his head. "I have no idea."

Susan doubted it. "What else?"

"Money buys things."

"Taylor also accused Brent."

"He tried. Brent said, in effect, 'Back off or you're in trouble.'"

"What did that mean?"

"I have no idea."

Right, Susan thought. "Why did you drive Vicky home?"

"Willis got a call. She didn't have a car."

"How did she seem?"

Carl's response was to close his eyes; when he opened them, she saw pain and worry.

"What did you talk about?" she asked.

"Six blocks. Hardly time for conversation. I drove her here, walked her to the door, drove myself home. I was there until Ellie called."

"What was Vicky's relationship with Dorothy?"

"She avoided her whenever possible, was slightly afraid of her. Dorothy thought she wasn't good enough for Willis."

"Why?"

"It wasn't true. She was a quiet little thing. Not real bright, but not as dumb as Dorothy thought. She never said much, mainly because she was made to feel whatever she had to say wasn't worth listening to."

"Did she like Dorothy?"

"No."

A loud voice came from the front of the house. Susan went to see what that was about. Willis Barrington had come home.

"What is going on?" he demanded. "Where's Vicky?"

"Dr. Barrington," Susan said, "I'm afraid we have some bad news."

TWENTY-ONE

"PLEASE," SUSAN SAID. "Dr. Barrington, if you could answer a few questions, it would be helpful."

With a hand on his elbow, she guided Willis Barrington toward the leather couch in the room off the kitchen. He dropped heavily.

"Can you tell me where you've been?" She sat back on the overstuffed chair.

"At the hospital. A patient. I must go to Vicky."

"I understand, Dr. Barrington. But right now we're trying to find out what happened. We tried to reach you at the hospital and were unable to get you. Where did you go when you left there?"

His face was slack and gray, eyes dull and unfocused. His hands trembled slightly on his knees. He squeezed them into fists.

"Where were you, Dr. Barrington?"

For a moment, she thought he was going to lash out at her. He took in a harsh breath, his eyes sharpened, angry and clear; then he lost the impetus, bent his head, and spoke to the floor, his voice slurred. "I was down at the river. We used to play there when we were children. Dorothy and I. I—" He raised his head, seeing something in the past. "I miss her. I thought I could feel her near—" Somewhere deep inside, he found strength to pull his mind into focus. He did not like the direction her questions were going, and straightened up his thoughts along with his spine. "What happened to Vicky?" The words were steady.

"We're not sure yet. Apparently an overdose. Did she ever take codeine?"

"Codeine? Certainly not. She was extremely allergic to

it. We discovered that when she had neuritis last year. Vicky would never take codeine.''

Susan couldn't move him beyond that point. Was Vicky depressed? Certainly not. Vicky was never depressed. Did she know something about Dorothy's murder? Certainly not. A drug addict killed Dorothy.

If Vicky hadn't taken the codeine voluntarily, what could have happened?

He refused to answer any more questions.

Susan told Parkhurst to track down Taylor Talmidge. She took Officer Tullick and went off to question Marlitta and Brent.

MARLITTA, in a dark-green robe that made her skin look sallow, rocked barely perceptibly in the wooden rocking chair. It creaked softly. Lights from the crystal lamps on the tables turned her fair hair to gold.

Brent, dark hair attractively tousled, had pulled on black pants and a black T-shirt. He stood in front of a bookcase built into the wall next to the fireplace. Susan's eyes were immediately drawn to him. The man had presence, she had to give him that. With the lights all on, a coffee cup on a table near the wing chair, a book open face-down beside it, the room looked like a stage set. Man awakened from sound sleep and given bad news: just the right display of shock.

He went to his wife, stood behind her chair, and put a hand on her shoulder. She reached up and placed her hand over his. Uninvited, Susan sat on the sofa and spoke quietly to Marlitta. ''Dr. Barrington, do you understand why I'm here?''

Brent squeezed his wife's shoulder, stepped around, and crouched in front of her, looking at her with concern. Susan asked him if he would mind waiting in the kitchen with Officer Tullick. He obviously did mind, but he rose and left without comment. Marlitta's eyes followed him.

"Dr. Barrington?" Susan wondered whether the woman's mind was tracking.

Marlitta blinked. "You said Vicky was dead."

"Can you tell me about this evening, when you were at Dorothy's house?"

"Ellen. She said Dorothy was killed because someone had stolen a painting. A painting." Marlitta shook her head, bewildered, and stared at the tips of her frilly green slippers, as though they didn't make any sense either.

"You think that's why Dorothy was killed?"

Marlitta rubbed fingertips over one eyelid. "I don't understand anything."

Susan started Marlitta at the beginning: What time did you get there? Where did everyone sit? What did Vicky say? What did each of the others say? The only thing Marlitta seemed to remember for certain was that it was Ellen who'd asked them to come.

"What time did you leave?"

"It must have been—" Marlitta looked around in confusion. "Close to eight o'clock."

They came straight home. She drank a cup of tea and went to bed.

Brent?

"He had something he had to do, and then he was here."

Brent sat at the kitchen table sipping coffee. The ceiling light sparkled on white appliances and cabinet tops, bright enough for surgery. Officer Tullick, standing just inside the door, stiffened to attention when Susan came in. She gave him a nod, and he left to keep an eye on Marlitta. Susan sat across the table from Brent.

He studied her over the brim of his mug, then set it down. "Coffee?"

"No thank you."

"Not really the best thing to drink at two in the morning, I guess." He sighed. "Sleep is out of the question anyway."

"Tell me about this evening, Dr. Wakeley."

He looked at her and smiled a quick smile with no humor. "Seeing if my story matches?"

"I need to get all the information I can."

He turned sideways in the chair, stretched out his legs, and propped an elbow on the table. He sipped coffee, looked down at his mug, and tipped it back and forth. "You've already talked with the others?" It was more a statement than a question.

"Does it make a difference?"

Another quicksilver smile. "Only that it might clue me in on what to say."

"This isn't a game, Dr. Wakeley."

He sobered instantly. "No. I'm sorry about Vicky."

She started him out with what time he and Marlitta had arrived at the Barrington house, where they were in the house, who said what. He answered with no evasions that she could spot until he got to Taylor's remarks; then she could see him sort through, choose, and discard.

"What time did you return home?"

"I'm sure Marlitta's already told you. Somewhere around eight o'clock."

"And then?"

"I'm sure she's already told you that too." There was a little hint of impatience in his rich, resonant voice. He waited a moment, then said. "I always swim on Tuesday evenings. My only bow toward exercise." He slapped his flat stomach.

She didn't believe it for a minute. He probably watched every calorie that went in his mouth, rode a stationary bicycle, and did isometrics at idle moments.

"Then I went to the clinic to catch up on some professional reading. You wouldn't believe the amount of journals that come out."

"You got home at what time?"

"Shortly after eleven, I'd guess. Marlitta was asleep."

She took him back to the conversation in the Barrington music room. "Taylor accused Vicky of shooting Dorothy?"

"I think he was simply scattering words to shift the focus from himself."

"Vicky got upset, angry?"

"Angry, perhaps frightened. Responded before she thought. She did that often."

"She mentioned seeing somebody parked by the side of the road. To whom was she referring?"

Brent did everything but squirm to indicate his reluctance to answer. If he hadn't been such a showman she might have been more quick to accept it, but he overdid it a hair in his attempt to make sure she got the point.

"She may have meant—" he drew out each word, a man uncomfortable but, under the circumstances, obliged to relate what he knew "—Taylor."

"Why Taylor?"

Brent got up, went to the coffeepot, refilled his mug, and set the pot back on the warming plate. He sampled the coffee before he spoke. "I happened to see Taylor parked on a country road."

"When?"

"Last week sometime."

"Where?"

"Near Ellen's place."

"Who was he with?"

"Holly Dietz."

For a moment, Susan didn't know who Holly was; then memory kicked in. Holly was the woman gathering old photos for a book about early Hampstead. Taylor and Holly? Love by the side of the road? Thus far there'd been no whiff of Taylor straying from marital bliss. Brent, on the other hand, smelled like a veritable bouquet. A little misdirection?

Rain sprinkled on the roof of the squad car when Susan and Tullick drove back to Willis Barrington's house. Jagged streaks of lightning crackled through the black sky, and Susan tensed in anticipation of thunder. It boomed like a cannon, rumbled away, to be followed by another crack and rumble. And she used to love rain. One thing she could say about Kansas, it knew how to put on a thunderstorm.

Carl and Ellen had gone off with Willis. She found Osey in the master bedroom, going through drawers. It was a large room with a four-poster bed, bright flowered bedspread with ruffled edges, two dormer windows with matching ruffled curtains. The sterility of the downstairs had been carried on up here. The room was neat, bed made, two white provincial chests with the tops bare, one large picture of three herons.

Osey shoved in the bottom drawer of a chest, swiveled around still in a crouch, noticed her, and uprighted himself in jerky movements like unfolding a ruler.

"Anything?" she asked.

"No, ma'am. 'Less you want to hear about Miss Vicky's underwear. Pretty fancy."

"No suicide note?"

"No, ma'am."

"You about finished here?"

Osey raked straw-colored hair off his forehead. "Downstairs. Still got a ways to go up here. Haven't checked on the bathroom yet. Reckon we might find a few meds."

"Bag everything."

"Yes, ma'am. I figured I might do that."

She smiled apologetically. She was simply holding him up. "Any word from Parkhurst?"

"Not since he left to find Taylor Talmidge. You want me to get him for you?"

"Never mind." She went back downstairs and started to speak to Yancy, stationed at the front door, when Parkhurst's Bronco pulled up outside. He sprinted through drizzle to the house.

"Did you find Taylor?" she asked.

He ran a hand down his face, wiping away water. "Yeah. He drove up just as I got there."

Hail peppered the porch roof, and she moved closer to hear better. "Where had he gone?"

Parkhurst grinned, with a flash of white teeth. "When I asked, he told me to get lost."

"I assume you asked him again. Politely."

"Only when I pointed out the serious interest I had in his whereabouts, and that if I didn't get an answer he was not going to be thrilled with my displeasure, did he say he'd been with a friend."

"What friend?"

"Holly Dietz."

"He say why he went to see her?"

"After an evening with his in-laws, he needed to be with someone who didn't look at him cross-eyed about Dorothy's murder."

"Times?"

"He got there about nine-fifteen."

Hell. Nobody had an alibi worth shit. Vicky was last seen alive at nine. Ellen found her body at close to eleven. Carl claimed to be home. He could have come over and fed her poison. Ditto for Marlitta or Brent. Ellen could have come earlier, then come back to find the body. Taylor could have stopped off before going to see Holly. Willis could have poisoned her before he hightailed it to the river to commune with memories.

Assuming Vicky was poisoned. Speculating ahead of the evidence again.

Lack of sleep was catching up with her. Her mind started thoughts that turned to smoke before she could finish them. She told Parkhurst about her questioning of Carl, Marlitta, and Brent.

He raised an eyebrow. "Am I hearing a few doubts about this handy suicide?"

"Why would she kill herself?"

"All overcome with remorse, felt we were snapping at her heels."

"I'd be more inclined to buy that if we had any teeth to snap with, or if she'd left a note."

"Suicides don't always."

"I know that."

She stared out at the rain spilling over the porch eaves. "What's the name of the janitor?"

"Who?"

"Maintenance man of the medical building. Kreps?"

"Murray, yeah. Why?"

"Ask him if he'd let us into the building. I'll meet you there."

MURRAY KREPS didn't mind at all being roused at almost four on a rainy Wednesday morning to let them in. He was bright-eyed and interested, all set to be helpful. Only Parkhurst's firm assurance for the second time that they would secure the building before they left sent Kreps back out in the rain.

Parkhurst hit the lights in the waiting room. "You feel like telling me what we're doing here?"

The bloody carpet where Dorothy's body had fallen had been replaced, in the same pale-oatmeal color. Not just one section, but the entire corridor.

"Brent said he was here for two hours," she said. "He could have dropped in on Vicky before he came here." She moved down the corridor, opened the door to Willis' office, and snapped on the light.

"You do realize," Parkhurst said, "we have no legal right to go anywhere but Dorothy's office."

"I'm not searching, I'm just looking." They had not yet

released Dorothy's office, so they were still covered under the search warrant.

"Willis and Vicky, Carl, Marlitta and Brent, Ellen, Taylor. They had an emotional gathering this evening. Anxiety, suspicion, grief all got mixed up together, and some of it spilled over. They took pot shots at each other."

"Normal."

"Yes." She opened the door of Carl's office. "Marlitta was whacked, barely knowing which end was up. Brent takes her home and says, 'Here's a cup of tea, dear. I have to go swimming and then to the office.'"

"So, he's a sensitive guy."

"I just wondered if there was a reason he needed to be here." She opened the door of Brent's office and let her eyes take in the room: oak desk under the window, blind slats closed, stack of nine-by-twelve envelopes sitting in the center ready for mailing, bookcase full of books, desk chair, patient chair, print on the wall of a skier flying down a slope.

She backed out, closed the door, and went to Dorothy's office. "The seal's been broken."

Parkhurst shrugged. "You're surprised? A crime scene works like a magnet. Each one of them probably went in to look. Only way to prevent it was stake a man at the door. We didn't do that; we didn't think there was anything left to find."

"It occurred to me to wonder if Brent wanted to remove something, destroy something."

"Something we were so stupid as to overlook?"

Dorothy's office looked no different than when Susan had last seen it: desk blotter, marble pen holder with two pens, desk chair slightly pulled out as though the occupant had just gotten up, telephone, medical texts stacked on one corner. Even the tulip in the cut-glass vase was still there, wilted and brown.

Everything looked exactly the same. Oh, hell. Maybe it's

time to pack it in. The long day's task is done, and we must sleep. Or something like that.

Parkhurst had the intent look of a cop taking in the surround, comparing with the mental picture.

"Anything different?" she asked.

"Not that I can see."

Did you write it down? The voice belonged to Captain Reardon, San Francisco cop and former boss. *Get this in your head and get it good. Ten rules for investigation. Rule number one. Write it down. Got that? Plant it firmly. Rules number two through five. Write it down. Rule six. Write it down. Rule seven, eight, nine, ten. Write it down. Write it down. Write it down. Write it down. The first question out of the mouth of the defense attorney is going to be whatever the fuck you didn't write down. Screws all to hell credibility with the jury. The hell with whether it's pertinent. Cases are lost in court because some cop didn't write down whether the curtains were dark blue or dark gray. If you can't even remember the color of the curtains, how can you be trusted in anything else?*

The habit was so instilled, it was automatic. Digging through her shoulder bag, she found her notebook and flipped back pages to find the rough sketches of Dorothy's office and the jotted notes. Two medical texts, lower right corner of desk. Prescription blanks used as bookmarks. Porphyria.

She picked up the top book—*Mendelian Inheritance in Man*—and opened it where it was marked. Adrenal Hyperplasia IV. Adrenal Hyperplasia V.

Arms crossed, leaning against the door frame, Parkhurst watched patiently.

"Know anything about adrenal hyperplasia?" she asked.

"Can't say I do. Can't say I want to."

She picked up the other book—*Genetic Diseases*—and opened it. Guillain-Barré syndrome. Acute febrile polyneuritis, neuronitis. Uh-huh. Well, then. "The day Dorothy

Barrington was shot,'' she said, ''prescription blanks were inserted in the section on porphyria.''

He raised an eyebrow. ''Mean something?''

''I can't think what the hell it might.''

''Somebody looked up something, then replaced the bookmarks in a different spot.''

''Probably. Let's go home.''

No LETUP in the rain. She rattled down the garage door, with head bent splashed to the house, and got drenched fumbling the key in the lock.

As she groped for the light switch, something small flew at her in the dark. She flung up an arm and smacked at it, connected with a ball of fur, and sent it flying.

''Oh, shit.'' She turned on the ceiling light, squinted in the glare, and looked around for the kitten. Perissa crouched under the table, fur standing on end, and hissed at her.

Susan shrugged off her dripping raincoat, slung it over a chair, and squatted to murmur apologetic noises. Perissa inched away warily. Susan duck-walked closer, hand outstretched. Just before her leg muscles gave out, Perissa decided Susan wasn't an axe-wielding cat killer after all and tippytoed toward her.

Susan scooped her up and cuddled her against her chin. Perissa clawed onto a shoulder and spoke loudly of hunger.

Susan opened a can, spooned fishy stuff in a bowl, and put it on the floor. Perissa fell all over herself getting to it.

Upstairs in the bedroom, Susan shed her clothes, pulled on one of Daniel's T-shirts and dropped face-down on the bed. She wasn't sure she had the strength to turn over. Jesus, what's the matter with me? Too old to pull an all-nighter? And it hadn't even been all night.

She was bobbling along toward sleep, when a horse galloped into the bedroom. Perissa swarmed onto the bed, stomped around on Susan's legs, and curled up in the small of her back. Rain pattered against the roof.

THE PHONE RANG, jarring her awake. She fumbled for the receiver.

The dispatcher at the department said, "Brookvale Hospital just called."

TWENTY-TWO

SUSAN LEFT the pickup at the emergency entrance at Brookvale and raced through the rain to the sliding doors. She
took the stairs two at a time. Outside Jen's cubicle, the
medication cart stood shoved to one side for a portable
EKG machine and a code cart, top littered with glass am-
pules and instruments and a black rubber resuscitator bag.
Off to one side, trying to stay out of the way and looking
angry and frightened, stood Officer Saylor, the cop who
was supposed to guard-dog Jen.

Dr. Sheffield, solid and stocky in gray sweatpants, caught
sight of Susan, broke off his conversation with the nurse,
and hurried to her side. Chest and shoulder muscles bulged
under a tight white T-shirt. Pugnacious jaw bristled with
stubble. "It's all right," he said. Even his voice had muscle. "Now. Looked pretty dicey there for a minute."

Jen lay motionless, splotchy face red against the white
sheets. The nurse was watching her cautiously.

"What happened?"

"That's what I'd like to know." Sheffield clipped the
words and aimed a look at the nurse. "The patient got an
overdose of morphine."

"What? How—"

"Ms. James was just following orders."

Susan glanced at the nurse; the name pinned to her chest
read "Nora James, R.N." She looked about twenty-five,
with short brown hair. She also looked very frightened.

Sheffield took a breath and spoke in a voice less damn-
ing. "At least she got on it right away."

"Dr. Sheffield—" Susan began, voice hard.

He stomped—loafers, no socks—to the nurses' station,

grabbed a chart, and opened it in front of her. She squinted at it, her heart still leaping around, adrenaline jagging through her system. He stabbed a blunt forefinger on the page. She bent over to read the squiggles.

He tapped the finger impatiently as though she were being exceptionally dense. She tried to focus and made out "3 squiggle squiggle q 4 h."

She straightened. "You want to tell me just what you're talking about?"

"Dosage for medication," he said. "It's been changed from one milligram to three milligrams."

She peered closely and, now that she knew what she was looking for, could just make out that a broad-tipped pen had turned a one into a three. She straightened. "When was this done?"

He let go of a breath, rasped a hand over his jaw, shrugged, and shook his head. She felt rage build inside her.

"I don't know," he said. "It had to be recent."

"Q 4 h?"

"Every four hours."

"That means this was done within the last four hours."

"No. Ms. James gave her medication at midnight and again at four."

"Twice? Jen was given triple the amount two times?"

He crossed his arms and rested a hip against the edge of the desk. "I've spoken with the nurse who administered the eight p.m. dose. It's charted here." He jabbed at the chart. "She says one milligram. That's what she noted. But that's the dose she gave previously, at four p.m., and she knew the amount. So even though she looked at the chart first, she can't say if she looked that closely."

"You're saying this could have been altered anytime within the last twelve hours."

"Probably."

"Who has access to these charts?" Even as she said it,

she knew the answer. Anybody who walked up and slid the chart out of the slot. It would have taken only a moment. The charts were all clearly labeled with the patient's names.

"It would have to be somebody who looked like he belonged," Sheffield said.

Yes. Or she. Nonmedical personnel would be noticed and challenged. A doctor. Possibly a nurse. Or possibly someone who looked like one or the other. Just possibly someone who chose his time carefully, when nobody was looking, and was quick. "This nurse, Nora James, was she unaware this dosage was three times the normal amount?"

He sighed. "We're understaffed. She's not experienced in working with children. She looked at the orders, did what they said. She only started to question them when the patient began showing signs of distress."

Distress. Susan clamped her teeth. "Would this have killed Jen?"

"Hard to say. It might have. That's a lot of morphine for someone her size. She's all right now," he hastened to add. "Just sleepy."

The rage in the pit of her stomach flared up and spread like a forest fire through her chest with a hot, intense heat that just kept growing. Pure rage, she thought, beat heroin all to hell. She wanted to tear this place apart, batter Dr. Sheffield, pound the nurse, shred the cop who was supposed to prevent exactly this sort of thing from happening. She wanted to scream at everybody who was standing up and walking around. How dare they, when Jen was lying on that bed.

Fatigue, adrenaline, and jangled nerves all combined with rage to create a high, thin humming in her ears.

"She's okay," Sheffield repeated.

Susan went to the cubicle and picked up one of Jen's hands. Jen opened her eyes for a moment, then sleepily closed them and settled into the pillow with a soft sigh.

Susan chewed on the inside of her cheek to keep from crying. With a gentle squeeze, she replaced Jen's hand on the white sheet and left.

A doctor. Possibly a nurse. She didn't know a nurse who might want to harm Jen. But she had four doctors: Willis, Marlitta, Brent, or Carl. Any one of them could have pulled the chart, made a stroke, and replaced it.

She got on the phone and told the dispatcher to get hold of Parkhurst and have him call her. Three minutes went by before the phone rang. She snatched the receiver.

It took him ten minutes to get there. The two of them questioned staff: doctors, nurses, aides, orderlies, housekeeping, and anybody else they could find. They got nothing definite. Willis, Marlitta, Brent, and Carl were all familiar figures. Nobody could remember definitely seeing one of them looking at charts. Nor could anyone definitely say that one of them hadn't been there.

At seven-thirty they packed it in. She was so tired the only thing holding her up was the wall of the elevator.

"This brings us closer to the Barrington Physicians," she said. "Or Dr. Brent Wakeley."

"Yeah. Except there's another physician, right handy, who could make changes on the chart in front of God and everybody."

The elevator doors slid open with a soft hiss, and they walked through the emergency section and out the sliding doors. Rain was still pelting down.

"Adam Sheffield," she said.

"Yeah."

"What's his motive?"

Parkhurst looked up and held out a cupped palm. "You think we might discuss this somewhere a little drier?"

Her mind darted from one thing to another, never catching hold of anything. She glanced back at the hospital and rejected that idea; hauling into the department seemed an unnecessary effort. The Coffee Cup Café opened at six but had cheery waitresses with curiosity. "My house," she said.

He nodded and trotted off through the rain. Lightning forked across the sky as she kicked herself into a shambling lope to the pickup.

At home, she pulled into the garage, plodded flat-footed to the house, fumbled for the key, unlocked the kitchen door, and snapped on the light. She had time to change into a dry pair of black pants and a white sweatshirt, and start the coffee, before she heard a soft tap on the kitchen door.

Parkhurst dropped the square white box on the table and shrugged off his raincoat. "Doughnuts."

She hung his coat over the shower rod in the bathroom and brought him a towel.

"Thanks." He rubbed his face and vigorously toweled his hair. In a tired sort of way, he looked rather handsome, rugged, damp, unshaven, in jeans and a denim shirt open at the throat.

She took down two mugs from the cabinet, filled them with coffee, and handed him one. As he took the mug, his hard eyes did a fixed, impenetrable surveillance of her face. All of a sudden, he seemed too close. She felt herself take a breath. Hail clattered on the roof, smashed against the window.

The kitten galloped into the kitchen, saw a stranger, and fell all over herself skidding to a stop. She arched her back and hissed. He laughed, crouched, and held out a hand.

"Uh— I don't—" she began.

Daintily, Perissa minced up to him, sniffed his fingers, then rubbed herself against his hand. He picked her up. She clambered up his shirt and bit his chin. He jerked his head back. "Hey."

Ripping her from his shirt, he set her on the floor, and she skittered away. He looked at Susan a little uncertainly and rolled up his sleeves.

She felt awkward and uncomfortable, took a sip of coffee, then realized maybe they could sit down. Get your mind in working order. Fatigue and worry had thoughts scattering like glass falling on concrete.

"Have a seat." She got plates and napkins, sat down across from him, and selected a doughnut.

"The kid's all right." He snared a doughnut, took a bite, chewed, and swallowed. "You all right?"

She nodded. Light from the ceiling fixture glinted on his damp hair and angled across his nose and cheekbones, emphasizing the tiredness around his eyes.

"Piling on guilt," he said. "Too much of that garbage and you can't move for the weight."

"I know that."

"Your fault? You're responsible for the actions of this scumbag?"

"In a way."

"Susan—" His tone crackled with irritation.

"If we'd caught the bastard, this attempt on her life wouldn't have happened."

"That's as rational as bat shit."

She waved that aside. "Motive for Sheffield?"

He eyed her a moment as though assessing her mental state. "We don't have to prove motive."

"I'm aware of that. I'd still like to see one. For Dorothy's murder. Motive to snuff Jen is obvious. She saw the killer."

"Did she?"

"She can't remember, and she's too sick to question closely, but memory might come back. Bits and pieces. Or even all of it."

"Ellen's not a doctor. You suggesting we leave her out?"

Susan pressed a fingertip against a glazed sugar crumb and stuck it in her mouth. "No. She's been around medicine all her life, would know enough to change one milligram to three milligrams."

"I'd say that goes for anybody."

"Yeah, Taylor too. But it would be riskier for either of them."

"I don't think our killer shies away from risk. He walked into an office building Saturday afternoon, shot Dorothy with a witness at hand, and walked out. What could be riskier than that?" Parkhurst got up to refill his mug and refilled hers while he was at it.

"If." He sat back down and reached for a doughnut. "And I'm just playing along with your fancies here. If Vicky was a homicide, why was she killed? Why now?"

Susan sat back, cradled the mug in her lap, and rubbed a thumb over the rim. 'To give us an answer," she said, trying to get thoughts to come together. "Realized we weren't going to stop until we had one. Realized the drug-addict explanation wasn't going to fly. Okay then, here. Murder and suicide. All wrapped up. Take it and go away."

She raised the mug with both hands and peered into it.

"Or?" he said.

She took a sip. "Or Vicky said something when they were all together that alarmed our quarry."

"What?"

She smiled sourly. "That's the hard part. Vicky said she wasn't so stupid she didn't see things. Would that make you nervous if you'd shot your loved one?"

"It's your fairy tale."

"She said money buys things."

"That probably wouldn't put me in a panic."

"She knew you wear a raincoat when it rains."

"I can ask each one of them if he or she ever went out in the rain without a raincoat," he said. "Slap cuffs on whoever did."

"You're not helping me here." With a loud scrape, she shoved out the adjacent chair and propped both feet on it.

"Good. I hate to feed illusions."

"Vicky said when people meet on a country road it's

not to pick wildflowers. Brent, with a becoming show of reluctance, suggested that meant Taylor and Holly Dietz.''

''Love in an empty pasture?''

''Core samples,'' she said. ''Find out what Vicky meant by that. Who's collecting core samples, of what, and why.''

''Yes, ma'am.''

The clock in the living room chimed eight times. She suddenly realized she could hear it. At some point the rain had stopped. The sky outside the window had gone from gray to blue-gray.

''Go home.'' With a thud, she dropped her feet to the floor and pushed herself upright. ''Get some sleep before you go in.''

He stood, drained the mug, and set it on the counter. He looked at her, paused, then said, ''You might do the same.''

TWENTY-THREE

TWO HOURS LATER Susan viewed the world with dark mutterings, staggered her way into the bathroom, and stood comatose in the shower. She managed to find all the belt loops on the beige pants and line up the buttons in the right order on the white blouse. As she drooped over extra-strength coffee, she glanced at the *Herald.* "Storm Leaves Trail of Destruction." Winds reported at eighty-five mph. A tornado touched down between the Hampstead Municipal Airport and the Kaw River, and remained on the ground for less than a minute; no report of injuries. Hail ranging in size from pea to golf ball did all kinds of damage. Trees were down, power lines were down. Forecast: more rain.

She rinsed the cup, put it on the cabinet, found her linen blazer, and headed for the hospital.

The sky was a vivid blue, but banks of sinister clouds hung around the edges. At the moment, the sun was bright enough to make itself known even through dark glasses. Streets were flooded with rushing water that fountained over leaves and tree limbs. She avoided State, which was impassable due to water and a fallen tree, and turned up Kentucky. City crews were out in force, trying to cope with overloaded drains, downed power lines, and stalled motorists.

At ten-thirty, it was already hot and muggy; the air felt too thick to breathe. She was sticky, blouse clinging to her back where she leaned against the seat.

Officer White, looking bored, was sitting on a chair outside Jen's cubicle. When he saw her, he shot to his feet. The youngest and newest of her officers, he was blond-haired, apple-cheeked, and had the misfortune of blushing when flustered.

"Anybody been in this morning?" she asked.

"No, ma'am. Just Dr. Sheffield and the nurses. Oh, and her mother's here now."

Terry Bryant was standing at her daughter's bedside, leaning over and caressing Jen's hair. She looked up, spotted Susan, and came out. "I hope you're not going to bother Jen. She needs to rest."

"I know."

Terry dug through her straw handbag for a tissue to pat her nose. Her makeup intact, she looked tearily attractive, with brown hair tumbling in curls to her shoulders, a bright-yellow full skirt, and a yellow blouse with ruffles down the front. She threw the tissue back in the bag and snapped it shut.

"She's a sturdy little girl. She's doing very well."

Terry gave her a look that said, no thanks to you. "They let me stay for only five minutes."

Terry turned and clicked off down the corridor in her high heels, skirt swirling.

Jen was lying on her back, eyes closed.

"Hi, Jen," Susan said softly.

Jen's eyes opened.

"How are you feeling?"

"Okay." The word was toneless. Jen closed her eyes.

"I need to go do some work. I just wanted to see how you were. I'll be back later."

Jen opened her eyes, said, "Okay," in the same flat voice, and closed her eyes again.

Susan's throat closed; she patted Jen's hand and made her way to the elevator.

Any lightness and charm the hospital might have was relegated to the upper floors. The basement was strictly utilitarian—scarred and scuffed white walls, brown-tiled floors—and housed all the functions for keeping the system going: housekeeping, laundry, heat and air-conditioning, lab, and Dr. Fisher's domain.

She could have sent Parkhurst or Osey, but she wanted to be here herself. Being too personally involved—the voice in her head had the cadence of Captain Reardon's—leads to errors in judgment.

An officer needed to be present for autopsies of homicide victims, she justified. Any possible evidence could be obtained directly, to shorten the chain of custody. The officer on hand can receive information immediately, not have to wait for the official autopsy report. And as far as she was concerned, the most important reason was the opportunity to ask questions. Sometimes information resulted that didn't get included in the formal report, information that could be extremely important.

At her first autopsy, she'd wedged herself in a corner, afraid if she moved, she'd fall on her face. The sight, grim as it was, wasn't the problem. The smell. Like no other. It got deep in the throat and stayed there for days. Once smelled, never forgotten.

Dr. Fisher, in scrub greens, glanced at her briefly as he snapped on a pair of latex gloves and spoke into the tiny microphone clipped to his chest. He recited the case number and name: "Victoria Barrington...body that of well-developed, well-nourished, thirty-one-year-old Caucasian female. Blond hair, blue eyes. Body sixty-three inches long, weight 112 pounds."

With deliberate attention, he examined the hands and fingernails for skin or blood or fibers that could provide evidence of an assailant. Hands and fingernails were clean.

Vicky lay on her back on the stainless-steel table, the bright overhead light harsh on her blue-gray skin.

Picking up a scalpel, he made a deep Y incision, starting at a shoulder, to a point midway in the chest, then the other shoulder, and a straight line to the pubic area. He examined the chest, lifted out the block of organs, weighed each, sliced sections for lab evaluation, moved methodically to the pelvis, then grunted and muttered, "Gravid."

"She was pregnant?"

"Five to six weeks gestation. Embryo ten millimeters."

Slightly larger than a bb shot. Had Vicky known she was pregnant? Five to six weeks, only just begun. A fetus weighing less than 500 grams—usually five to six months—didn't require a separate death certificate, but two lives had been taken here. Licks of anger like small flames flared in Susan's chest.

Fisher removed the bladder. Any urine would be carefully removed and sent, as would the dregs of hot chocolate from the mug in Vicky's living room and the vial labeled codeine, to the KBI lab in Topeka for toxicology. Many drugs, including barbiturates and sedatives, were excreted by the kidneys. Urine was the way to find them.

Dr. Fisher peeled off the latex gloves. "Not much to help you with." He turned on a spigot in the deep sink and washed his hands. His hands were actually quite beautiful. They fascinated her. Even working on somebody long past caring, they were gentle. His touch on a body was almost a caress, as though knowledge was absorbed through the fingertips.

"What can you tell me about porphyria?" she asked.

"She didn't have it."

"It's a disease," Susan said to get him started.

"Not one. A constellation of seven different inheritable diseases." He shook water from his hands and reached for a towel. "Some forms are more debilitating than others, some life-threatening."

Dr. Fisher was a man happy in his work, enthusiastic about the job, with the attitude "Oh, boy, I'm fortunate to be given this opportunity" and "Well, well, what do we have here?" whenever he pulled on latex gloves. Sometimes his enthusiasm spilled over and he had to share it with whomever was at hand. Like the time when he'd sliced open the heart of a young man and traced the flow of blood through the chambers. In great detail. There might have been some purpose if the kid had had heart disease, but he was a healthy young male who'd died of a head injury sustained in a motorcycle accident. For a long time after that she'd been aware of her every heartbeat.

Questions never irritated him, no matter how irrelevant. Information about the human body came pouring out, like turning on a tap.

"Extremely rare." He tossed the towel at a hamper and leaned back against a stainless-steel cabinet. "A group of inborn errors of metabolism caused by mutations in genes that code for various enzymes of the heme biosynthetic pathway."

Right. One difficulty with all this information that poured out was she usually needed a medical dictionary to interpret it.

"The rarity makes it hard to diagnose. Each form has its own symptomology. Appropriate lab tests give an unequivocal diagnosis, but the symptoms simulate a multitude of illnesses, even including mental illness."

"What are the symptoms?"

He drew his heavy, dark eyebrows together and peered at her from under them. "Seven different kinds." He held out the index finger of his left hand, tapped it with the index finger of his right hand, and recited, "Congenital erythropoietic porphyria. Characterized by severe cutaneous lesions, hemolytic anemia, large amounts of uroporphyrin 1 in the urine. Onset of symptoms usually in the first year of life. Treatment here, often blood transfusions. The photosensitivity can lead to scarring to the point of mutilation affecting nose and fingers. Teeth can get pointed and red. Increased hair growth sometimes."

Dr. Fisher broke off his discourse and rubbed a finger down his forehead between his heavy eyebrows. "Matter of fact, some scientist somewhere hypothesized that vampires might have been porphyria victims.''

"Vampires.''

"They go out only at night. The teeth get pointed and look larger because mouth and gums are tight. The need for blood.'' He even brought in the bit about garlic. Theory being garlic was dialkyl disulfide, which destroys heme and increases the severity of an attack.

"Heme.''

"Porphyria's a metabolic disorder, comes from a deficiency of an enzyme involved in the synthesis of heme. Bunch of nonsense, this vampire stuff. All it did was cause people suffering from an incurable disease a whole lot more suffering by making them the victims of nasty jokes.''

He held out his middle finger and tapped it. "Protoporphyria. Characterized by acute photosensitivity, no urine abnormalities, often serious liver disease.''

He held out his third finger. "Acute intermittent porphyria. Can exist in latent form. No cutaneous manifestations, but acute attacks of neurologic dysfunction—''

"Never mind.''

"—chronic pain, muscle paralysis in arms and legs, seizures, blindness, tachycardia. Purple urine. Then there's porphyria cutanea tarda. Excess iron in the blood, needs to be periodically removed by phlebotomy.''

"Never mind.'' The problem with turning on Fisher's flow of information was that it was hard to turn off. "Was Dorothy Barrington likely to see a patient with porphyria?''

"Not likely, no. I told you, it's extremely rare.''

"Tests can be done to find out if a patient is suffering from this illness?''

"Didn't I just say that? But because of its rarity, it's not considered until other things are ruled out.''

Had Dorothy thought she might have a patient with porphyria? Had she been reading about it to see if she might be right? Which patient? Susan had never had the need to get a court order to look at patient files, but she knew there was no way a judge would sign an order on the basis of her vague speculations. Fishing expedition. She didn't even have a name, would have to go through all the patient files. The possibility—if it even was a possibility—of a patient having porphyria could have no bearing on the murders anyway. Probably didn't. A bookmark inserted in a different spot probably meant, as Parkhurst had suggested, someone used the book and put the bookmark back at random. Maybe.

"Have you ever seen a patient with porphyria?"

"By the time I see them, it wouldn't matter. I haven't seen any evidence that might indicate porphyria. Unless I missed it."

"You ever know of anyone who had it?"

"No. I told you it's rare." He massaged his chin. "One interesting particular. Sometimes a genetically affected individual is asymptomatic. Raises some questions concerning the simple, Mendelian, dominant mode of transmission, doesn't it?"

Is that what it raised? In her mind, it simply raised confusion.

TWENTY-FOUR

SUSAN NO LONGER needed sunglasses when she left the hospital; the clouds had taken over. She turned right on Railroad Street—passable, but with standing water in the gutters—and drove past Bobcat Canyon Park, which was a big lake with trees rising from it, wooden benches covered with water, the old railroad locomotive in water up over its wheels.

Outside of town, the farm road was passable, but the fields on both sides held standing water. In one, nine mahogany-colored cows stood in a line, water up to their knees. They all had their rears turned toward the road, except one white-faced freethinker in the center who blandly watched the pickup drive by.

At the crossroads, she went left. Ellen Barrington's land lay to the right. Not much was getting accomplished in the way of plumbing repairs, most likely. Susan slowed at a row of six mailboxes. Two redwing blackbirds perched forlornly on one, surveying the flooded fields like leftovers from the ark.

She made a left to the Dietz farm and pulled up behind the house. A large walnut tree, uprooted by high wind, lay across the ground, limbs split and broken.

Heat and mugginess made the air seem like something you had to push through. Her white blouse stuck to her back, her beige pants clung to the back of her legs. Shrugging off the linen jacket, she tossed it on the seat beside her.

The Lab, the collie, and the hairy mutt eyed her from inside the kitchen. As watchdogs, these three were a washout. Not even a mild growl until she rapped on the screen door, then they gave excited little yips and whipped their tails so hard their rear ends wiggled.

Holly came into the kitchen. There was no surprise on her face at seeing Susan. The corners of Holly's mouth twitched as she was deciding whether or not to smile; she opted for a smile. The dogs crowded in front of her, prancing and yelping.

She held open the screen. The dogs rushed out and swarmed around Susan, nudging and sniffing. "Come in." Holly had on baggy cotton shorts and a green shirt. Her loose brown hair stuck up in a clump in back, as though she'd been resting her head on a pillow.

The living room still had stacks of photos in piles on every flat surface. Without waiting for an invitation, Susan made her way to the couch and plunked herself down. The Lab stood by her knees, eyeing the spot next to her with the clear intent of leaping up beside her. Holly snapped a finger. With a sigh, the Lab lowered itself to lie across Susan's feet. She reached down and rubbed its chest. It locked her hand and snuggled closer.

Holly sat across from her in the overstuffed chair. "Can I get you something? Iced tea? Coffee?"

"No thanks. What time did Taylor Talmidge get here last night?"

Holly flinched as though she had a headache and Susan's voice was too loud.

"He was here last night? Is that correct? What time did he come?"

"I've already told Ben Parkhurst."

"I understand that. If you don't mind, I'd like to hear it again."

"Around nine-thirty."

"You were expecting him?"

With a fingernail, Holly scratched at the frayed arm of the chair.

"Your husband was home?"

"No. He went to see a friend in Kansas City."

"He got home at what time?"

"I don't know. One maybe, one-thirty."

"Did Taylor know he wasn't home?"

"Yes. I guess. I don't know." Holly glanced at her watch. "I don't have much time. I need to get ready for work."

"Work?" Susan was surprised; she assumed farmers' wives spent all their time gathering eggs and milking cows.

"Of course, work. How do you think we make it? Farmers' wives work wherever they can. Even farmers have second jobs. And this year, with the rain and the flooding—" Holly zipped her mouth shut.

"What time do you need to be there?"

"Three," Holly admitted.

Since it was only one-thirty, there was no risk of being late.

"Where do you work?"

"At the hospital. Nurse's aide."

Oh, for Christ's sake. Asses needed to be chewed about this one. Primarily, her own. She'd talked with Holly two days ago and hadn't gotten this little nugget of information.

"You knew Taylor was coming to see you last night?"

"No. Not really. I mean— Well, we're friends. He needed a friend to talk to."

"I see."

Holly had a half-tense, half-wary look of expectation, waiting for a question and hoping it wouldn't come. What the hell was it she didn't want to be asked?

"How long have you been friends?"

"What do you mean?"

"Maybe you can tell me about your friendship."

"What business is it of yours?"

"None. Unless there is a connection with the murder." Susan almost had a thought here, but it got away. She hadn't had enough sleep to be doing this.

"I don't know anything about Dorothy's murder."

Dorothy's, not Vicky's. "What time did Taylor arrive last night?"

"I told you, nine-thirty."

"Your shift doesn't last until eleven?"

"I was off yesterday."

Taylor could have gone to Vicky's house, fed her codeine, then come here. The time would have been tight, but it was possible. An attempt to set up an alibi? The thought teased and vanished before she could catch it. "How long was he here?"

"A couple of hours."

"You must be very good friends. He came without being invited, stayed late. Your husband wasn't here."

Holly didn't respond. Susan waited.

Holly fidgeted. "We're good friends."

"How good?"

"I don't know what you mean."

"Lovers?"

"No!" Holly's face turned a hot pink. "Let me tell you something. I am not some bored housewife just dying for excitement, fluttering over romantic looks, snatched murmurs of love, and forbidden afternoons of lust. Taylor and I are friends."

Susan believed her, reluctantly. If Taylor wasn't trying to rig up an alibi, hadn't come to ease into the sack with Holly, then why? The thought fragment slipped into her mind and out again. Damn it, what was she groping for? "What did you talk about?"

"Nothing." Holly took an instant too long to answer.

Ah. Whatever they'd talked about was the very thing Holly wanted to avoid.

"I mean we just talked. It's hard for him. The Barringtons never really liked him all that much, and they think he— He just needed a friend."

"Did he mention Vicky?"

"No. Why would he?"

"Did he tell you why the Barringtons got together last night?"

"No." The word came too fast and got caught on an indrawn breath.

Stolen painting. That's what Holly was trying to avoid. Susan finally got hold of the errant thought. Taylor had come to tell Holly the theft had been discovered. Why would he do that unless Holly was involved somehow and he wanted to tell her to expect cops with questions? "He told you they were all there because Ellen asked them to come?"

"He may have. I don't remember." Holly reached up, smoothed down the clump of hair, and for a moment held her hair back in a ponytail. She looked ten years younger with the hair off her shoulders and curly wisps around her face.

"And the reason Ellen asked them was because she thought she knew why Dorothy had been killed."

Apprehension pinched Holly's face, a thin white line appeared at the corners of her mouth. Susan had seen the look before, usually just a moment or two before the person dropped over in a dead faint.

She went to the kitchen, found a glass, and filled it with tap water. She handed the glass to Holly and watched her take a sip; then, when she was sure Holly wasn't going to pass out cold, she sat back down. "You want to tell me about it?"

"About what?"

"You must have known you were breaking the law," Susan said gently. "You could go to jail." Not unless some charges were made.

"I don't know what you're talking about."

"The painting is valuable. You're facing a felony charge."

Holly gripped the glass with both hands. "I didn't steal it."

"You know who did. It was Taylor, wasn't it? That's why he came to see you last night. To warn you we'd be around asking questions."

Holly stared at the glass.

"Is that why Taylor killed Dorothy? He took the painting and she found out."

Holly looked up, stared at her with eyes like flint.

"You helped him steal it."

"No."

"Mrs. Dietz, you're in a lot of trouble. Your best bet is to tell me about it. Maybe I can help you." She waited. Holly sat like a rock. "You told the owner of the gallery you were Ellen Barrington."

"No."

"He can identify you." Susan wasn't sure he could, if his eyesight was as poor as Osey thought. Doubts niggled in. Why would Holly help steal a painting? Why would Taylor steal it in the first place? Money, of course, but an urgent need? She was speculating ahead of the evidence again—her biggest flaw, according to Captain Reardon—but she felt the kick of adrenaline that happened when a case starts to come together.

"I don't want to talk to you anymore," Holly said.

Short of reading her her rights, taking her in, and booking her, there was nothing Susan could do. Ha. Book her for what? There was no evidence linking Holly to murder, no evidence linking her to theft. Which they didn't even officially have.

Susan stood up. "When will your husband be home?"

"Harlen? This afternoon sometime."

"I'll be back."

In the pickup, the radio chattered. She reached for the mike. "Yes, Hazel?"

"Ben's trying to get you. Hang on, I'll patch him

through.'' A minute later, Parkhurst's voice came in over a lot of static. Birds again, sitting on the communications tower; something had to be done. Beyond the odd word, all she could hear was fuzz. They did manage enough contact to work out a meet at the Best Little Hare House in Kansas.

The diner, on the edge of town, featured rabbit on the menu: fried rabbit, rabbit stew, ground rabbit. It was busy and loud, jukebox blaring a country-and-western tune, a haze of cigarette smoke hanging heavy, cement floor, rough wooden booths with unpadded benches, truckers arguing, laughing, slapping each other on the back. Antlered deer heads and bobcats were mounted on the walls. Pictures of muscular young males in various stages of nudity were plastered all over the walls and ceiling of the ladies' room. She assumed the men's room had the opposite adornment.

In a booth at the rear, Parkhurst was working on a glass of iced tea. She slid in across from him and felt the rear of her slacks snag on the rough wood. She'd never tried the specials, and never intended to. Bunny rabbit was something she'd never cared to eat. She ordered a chicken sandwich and iced tea, closed the menu, and handed it back to the waitress.

''What have you got?'' she said.

Parkhurst propped his elbows on the table and leaned forward to hear over the babble. ''Core samples.''

''Ah. What?''

''Harlen Dietz is getting into all the activities that precede drilling himself an oil well. Aerial photographs, geological surveys, core samples.''

When she thought of oil wells—if she ever did—she thought of Texas, but beam pumps, like giant bobbing chicken toys, raised their heads any number of places in northeast Kansas: cornfields, sorghum fields, by the side of the road. ''I thought the oil business went in the dumper.''

''Pretty much has. Used to pump millions into the state

coffers, but oil prices slid way off. That meant production went down, which led to fewer new wells and existing wells plugged, then layoffs and companies going belly-up. And crude here is heavier than the imported stuff, so it sells for less.''

"Then why is he doing this?"

The waitress brought Parkhurst's cheeseburger and her chicken sandwich in red plastic baskets, added bottles of catsup and mustard, and asked if they needed anything else.

When she left, he dumped catsup on his French fries. ''I think it's a last-ditch effort to save the farm. Harlen's in bad trouble. Owes money everywhere. He hasn't been able to pay the back taxes. If he doesn't take care of that, he's going to lose the land. He loses Holly's land, she's apt to drill him.''

"Holly would do a lot to save that farm?"

"Yes, ma'am, she would. People get rabid about land that's been theirs for generations. Anything short of murder, and I'm not real sure about that." He looked at her. "What have you got cooking in your head?" He bit into the burger and chewed.

"I assume this is an expensive proposition, drilling a well.''

He swallowed. "Very."

"Does he expect to get it back, make a profit?"

"He must. And according to the geologist, he's got a promising site with great potential. Estimate in the millions of barrels. The section of Dietz land that abuts Ellen's place. The assumed oil pool runs under her land too.''

The waitress came up and refilled the iced-tea glasses.

"Where is Harlen getting money for photographs and surveys and whatnot?"

Parkhurst took a slug of tea. "Why do I get the feeling you're about to tell me?"

She pulled a piece of lettuce from her sandwich and stuck it in her mouth. "Harlen Dietz wasn't at the Barringtons' when Vicky threw out her barbed comment about core samples.'' She frowned as a thought struck her. ''How would Vicky know?''

''Her family and Holly's have been friends for years. She sees Holly now and again. Holly could have told her. You want to come right out and tell me what you're talking about, instead of dancing all around it?''

''Taylor.'' Susan broke off a chunk of sandwich and popped it in her mouth. When she swallowed, she took a sip of tea to help it down. ''He got annoyed with the Barringtons pointing their fingers at him and pointed one at Vicky. She said, 'Don't point at me; I know about core samples.' Why would she say that unless it meant something to him?''

''And it meant?''

''Taylor was providing the money for Harlen's oil well. Taylor didn't have enough, or the whole deal cost over the estimate and he had to come up with more or lose what he'd already invested.''

''Uh-huh. So he grabbed a painting and sold it. Holly then waltzed it into the gallery and said, 'Hi. I'm Ellen. Fork over the dough.''' Parkhurst raised an eyebrow. ''Anybody ever say you got a fancy imagination?''

''It's been mentioned.'' That fancy imagination had been as useful as an informant at times. It never made a case, but it gave her direction. Those leaps of fancy, more often than not, proved right on when evidence was turned.

''Why pick Ellen to blame?'' Parkhurst said in a voice cluttered with doubt.

''She's the only Barrington with dark hair. Holly has dark hair. To someone with poor eyesight, it could look short if she had it pulled back. Maybe Ellen was the only one Dorothy could be convinced was lying, if the theft were discovered. It's conceivable Dorothy would believe Ellen would take it and then lie.''

The waitress drifted up to remove the baskets and topped off the tea glasses.

"Taylor had a piece of bad luck," Susan said when she drifted away. "If Dorothy hadn't spotted the filler in the paper, it might have gone undetected for who knows how long."

"Taylor was simply going to hope nobody would realize it was gone? Less than bright."

"There's Ellen. She could deny it until the sun went down. Taylor could whisper in Dorothy's ear, 'Ellen's lying. Look how much trouble she's always been. Maybe you should just let it go. Why cause a rift in the family?'"

"Dorothy called her family together to denounce the thief, and Taylor shot her," Parkhurst said, with his doubts still showing.

"I'm inclined to think she didn't know who took it and called them all together to find out."

"Then Taylor offed her before she could."

Susan could see he wasn't anywhere near sold on the idea. Neither was she, but she was convinced—almost convinced—that Taylor had snatched the painting and Holly had peddled it.

A man built like a tank rolled over to the jukebox and thumbed in coins. Music blared out; a nasal voice wailed in despair, "We only have to figure out where to go from here."

She couldn't have put it better herself.

TWENTY-FIVE

FIVE O'CLOCK in the afternoon, clouds moving in like a war party, the air hot enough to steam clams, and Nadine was adamant about going to the park.

Ellen pulled on the bottom of her T-shirt and flapped it back and forth. "Heatstroke," she said.

Nadine, looking wilted in white shorts and loose white blouse, ignored her and pushed on around the corner. She stopped and frowned at the lake that was Bobcat Canyon Park. A kid in a kayak was paddling across it. "Maybe this wasn't such a good idea."

"Why do you say that?" Ellen waved her arm. "We could swim out to that bench and huddle on it while we eat sandwiches. Pretend it's a raft."

"Don't be difficult." Nadine wrestled the stroller with a sleeping Bobby into a U-turn, bumped it over squishy ground to the sidewalk, and made off down Ninth Street. "Let's see about Broken Arrow Park. Maybe it's okay."

"Why do we have to have a picnic? It's going to rain any minute. We could eat at the house."

"Bobby needs fresh air."

"He could get fresh air on the way to the Coffee Cup. It's cool in there, and they have booths. That makes it real nice. When the rain comes, you don't get wet."

"I told you to bring your raincoat." Nadine's own raincoat with the gourd appliqué, identical to Ellen's except a bright blue instead of black, hung over the handle of the stroller.

"I can't find it."

"What happened to it?"

"I don't know. Nadine, what are you up to?"

"I told you. I want to talk to you."

"Bobby'll get wet."

Nadine strode firmly on with that bossy attitude she always got when she'd done something she knew Ellen would get pissed about.

Broken Arrow Park had a tree down at the entrance blocking the way. Undeterred, Nadine maneuvered the stroller around fallen branches and wheeled over to a bench. It wasn't exactly wet, but it wasn't dry either. Ellen could feel damp boards through the seat of her jeans.

"Nadine, this is stupid."

"Get up a minute." Nadine spread her raincoat over the bench and then busied herself getting sandwiches and cookies from a bag in the stroller. She handed a sandwich to Ellen.

Ellen unwrapped ham and cheese and tore off a corner. She chewed and swallowed. "All right. What is it?"

Nadine fussed over Bobby, poking and tucking.

"Nadine—"

Nadine peered studiously into the small bag. "I have chicken salad too, if you'd rather."

"Knock it off. Or I'm going to hit you."

"Well." Nadine carefully peeled plastic wrap from a sandwich and examined it. "I saw Adam."

"So?" Ellen chomped down on another corner.

"I mean I talked to him."

"Yesss?" Ellen said darkly.

"I just happened to run into him at the service station. You know, Pickett's, over on—"

"I know where Pickett's service station is."

"Right. Well, he was getting gas and I pulled in right behind him. I needed gas. And I could hardly not say anything. I mean, he spoke to me and said how cute Bobby was, and asked how I was doing, and how Bob was." Nadine nudged the stroller to and fro. "And anyway, I asked him."

"Asked him what?"

Nadine aimed a sideways glance at her. "Why he left."

"You did what! My God, Nadine, I may hit you just on general principles."

"Well, I kind of knew you'd feel that way. That's why I thought it'd be better if we were somewhere nobody'd hear when you yelled at me. He didn't do it, Ellen."

Ellen glowered. "Do what?"

"Take money from Dorothy."

Fizz started to bubble up in her chest. She slammed a lid on it. "How do you know?"

"I asked him."

"You *what?*"

"Dorothy offered. If he'd leave. He turned her down."

All of a sudden Ellen found it hard to breathe. Things inside seemed to be fighting with other things. "Dorothy didn't lie," she said when she could grab hold of words.

"I know, but—" Nadine twisted the cap from a thermos and handed her something red. "What exactly did Dorothy say?"

"Lots. And at the end she said she—" Ellen drank whatever was in the cup and grimaced. "What is this?"

"Kool-Aid. You see, she *offered* him money. She didn't say he took it."

Ellen was so flat-out steam-rollered, she couldn't remember what Dorothy had said. Nadine had really done it this time. She had no right. Always sticking her nose in.

Nadine eyed her warily. "Dorothy tried to do what she thought was best for you. That's what happens when you have too much control. You start thinking you know what's best. Then you start manipulating to get what you know is best to come about."

Ducks from the swollen pond waddled up, quacking and grumbling. Ellen crumbled bread and tossed it to them. They squabbled and darted.

"So anyway, I just thought you should know." She

looked at Ellen, waited, and finally asked, "So you going to yell?"

"Damn right, I'm going to yell. Just as soon as I—" She burst into tears.

"Hey now, Ellen—"

"I'm going to be arrested."

"Of course you're not. Why would you?" Nadine rooted around in the diaper bag and came up with Kleenex.

"I found Vicky's— I found Vicky. The cops think I killed her. And stole a painting. And—" I'm losing it, she thought, scrubbed at her face, and blew her nose. "I'm scared." She hauled in a long, shaky breath. "One of my family hates me."

"Oh, Ellen, no. Why would you think that?"

"Because—" She almost told Nadine about Daddy's gun. Instead, she explained about the painting and the phone call that had gotten her to Vicky's. "I can't stay at the house anymore. It's too weird with Dorothy not there. I'm scared of everybody. What if Taylor did it? What if he creeps up and stabs me in the back? I've go to leave."

"And go where? Carl's?"

She couldn't even do that. Afraid to trust Carl. Everything was wrong and crazy. "Home. My place."

"You can't. There's no plumbing."

"So I'll camp out. No big deal. I can't stay at the house anymore. I'm going. I have to."

"It's not safe, all by yourself."

"Safe?" Ellen heard the high wail in her voice and got a tighter grip. "I'm not safe anywhere. At least, out there I can hear them coming." I'm safer there than where I am.

"Ellen, there's another storm on the way."

"So I'll wait out the wind." Ellen gathered cookie crumbs, tore up leftover pieces of bread and squished toward the duck pond, swollen almost double. The ducks saw her coming and noisily squabbled around her. She scattered crumbs, dusted off her hands, and wiped them on the seat of her jeans.

"I'm not going to let you do it." Nadine packed wrappings back in the paper sack and stowed it in the diaper bag.

"You can't stop me."

They left the park, Nadine shoving the stroller over the uneven ground. "Then I'm coming with you."

"With Bobby? Don't be ridiculous. And what would Bob say?" Ellen lifted the front end of the stroller up onto the sidewalk.

"Please don't go."

"I have to."

"Ellen, no—"

After Ellen made promises to be careful, they split at the intersection. Ellen plodded along Ninth Street, then over to Indiana, and let herself into the old family home. Ha. Where, if you have to go, they have to take you in. Taylor wasn't around, and she wondered where he was.

Upstairs in her bedroom, she gathered clothes, toothbrush, and comb and jammed them in the backpack. After all that firm talk, it suddenly didn't seem like such a good idea. Foolhardy. Dorothy had always said she was foolhardy. Ellen sat sideways on the window seat, elbows propped on her bent knees, and stared out at the flowers and the latticework gazebo where she used to read as a kid. Her throat got tight, and tears dribbled down her face. Leaving home. She seriously didn't want to go.

Then what? Stay here and snivel? She hauled herself to her feet and slung the backpack over one shoulder.

Leave a note? Call Carl? She didn't want anybody to know where she was, but if she simply disappeared, panic and bloodhounds would be in order. She scribbled a note and left it on the kitchen table.

It was after seven-thirty when she tossed the backpack onto the passenger seat of the Mustang and stuck the key in the ignition. The cranky old car was always developing freaky problems that couldn't be diagnosed, but it started right up and idled roughly. Hands on the wheel, she sat looking at the house: a symbol of safety, belonging, a haven in times of dire trouble. Looking at it now made her cry again. Nothing had been what she thought, not family unity, not loving relatives, not even safety. It was a place of danger and betrayal.

Shoving the car in gear, she backed out of the driveway. Adam she didn't even allow headroom. If she were arrested, there'd be plenty of jail time to think about him. Find out who was trying to frame her. Stop this quivering in fear and waiting for the axe to fall.

Willis. Of them all, he was the most devastated by Dorothy's death. The two of them had always been close. With a crazy father and a mother too busy and psychologically unsuited for motherhood, they had clung to each other. Vicky's death coming on top of Dorothy's shattered Willis to the point of nonfunctioning.

Marlitta. Plodding along doing everything by rote. Like her mind was zapped by electricity and her body went on without it. Brent. Slimy creep. Pawing anything young and female. God's gift, for Pete's sake. Marlitta loved him. Why? Couldn't she see what he was? Obviously not. Besotted.

Carl. The smartest. Would he kill and try to frame her? That hurt. That hurt a lot. So much, she could only come at it sideways. No matter how this all turned out, there'd be pain. Maybe too much, and it would tear away even the pretense of togetherness.

Unless Taylor was guilty. Nobody would be too grief-stricken then. Which was, of course, why everybody wanted him to be it.

A hawk flew against the gray sky, banked in a wide arc, and floated gently down to a tree limb. Freedom. Ha. Freedom was a myth. The world consisted of predators and prey. You were either hunting or running.

Far to her left, floodwater surrounded outbuildings and the roofs looked like small islands. A farmer in a rowboat was ferrying a pig to higher ground. The pig gazed imperiously ahead like an emperor surveying his kingdom.

Two miles further, she turned off on the road that led to her place. When the old stone house came into view, her heart lifted. She loved this place; just being back gave her some hope. Maybe she could figure out what was going on.

The house sat on top a hill, and even though there were patches of standing water, the house itself was in no danger of flooding, though the trenches the plumbers had dug were brimming. Her very own swimming hole. So it was long and narrow instead of round. She'd always been a nonconformist. Would she ever have workable plumbing? She sighed. Not until the weather cleared up. She pulled up in front.

Slinging the backpack over a shoulder, she slid from the Mustang, unlocked the door, and let it stand wide. Dim inside. Musty smell. She shoved up the two windows in the living room and trudged upstairs. Didn't smell as bad up here. She opened windows and went back down.

Worry tugged frantically at the edges of her mind. Some small animal, maybe a field mouse trying to get away from floodwater, had gotten inside and died. Didn't smell too bad in the living room. Stronger in the dining room. Apprehension catching hold, she eased toward the kitchen.

Her heart banged around in her throat.

Blood. Dark against the scuffed linoleum. Taylor crumpled like a felled steer. Legs bent, arms flung out, knife handle in the middle of his chest. Gray suit jacket open, white shirt soaked black.

Flies. Oh, God, flies. Horrible, big green flies. Buzzing.

Crawling. Taylor wasn't moving. He wasn't moving at all. The knife handle was ivory. It came from the wooden block on her cabinet.

TWENTY-SIX

"WHY WAS TAYLOR here?" Susan sat in a white wicker chair with flowered cushions. Dr. Fisher had come and gone; the body had been bagged and taken away; Parkhurst and Osey were working the scene with a sheriff's deputy, since technically this was the sheriff's jurisdiction.

"I don't know," Ellen said. Huddled into herself, she sat on the hearth of the stone fireplace that reached the ceiling, with knees tight together, sneakered feet pointed in with the toes touching, and the relative calm of being pushed so close to the edge the slightest movement would send her over.

Lamps on small tables lent a gleam to the wood floors. Brightly colored rugs—by the small paisley couch and blue chair and in the entryway—gave the room a cheery note. On white walls were framed photos of woodland scenes: a deer, an eagle in flight, a coyote against snow.

"Why were you here?" Susan asked.

"It was strange at the house with everything—"

Susan could tell from her tone her mind was cluttered. "When did you decide to come?"

"I've been thinking about it."

"Staying here? With no plumbing?"

A mulish look settled over Ellen's face.

"When did you get here?"

"Seven-thirty. Maybe later. It wasn't dark yet."

"Why didn't you notice Taylor's car?"

Ellen glanced around as if she might spot it. "His car is here?"

"It's parked behind the house. Did you see anyone on your way out? Cars?"

"I don't remember. Maybe."

"Where were you earlier this afternoon?"

Ellen rubbed her face. Susan could see her mind still wasn't tracking too well, but in a shivery voice she gave a fairly coherent account of her day at the Barrington house and seeing her friend Nadine. She was sketchy about the conversation with her friend, whether by choice or from mental chaos, Susan couldn't tell.

"What reason would Taylor have for coming out here?"

"None. Why would he? He's never been here."

"To talk about something?"

Ellen moved her head deliberately to one side and then to the other. "He doesn't have anything to talk to me about. Even if he did, he could have said it at home. I mean at— What would he have to say? He never had anything to say to me."

He was here. This was too much out of the way for just going by. He must have had a purpose. "When did you last see him?"

"When he left this morning."

"Where was he going?"

"I don't know. I assumed to work."

Susan made a note to have that checked. So far what she had amounted to damn all. Ellen had decided to come home and found Taylor with a knife in his chest. That was it.

"Have you had any trouble here? Other than the plumbing problem?"

Ellen shook her head, more tiredness than negative response. "Nadine lost her keys. She's always losing keys. Then she found them. There were times when I thought somebody had been in here, but I could never be sure."

"Anything missing?"

"No." Ellen came out with the word too fast and leaned forward as though she had a sudden pain.

Something was taken that Ellen didn't want to talk about.

A second or two of silence crept past, and then Ellen said, "Harlen Dietz."

"What about him?"

"He keeps trying to buy the place. No matter how many times I tell him I won't sell."

"Chief Wren?" Sheriff's Deputy Meyer, hat in hand, came through the dining room.

She went over to him.

"Miss Barrington's brother and sister are here. The brother's getting insistent about seeing her."

Once again, evidence of how news traveled. She was finished anyway—for now—with Ellen. These two had just saved her the time of tracking them down. Let's see what they have to say. She gave a nod to the deputy.

Carl shot her a glance, went directly to Ellen on the hearth, and crouched in front of her.

Marlitta followed more slowly, plodding and awkward, and sat beside her. Ellen didn't seem reassured to see them.

Carl touched a finger to her hand and looked hard into her face. "You all right, darlin'?"

She nodded. "Yeah."

Leaving Meyer to keep an eye on Ellen and Carl, Susan questioned Marlitta in the room behind the kitchen that Ellen used as an office, then switched Marlitta with Carl. Neither had an alibi. Marlitta had been at the medical clinic until five, when she went home. Husband Brent had left at the same time and gone swimming. Carl had stayed, alone at the clinic until seven-thirty, then gone home, later had dinner with Comach Meer, gallery owner.

Susan told all three Barringtons they were free to go and went to the kitchen, where Osey was crawling around on the floor. She jerked her head at Parkhurst and went on out the back door.

"You seem a tad irritated," he said. "Ma'am."

"Knock it off. Let's pay a call on the Dietzes."

She climbed in the Bronco and snapped the seat belt. He

started the motor and maneuvered around the other vehicles and they jounced and splashed down the rutted driveway. She rolled down the window. The night air was silky-soft after the rain, the sky clear and endless, the stars brilliant, the moon full.

"Got anything you need to say?" Susan asked.

The dash lights showed a bright flash of teeth as he smiled. "Only that I'm a mite surprised you didn't haul her ass in."

"Why would she kill Taylor in her own house? With her own knife?"

"Not too bright."

"Her family seems to think so. She seems bright enough to me. She's afraid."

"Dead man in the kitchen will do that."

"Yeah." Susan stared out at the headlights making tunnels on the road. A jack rabbit tore across in front of them, and she stomped on imaginary brakes.

Parkhurst slowed and swerved. "I'm driving."

"Yeah. And a good job you're doing. Just don't hit any bunnies."

"Vermin."

She leaned back. "We've had one person shot, one poisoned, one stabbed. Our killer certainly doesn't like repetition."

"Versatile. Uses whatever means are at hand."

"Mmm. Why was Taylor killed?"

Parkhurst snorted. "Because he knew something? We'd be further along here if we knew why Dorothy was killed."

"You don't go along with my theory Taylor stole the painting and zapped Dorothy because she found out?"

"I was leaning that way until Taylor got iced. Harlen Dietz could have stabbed him, not needing him anymore now that he'd come up with the money for oil speculation. Wouldn't have to share any of the profits. Figured Taylor's death would be lumped in with Dorothy's and Vicky's."

Parkhurst was silent for a moment. "Not likely Harlen, or Holly either, would kill him. Killing the goose that lays the golden eggs."

"Falling out among thieves?"

"At Ellen's house?"

"Yeah."

At the Dietz farm, a start had been made on cutting up the fallen tree. The headlights swept over foot-long logs stacked at one side of the drive. Parkhurst knocked. An outside light came on.

Holly, clutching an ankle-length robe together at the throat, opened the door. The dogs crowded around her in joyous eagerness.

"Sorry to bother you so late," Parkhurst said. "Mind if we come in?" He took a step forward without waiting for her response.

Automatically, she moved back.

"Hol, what's going on?" Harlen came into the kitchen, stuck a cigar in his mouth, and looked at Parkhurst, then at Susan.

"What can we do for you folks?" He displayed all his teeth, but the smile didn't reach past his cheekbones.

Late as it was, he was still dressed in denim pants, a western-style shirt, and cowboy boots. Didn't farmers go to bed with the chickens?

"A few questions, Mr. Dietz," Susan said. "Can you tell us where you were this afternoon and early evening?"

Harlen took the cigar from his mouth. "Well, I reckon I could. You want to tell me any reason why I should?"

The look Holly flicked over him was a far way from loving.

"Obvious something's going on. All the vehicles, ambulance, out to Ellen's place. Something happened to her?" Harlen stuck the cigar in his mouth, puffed. "Maybe you good people would like to sit down."

They moved into the living room, and he turned on lamps.

"Hol, how about some coffee?"

"No thank you, Mr. Dietz." Susan sat on the couch.

The dogs milled around, darting from person to person, until Holly snapped a finger, then the collie and the Lab trotted to her chair and dropped to a crouch. The black, hairy mutt went straight to Parkhurst propped against the wall, and sat at his feet gazing up with adoring eyes.

"Just a few questions," Susan said, "and then we'll get out of here and let you go to bed."

"Before I answer any questions, I'd like to know what's going on. What happened to Ellen?" Harlen settled back in a chair and laid the cigar in an ashtray on the table by his elbow.

"Ellen is fine, Mr. Dietz. It's Taylor Talmidge we're concerned about."

Holly sat straighter. "What happened to Taylor?"

"Did you see him today, Ms. Dietz? What time was he here?"

"Here?"

"Holly, pull yourself together." Harlen looked at Susan. "What makes you think he was here?"

"Was he?"

"Yes. Late this afternoon. About what?" He looked at his wife. "Five-thirty or so?"

"Why was he here?"

"We got a business deal going, that's why. Anything wrong with that?"

"A business deal involving speculation in oil wells?"

"Anything illegal about that?"

"No, Mr. Dietz. So far as I know there's nothing illegal in that."

"Then what business is it of yours?"

"Taylor Talmidge is our business, Mr. Dietz. He was stabbed this evening."

"Ellen stabbed him?"

He seemed genuinely startled. Holly was watching him.

Susan caught an ugly glimmer in her eyes. She was the tough one, Susan realized. For all his bluster, Harlen Dietz was a basically weak man.

"How long was he here?"

"'Bout an hour, I'd say. That right, Hol?"

She reached down and ran her fingertips over the collie's silky ears.

"Where were you between five and eight?" Susan asked her.

"She was right here with me," Harlen said firmly. "Ain't that right, Holly?"

The Lab, feeling slighted, pushed his nose under Holly's hand.

"Answer the woman, Hol," Harlen said.

"Yes. Here."

"Did Taylor say where he was going when he left here?"

Holly shook her head.

"Did he mention Ellen?"

"No."

"Can you think of any reason why he'd go to Ellen's? No? Mr. Dietz, I understand you made an offer to buy Ellen's land."

"Perfectly good offer. Good price. What's that got to do with Taylor?"

"Not much good for farming," Parkhurst said. "Is it maybe what you think might be under it?"

"That's none of your business," Harlen said.

Susan asked a few more questions, then thanked them for their time and told them that was all for now. The hairy mutt gave a mournful wail of desertion when Parkhurst left.

He started up the Bronco and turned toward her. "Where to?"

"Willis Barrington."

Dr. Willis Barrington, bleary-eyed and unshaven, answered the door wearing rumpled pajamas and a robe. She got the impression he'd worn them all day. The living room no longer looked pristine; it looked neglected: cups and glasses, plates with uneaten food. The air smelled stale, felt still, as if it had been hanging in the same spot for days. He seemed barely coherent, said he hadn't left the house since Vicky's death.

It was midnight when they left Willis Barrington alone in his depression, the kind of depression that wrapped around the body like a great gray octopus and sucked away the spirit until life became unbearable. She made a note to talk with somebody about him, before the long jump suggested itself with brilliant focus as the only relief.

Parkhurst clicked in his seat belt and put the Bronco in gear. Her eyes felt gritty, her mind was slushing through fatigue, and she was mad. With the heels of her hands, she rubbed at her eyes and tried to remember when she had last eaten. Sometime before noon?

"Food?" Parkhurst asked, picking up her thought.

"Nothing is open."

"Maybe." He set a course toward the campus. The streets were dark and deserted, streetlights reflected in puddles of rainwater along the curbs. At Poppy's Pizza, he pulled up. A lone car was parked near the door. Neon lights flickered across the empty parking lot, bleeding reds and yellows and blues over the wet, oil-slicked pavement.

When he opened the door for her, noise hit her like a physical assault. This was a student hangout. Music blared from speakers mounted near the ceiling, video games beeped and flashed. Long wooden tables occupied the square room, but the only customers were five males clustered around one, arguing, laughing, and drinking beer. One of them was Ed Cole. She squinted at him, wondering how much alcohol he'd consumed and if he'd knock Debra around when he got home.

"Sorry," the skinny kid behind the counter said. "We're closed."

Parkhurst raised an eyebrow and turned to look at the group of students. They got to their feet, swigged down what was left in the glasses, and, with a good deal of jostling and shoulder-punching, got themselves moving toward the door.

"Hold it," Parkhurst said, soft, courteous, menacing.

The bunch stopped.

"Who's driving?"

"Nobody, man. We're on foot."

Parkhurst nodded, and they took their boisterous energy out the door. Parkhurst turned back to the kid behind the counter. "I'm in great need of a pizza."

"Hey, I'm sorry. The ovens have been turned off. There's no way."

Parkhurst looked at him long enough to make the kid jittery. "I've got one somebody ordered and didn't pick up. I can give you that if you want."

"What kind?"

"Salami."

"I'll take it."

Susan pulled out some bills for her share and laid them on the counter.

In the Bronco, she got on the radio and told the dispatcher to have a squad car cruise by the Cole place periodically. Maybe its presence would help Ed keep his fists in his pockets.

Ten minutes later, she got out plates and uncapped two bottles of beer, which she set in front of Parkhurst at her kitchen table. Then she checked the messages on her machine: three from the mayor demanding she call him immediately and one from her father in San Francisco. Both could wait. She zapped the pizza in the microwave.

Parkhurst separated a slice, dripping cheese, dropped it on a plate, and handed it to her. The kitten, much interested, watched from the doorway. Parkhurst sailed a salami disk toward her. All her hair stood on end. She stalked it with ferocious growls, wrestled it to the mat, and kicked it to death.

Parkhurst loosened his tie, unbuttoned his top shirt button, and rolled up his sleeves. The light brought his face into sharp relief: lines and planes that were hard and uncompromising, full mouth, creases at the corners of his eyes that worked such a transformation when he smiled. She took a slug of beer. He picked up a slice of pizza, gathered up the strings of cheese, and chomped off the end.

She rubbed her forehead. "We're not making a very good showing here."

"All part of the job."

"Oh, shut up." She picked off a piece of salami and popped it in her mouth.

"Whoever this shit is has got to run out of luck sometime. We'll nail him."

"Yeah. Right. Any of these Barringtons could have done it, from what we've got." Although she wasn't so sure about Willis. He seemed destroyed, sick with grief, his mind not functioning. Didn't seem to have the mental capacity to brush his teeth. Unless he was a whole lot better actor than she thought. "Willis hasn't been to the clinic since Vicky was killed. Home. With nobody to monitor his comings and goings."

"Not an impulsive man."

"True." Impulsive was maybe not the right word here. Desperate was more like it. Grabbing the opportunity no matter the danger. Ha. So far he hadn't been in any danger from them. "Marlitta doesn't seem to be thinking at top capacity, but as far as times go, she could have done it. Left the clinic, driven to Ellen's place, stabbed Taylor."

"The big question: Did she, or whoever, go out there to kill him, or was he killed because he was there?"

Susan chewed on pizza crust, thinking her own mind wasn't working any too well either. She laid the crust on her plate and looked at Parkhurst.

"Flash of insight?"

"Our killer went there for a reason."

"I'll buy that. What reason?"

"I don't know yet."

"Uh-huh. And Taylor?"

"He was driving back from the Dietzes'. Saw the car, recognized it, recognized the driver. Knew Ellen wasn't there. Went to see what was going on."

"Uh-huh."

"Anything wrong with that?"

Parkhurst took a thoughtful swallow of beer. "On the surface, holes big enough to drive a combine through."

"Brent left the clinic and went swimming. He could have driven out there after swimming and before he went home."

"Beautiful Brent thinks he's smarter than everybody else, he'd be certain he could get away with it."

Susan picked off a lump of cheese. "Carl's the smart one. If it was Carl, we'll probably never get him for it. He *is* smarter than we are."

She thought about that a moment. Being so intelligent, would he have considered the risks in blasting away at Dorothy in broad daylight? It hadn't been broad, it had been dark and stormy. A memory floated up from the murk in her mind: Dr. Adam Sheffield saying he only killed people with knives, and there was Taylor Talmidge with a bloody big knife in his chest.

"That brings us to Ellen," Parkhurst said. "A perfectly good suspect. Caught redhanded, you might say. Evidence and everything."

Susan sighed and rubbed her forehead. "Not hard evidence."

"How hard do you need? Although the mayor wouldn't be happy if Ellen was arrested. She might be the least of them, but she is a Barrington."

"Yeah." She stood up, closed the empty pizza box and

moved it to the counter, picked up her plate and put it in the sink.

"Susan—" The word took all the oxygen out of the air.

He was standing next to her, holding a plate and the empty bottles. She gazed at their reflection in the window. He looked tired, eyes in dark shadows, a muscle ticking at the corner of his jaw. Her face had the panicked expression of a Gothic heroine. A full moon hung in the black sky beyond their images. How corny could you get?

She turned to face him. The tension in his jaw made her own jaw ache. His eyes were guarded, but not enough. Sadness was there too, as it briefly was on those scarce occasions when he was tired and not careful enough.

He set the plate on the counter, fumbled the bottles, and dropped one. They both knelt to reach for it. She looked at him.

For an instant, she thought he would kiss her, but he debated it too long and the moment grew cold. She didn't know if she was relieved or disappointed.

She stood up.

He snatched the bottle and planted it with a firm clink on the tiled counter. "We will nail this scumbag. And then we can celebrate. Dinner maybe."

TWENTY-SEVEN

MORNING SUN, high and strong, slanted gold light through the bedroom; a shadow of leaves danced back and forth across the glass on Daniel's picture, sitting on the chest. Susan closed her eyes against the grief and loss that threatened to overwhelm her. She cursed silently at the sly trickiness of grief. It would back off and wait, crouched and hidden, motionless except for a twitch of the tail tip. It would wait for that moment when you were off guard, completely off guard, when you opened your eyes one sunny spring morning and saw his picture. Then it would pounce, shake you, and whisper, "There is no Daniel. He's gone."

He's gone, and nothing matters anymore.

Doing this job that was his, one thing at a time, a job filled with people who knew him, was some great appointed task which would expiate guilt. That the guilt was irrational didn't matter.

The kitten zoomed up from the foot of the bed, leaped on Susan's hair, tried grooming it, gave that up as an impossible job, and snuggled up to her neck, kissing, purring, slapping, and nipping, her usual morning get-your-ass-in-gear routine. When Susan didn't stir, Perissa attacked her feet: rip, snarl. Still ignored, Perissa dived off the bed, skittered around the door frame, and galloped down the stairs.

Susan picked up the phone from the bedside table and punched in her parents' number in San Francisco. Nine o'clock here. Two hours earlier there. Too early? Her father answered, sounding fully awake. She felt a stab of homesickness.

"Morning, baby. How's home on the range?"

"Very quiet. Haven't had a shootout on Main Street for

near a week. We're all just hanging out on the porch in torn T-shirts drinking moonshine.''

"Watch that stuff. It'll make you blind. Easter's coming up pretty soon.''

'That it is.''

"It would be nice to see a little of you.''

Ah, that's what he was working up to. Come home for Easter. Get a reminder of how great it is in San Francisco. Maybe get socked with an irresistible urge to move back. As a kid, she'd thought his every action was calculated, planned right down to the last step, like a choreographed dance. Now, as an adult, she still wondered how aware of his machinations he was. Only in the last few years had she come to the realization that he operated on an instinctive level he was only partially aware of. ''Why don't you come and see me?''

"In Kansas? Tornadoes are destroying the state. What's wrong, baby?''

"Nothing's wrong.''

"I can hear it in your voice.''

His instincts seldom steered him astray. He knew how to charm her, be the adoring father she loved, let the coming home hang untouched, and swing back to it later from another direction. ''I have a homicide that won't get itself cleared. Well-respected physician.''

"Disgruntled patient?''

"Could be.'' She thought of Ackerbaugh and all his anger that the baby wasn't getting well. ''Money's involved, and a bunch of other physicians, all related. Victim was the titular head of the family and the medical practice.''

"Moral, upright man?''

"Woman actually, but moral and upright. And controlling.''

"I suppose you've looked into the possibility of error in the treatment of a patient. If one of your physicians did something grossly wrong, your moral, upright lady might have been on the verge of punitive action.''

Leave it to her father to spot a motive in a case he didn't even know anything about. She chatted with her mother for a few minutes, then listened to her father drop pebbles about how overworked he was and how the firm could use another brilliant attorney. An attorney she was. At least she'd gone through law school and passed the bar, although she'd never practiced law. His idea, law school, preparation for joining his firm.

After she hung up, she stripped off Daniel's T-shirt and stepped into the shower, then put on blue cotton pants, a white blouse, and a light-blue blazer that the temperature made already too hot to wear.

She fed the cat, made a mug of instant coffee, and sipped it while she scanned the latest storm damage in the *Herald*.

Driving in to the department, she let her mind play over what she knew, waiting for an idea to swim to the surface like a goldfish in a pond, waiting for unconnected facts to arrange themselves into a pattern.

''The mayor's on the phone,'' Hazel said when she walked in.

ELLEN PUSHED BACK the curtains on the bedroom window. Daylight. Even sunshine. She knelt on the ledge, rested her elbows on the sill, and looked out at the starlings and sparrows giving the lawn a good going-over. On top the gazebo, a goldfinch was singing his heart out. All that fine talk yesterday about living in my own house, and here I am back in the Barrington mausoleum.

All alone.

Hey, I'm still alive. She'd been stupid to insist on staying here, despite Carl and Marlitta telling her she couldn't. She was stupid and stubborn and had spent the entire night an inch off the bed scared out of her mind, leaping into horror fantasy with every creak of wind and rustle of leaves and movement of shadows.

So she'd survived the dark, sleepless, terrified, and reduced to a quivering pulp. Now she was sticky with nervous sweat. She did have a fully functioning shower, there was that. But if she turned it on, how could she hear someone creeping in with a knife?

This was really stupid. She should have gone home with Carl or Marlitta. Well, at least with Carl. He'd never hurt her. Come on, neither would Marlitta. Ellen rubbed her face. Well, somebody was working on it. One of her family—her loved ones, her nearest and dearest—had set her up. Daddy's gun. The phone call getting her to Vicky's. Taylor with a knife in his chest. She felt sick.

Don't think about him.

You have to do something. This big, old, creepy house. All alone.

Take a shower. Put on clean clothes. She'd slept in her clothes last night, feeling a skimpy nightgown made her more vulnerable.

I need a dog. A big, fierce dog with big, fierce teeth.

It was beautiful outside. All the rain made everything shiny-green in the sunshine. Quiet too.

All of a sudden it was so quiet she could hear her own breathing. Nothing else. Just breathing. She took in a noisy whoosh of air and blew it out hard, then got up, stomped across to the chest, and snapped on the radio.

"...more rain forecast for this afternoon. A heavy storm is moving..."

She snapped it off, tugged her T-shirt straight around her hips, and started down the stairs. Breakfast. Halfway down, she heard a car and scooted into the living room. Standing in the gloom well back from the window, she tried to see through closed curtains. Couldn't see a damn thing.

The knock made her jump.

"Ellie? Come on, let me in."

Relief unlocked her knees. Carl. Then she stiffened again.

"Ellie? You awake? Come on."

On legs that felt like pegs, she moved to the door. If Carl was going to do her in, the world had gone mad, and she might as well leave it.

"Ellie?" He came in, crossed his arms, and looked at her with an expression that said, I understand, and life is really absurd anyway, so what if misery swamps you? "Had enough?" he asked quietly. He wore khaki pants and a short-sleeved white knit shirt, the usual working clothes that had so annoyed Dorothy. She had thought he should wear a suit and tie.

Ellen wondered if he hadn't refused just to needle Dorothy. She shoved her fingertips in her back pockets. Life was a lot simpler before she started having all these insights. "Enough of what?"

"Clinging stubbornly to a foolish position, just because you took it."

"I don't know what you're talking about."

He smiled. "Don't be obtuse. Get any sleep last night?"

"No,' she said, then grinned. "All night long, I heard people creeping up on me with hatchets. What are you doing here?"

"I came to make sure you were all right and take you out of here. Come on. Don't dilly-dally. I have to get to the clinic. With Willis out of it and Marlitta's mind unconnected, chaos reigns."

"You don't look like you got a whole lot of sleep either." His thin face looked as if the skin were too tight; his eyes were slightly bloodshot, with dark shadows beneath.

"Not much. I was working."

"You were on call last night?"

"That wasn't what kept me awake."

Something about the way he said that made her ears perk up. "What then?"

"A lot of thinking and a lot of searching. Let's go. I don't have time for this."

"I have to go out to my place."

He sighed wearily. "Oh, little Ellie."

"Don't call me that."

"Can't you for once just come along without planting your feet and scowling with defiance? Come and stay at my house. At least then I'll know you're all right."

Ellen had never wanted to do anything more than she wanted to go with him. She hated herself for not trusting him. "I'm fine here. Really. Honest. I just—" She couldn't think of anything safe to say.

He shook his head at her. "Now, why did I suspect that's what you might say?"

"Nadine's coming in a bit. She's going to take me out to get my car." And be with me when I go inside.

He sighed, looked at his watch. "I have to get to work. I'll come back later."

When he left, she made sure the door was locked, went up to the bathroom, and locked that door too. Her shower was very brief. Pulling on her last pair of clean underwear, she thought she'd better remember to bring back some more. Some clean jeans wouldn't be a bad idea either. As she buttoned up a blue blouse, she glanced out the window. Clouds already. What the hell had she done with her raincoat?

By the time she'd swallowed coffee and forced down a half slice of toast, Nadine was at the door.

"Where's Bobby?" Ellen asked as she slid into the station wagon.

"With Bob's mother. She's thrilled." Nadine tilted her head toward the backseat. "I also brought some extra rags and cleaning stuff. And a thermos of coffee. Don't let me forget the thermos when we leave. It's Bob's, and I had to promise on my life nothing would happen to it."

"Oh, Nadine, you don't have to—"

"Of course I do. You think I'm going to let you be out there by yourself."

Ellen couldn't bear it if she was afraid to be in her very own house, if this—all this—changed her feelings about it. "Thanks," she said.

WITH AN EYE on her watch, Susan listened to Mayor Bake-over tell her how to do her job: stop harrassing important people, arrest someone, and do it now.

Yes, sir, Mr. Mayor, sir. I'll just go right out and arrest Ellen Barrington, whether she's guilty or not. Clean this right up.

When he finally ran down, she—with great restraint—hung up gently, grabbed her blazer from the back of the chair, took a look out the window, wondering if she could get by without a raincoat, decided she could, and dashed off.

If she hustled, she could stop in to see Jen before getting her presence down to the hospital basement and standing there while Dr. Owen Fisher did the autopsy on Taylor Talmidge.

Dr. Adam Sheffield, in scrub greens—did he ever wear anything else?—was at the nurses' station when she got off the elevator. "How's Jen doing?" she asked.

"Remarkably well." He pulled off the scrub cap and ran a hand through his dark curls. "Amazing kid. I'm still trying to be cautious here, but I think she's going to be good as new."

A smile spread all over Susan's face.

"She still has a ways to go. Don't subject her to hard questions. Right now she's asleep anyway. Don't wake her up."

Susan nodded and went into Jen's cubicle. Jen's face was

still splotched red, but she did look better. She looked alive. Like a very sick little girl with measles, but not like death on a respirator. Susan only stood by the bed and looked at her, didn't speak, didn't touch.

In the basement, Dr. Fisher, also in scrub greens, shut off the tape recorder in the midst of his spiel: "Taylor Talmidge. Male. Caucasian." He looked at her. "You're late. I thought I was going to have to start without you."

Taylor's nude body was on the stainless-steel table. The harsh light glared down.

Dr. Fisher finished the particulars of weight, height, and age, and picked up a scalpel. He sliced, peered, cut, and diced in his careful meticulous way, and when he finished, his considered professional opinion was that Taylor had been stabbed with a sharp instrument.

He turned off the recorder, peeled off the latex gloves, dropped them in a hamper, and washed his hands at the deep sink in the corner.

"Owen—"

"I can't tell you anything more than what I find." He grabbed a towel, turned to face her, and dried his hands. "You heard it all. I'll send you the preliminary as soon as I get it written up."

"Yes, thank you. If a child were suspected of having porphyria, what kind of laboratory tests would be done?"

He rested against the sink, crossed his feet at the ankles, and thoughtfully dried each long, delicately tapered finger. "You're not suggesting I run a bunch of tests on our friend here, are you? There's no reason to suspect he had porphyria. It's extremely rare. I'd venture to say most doctors have never even seen a case."

"It's rare. It's inherited. It's difficult to diagnose."

"Correct."

"What kind of tests are used for diagnosis?"

He rubbed a finger along one side of his nose. "Blood tests of various kinds. Urine. Fecal. Liver. Problem is, with the different types, some show abnormalities and some don't. It's complicated. What is this bee you've got about porphyria?''

''I'm not sure.''

Driving back to the department, she was vaguely aware the sunshine had lost out and black clouds were taking over. She was sure, very nearly sure—the adrenaline, the excitement, the tingling in her mind that happened when she was pulling the right threads—that she knew who had shot Dorothy and why. But there was not one sliver of evidence and not a chance in hell of getting any.

''YOU HAVE TO COME through for me, George.'' Susan stood in front of his desk and tapped her finger on the gray metal surface.

He leaned back and looked up at her. ''At least sit down.''

''Because if one piece isn't so, the whole thing falls apart.'' She backed into a chair.

''Give me a minute. The man died thirty-some years ago.''

''He had a chronic illness. What was it?''

George took off his glasses and pinched the red spots on the bridge of his nose. ''Well, Susan.'' He put the glasses back on. ''I may have to shoot you. You've asked a question I don't know the answer to.''

She grinned. ''Ha. One for my side. You know anybody at the county courthouse?''

''Sure. Minnie Oaks. Known her forever.''

''Would you call her and ask her to look up the death certificate?'' Susan could do it herself, but George could get it faster. ''Find out what it says and let me know.''

Ten minutes later, she was plowing through reports at her desk when he got back to her.

''Death due to liver disease,'' he said, ''due to porphyria.''

TWENTY-EIGHT

"AND SO," Susan said. "Dorothy's murder had nothing to do with August Barrington or his paintings."

Parkhurst paced in front of the desk to the door, turned, and paced to the window. He rested his rear on the sill, a hand on either side of him. "You have to have a reason to look at medical records. You don't have one."

The sky outside had angry-looking banks of black clouds, with an occasional thin zigzag of lightning. No rain yet, but it ought to be pretty spectacular when it arrived. The fluorescent ceiling fixture had one burned-out bulb, and she turned on the desk lamp for more light.

He pushed himself from the sill and padded to the door. "No judge in the world is going to issue paper on what you've got."

"I know."

"Jesus, you've got so many ifs you need to draw lines to connect them." He reached the door, turned, and paced back.

"Sit down. You're making me nuts."

He dropped into the wooden armchair and slid low on his spine. "His father had this whatever-it-is—"

"Porphyria. He told us when we questioned him after his very dramatic class at Emerson his father had been chronically ill. I thought at the time he meant alcoholism. He didn't. His father had porphyria."

"—and he inherited it. How come he doesn't show any symptoms?"

"Dr. Fisher said that happens sometimes."

"Uh-huh. You're speculating he had an affair with the Ackerbaugh woman and fathered a child—"

"He is the unfaithful type."

"...a child who is sick, and even the physician doesn't know what's wrong with him. Dorothy begins to suspect this child has the disease."

"She left bookmarks in medical texts, scribbled notes for lab tests." Susan paged through her notebook until she found what she was looking for. "Protoporphyrin. Erythrocytes. Plasma. Feces."

Parkhurst tapped his fingertips together across his chest. "Your theory is she realized what was wrong with the kid and immediately knew he was the father because the disease is so rare."

"That would tell her he'd had an affair with a patient."

"Uh-huh. She'd have been pissed and given him the boot."

"Right. Told him he would no longer be a part of the Barrington clinic."

"So he shot her."

Susan tossed her pen on the desk and leaned back in the chair. "Anything wrong with that?"

"Oh, not a thing." He drew in his legs and got up. "I've run with some pretty thin evidence at times, but this is so thin it's nonexistent."

"Right. Feel like talking to Brent the Beautiful?"

"Damn right."

"You want to tell us about it?" Susan pulled up a brown plastic chair and sat down across the long wooden table from Dr. Brent Wakeley.

He leaned back and smiled at her. "There are a raft of things that I might want to discuss with you, but I can't believe any of them are the reason you've dragged me in here to listen to." With a casual hand, he brushed through the lock of dark hair that fell appealingly across his forehead.

He looked less dramatic in an ordinary light-gray suit—

he must use the black for his dynamic-professor outfit—but she still felt the power of his presence. Beautiful, she had to admit. Arrogant, and reeking with a powerful magnetism.

The interview room had no windows, but the ceiling light picked up small flecks of gray at his temples and the tiny lines around his eyes.

Parkhurst took two steps, planted palms flat on the table with a sharp slap, and leaned over until he was three inches from Brent's sculptured nose. "We know you killed Dr. Dorothy Barrington."

Brent drew back with condescending amusement. "I'm afraid your knowledge is sadly faulty, Lieutenant."

"Faulty?" Parkhurst rolled the word around in his mouth as he pulled back and propped a shoulder against the wall. "Maybe you'd like to set me straight."

"Dorothy Barrington was a very principled woman," Susan said. "Ethical."

"I guess you could say that. You could add moral, upright, and virtuous if you like."

Susan nodded. "All of those characteristics would have made her disapproving of adulterous affairs." It's catching, she thought. I'm beginning to sound just as profoundly erudite as he does.

The amusement in his eyes dried up. "And where is all this leading?"

"'Affair' is the operative word here," Parkhurst said.

"Without making any admission, I hardly think my affairs are your business."

"Wrong, Doctor. Homicide is our business. And when your affairs end in murder, it's definitely our business."

Brent looked at Susan. "I think you'd better get out your whip and chair and put him back in his cage."

"You had an affair with Mrs. Ackerbaugh. Linette Ackerbaugh," Susan said.

For one instant his eyes went blank, like the fast click

of a camera shutter, then he shook his head with a conde-scending smile. "Even if that were true, which I'm not admitting for a moment, what makes you think Dorothy would know about it?"

"She didn't, not at the time. Or she would have con-fronted you then."

"Long afterward, she suddenly stumbles upon this? Come, come."

Susan looked at him. He held her gaze, but a tiny muscle under his eye twitched.

"Interesting how she found out," Parkhurst said, and waited until Brent looked at him. "The baby."

"What baby?"

Parkhurst smiled: soft, dangerous. "The Ackerbaugh baby. The one you fathered."

Susan heard Beautiful Brent inhale.

"You are getting dangerously close to a lawsuit." He gave up all pretense of charm.

"Passed along what you're carrying in your genes."

"You have absolutely no proof of this."

"Well, Doctor, a smart, educated type like you probably knows there are tests for this sort of thing."

"Well, *Lieutenant*, even an uneducated type like you probably knows you need permission to run those tests. From me, from the parents. You have that permission?"

A crack of lightning followed by a loud clap of thunder made him jump.

"I've listened to this nonsense long enough," Brent said. "Are you prepared to arrest me? And I must warn you if you do, I will immediately file suit for false arrest. Much more of this and I'll add harassment charges."

BY THE TIME SUSAN LEFT the department, it was after five, and rain hammered down with force. The windshield wip-ers barely kept ahead of it, giving her only brief glimpses of the street between ripples of water. The headlights poked through streams of silver coming down at a hard slant.

She eased into a parking space behind Erle's Market to pick up cat food. That was the trouble with dependents; you always had to stop and pick up something. Sliding from the pickup, she flipped up the collar of her raincoat and, head down, sloshed toward the store. Neon lights bled red and yellow onto the wet pavement. A car driving out fountained water in wide arcs.

Out of the corner of her eye, she glimpsed a dark figure slogging toward her from the right. In the gray light through the curtain of rain, she saw a long, belted robe with the hood pulled forward and no visible face; near the shoulder was a small skull.

Hair stirred on the back of her neck. She heard Jen's words: a monk in a long robe with a rope belt, no face, small skull on the shoulder.

The figure swerved and set course for the store.

"Excuse me," Susan called, trotting to catch up.

The individual in the monk's robe halted under the overhang jutting out above the doors and threw back the hood to reveal a round face with a thick braid coiled on top of her head. "Oh, Chief Wren, I didn't see you. Just trying to get out of the rain."

Nadine, Susan thought. Ellen's friend, Nadine something. Haskel. Nadine Haskel.

"Did you want to see me?" Nadine asked.

"I was noticing your raincoat. It's very unusual."

Nadine looked down at her blue coat, tugged tighter on the braided belt, and smiled. "It was Ellen's idea." Her fingertips touched the appliqué below her left shoulder. "Our logo. Advertising, you know."

Up close and with light overhead and spilling through the glass doors, Susan could see it wasn't a skull but an oddly shaped vegetable thing—no doubt a gourd—with a wide, round skull-like top and a narrowing-in, jaw-like, below. Dark splotches gave the illusion of eyeholes. "How many of these raincoats are there?"

"Only two, mine and Ellen's just like it. Except hers is black."

TWENTY-NINE

"THIS IS THE CLEANEST the place has been since I moved in." Ellen fished two cans of soda from the refrigerator and popped the tabs. She handed one to Nadine and dropped into a chair across the table from her. They'd spent all day cleaning and polishing and straightening, removing all residue of murder, cops, searches, trying to scrub away the awful sense of violence.

Nadine took a gulp, looked at the barely visible traces of blood that had soaked into the scarred linoleum, and grinned. "Well, the best we can do, anyhow."

Yeah. Ellen had always hated that linoleum: worn splotches of brown and green and yellow with dull silver bits like confetti. She rubbed her face in the crook of her elbow. She wanted her own place back, the feeling that this was all hers, home and safe, being here and loving it.

Wind slammed against the old stone house and, solid as it was, Ellen felt it shudder.

"Storm coming up," Nadine said. "You ready to go? I need to collect Bobby. Bob's mother is probably worn to threads by now."

"You go ahead. I want to get some clean clothes. Boy, am I looking forward to a shower."

Nadine stood up, drained the can, and set it on the table. "I'll talk to you tomorrow."

"Right. And Nadine, thanks for—you know, everything."

When she heard the rattletrap station wagon jouncing down the driveway, she noticed the thermos on the cabinet. Oh, oh. Nadine forgot Bob's thermos.

Ellen turned on the radio for company and carried it into

the bedroom with her. The local station was playing oldies. *I Left My Heart in San Francisco.* I left my heart here, and I want it to belong here, and I want it to be happy. Like it was before—

Just get on with it.

From a chest, she took out her last two pairs of clean underwear. Time to do laundry. She shoved the drawer shut and pulled out the one beneath. Jeans, shorts. She dumped everything into a plastic bag.

The wind picked up, fitful and teasing. Infrequent gusts sniffled around the window.

Tony Bennett faded, and the announcer's cheery voice came on: "Those weather-chasers say we might be in for a good one, folks. So get your emergency kits ready. Stock up on batteries, get your blankets, and start filling up water containers. This just might be the real thing. And while you're packing up your gear, a little 'Rocky Mountain High' by John Denver."

She opened the closet door in search of blouses and blinked.

Her raincoat.

Hanging right there. Clear as day. Couldn't be. It wasn't there. It wasn't. I looked. I looked. I went all through everything. She pressed the heels of her hands against her temples. I'm losing my mind.

She also realized this day wasn't clear; it was as dark as it could get without being night. She switched on the ceiling light. Outside, the sky boiled with clouds, black, purple, green, gray, and white. Livid streaks of lightning charged from one cloud to another, thunder exploded. Rain splattered against the window.

She got two blouses, stuffed them in the bag, and was reaching for the raincoat when she heard a *rap rap rap.*

It came again, louder. Nadine at the door, come back for the thermos. She went into the living room.

"Ellen?" The word was almost lost in a clap of thunder.

When she opened the door, the wind tore it from her hand and banged it back against the wall.

"What took you so long?" Marlitta, raincoat dripping, short hair pasted to her head, swept past her.

"Marlitta?" Ellen had to lean into the door to get it shut. The wind wailed around the edges, as though incensed at being kept out.

Marlitta plodded into the kitchen, leaving a trail of watery footprints. "This has got to stop."

"What?"

Marlitta whipped around to face her.

Jesus, she looked terrible, wet, bedraggled, face all gray and tight. "Marlitta, are you all right? Maybe you better sit down."

Marlitta looked around at the jumble of gourds in hanging baskets, ivy trailing down the side of the cabinet, the large hollowed gourd with apples in the center of the table. "How can you live out here?"

Irritation clogged up Ellen's throat. "I like it here," she said when she could untangle the words. "What are you doing here? There's a storm coming. You shouldn't be—"

Marlitta's face seemed to melt with grief, or sadness, or—Oh, Jesus, what was the matter with her?

"You're the youngest." Marlitta's voice was low and creepy, with edges of—something.

"Sit down," Ellen said. "Let me get you a Coke. Or some coffee."

Marlitta stared at the linoleum where Taylor's blood had spilled.

Ellen was getting scared. Something was sure bad wrong with Marlitta.

"I can't let Brent be blamed." Marlitta raised her eyes and looked at Ellen. "The police have him."

Brent? Arrested for the murders? Relief fizzed over Ellen like carbonated water, then she was ashamed of herself. No wonder Marlitta was so zonked. She loved the jerk.

"Please sit down," Ellen said. "I'll get you some coffee." She lifted Nadine's thermos and shook it, hoping there was some left. It sloshed reassuringly, and she managed to squeeze out two cups.

Outside the kitchen window, lightning flickered and zigzagged across the sky, then came the boom and rumbling roll of thunder.

THUNDER ECHOED away to nothing, lost in the wail of the wind. A crosswind pushed the side of the Bronco, and Parkhurst, sitting erect and gripping the wheel at ten and two o'clock, had to make quick, small compensating twists. Rain hit the road in front of them and rebounded a foot. The air smelled like ozone and gunmetal.

Susan looked at his hands as the car shuddered on a curve. He was holding it just on the edge of control. Trees along the side of the road and in the fields whipped back and forth, bent almost double, then snapped upright. She heard a rending crack, muffled by the wind and rain; a limb fell onto the road, bounced and rolled, was pushed fast across in front of them, and tumbled into a ditch. So much force filled her with a wild, high surprise.

She knew that some people were sensitive to weather: bright sunny days brought out happy, festive feelings of good cheer; winter snows caused an oppressive, pushed-down sense of hush; rain made them weepy. A low barometer touched off primitive warning instincts, memories that created nervousness and tension; it was time to seek out shelter. She'd never been affected by the moods of weather.

Now she felt a stir of irrational fear—we're traveling as fast as we can into the jagged teeth of disaster—so strong she wanted to tell Parkhurst, "Turn this buggy around; get us to a cave." She took a long breath to force herself to relax and looked at him. The Bronco bucked so violently he eased back on the accelerator.

"You're awfully quiet," she said.

"I'm thinking. You know how hard that is for me. You ready to let go of Brent the Beautiful?"

"Whoever clipped Dorothy wore that raincoat. It couldn't have been Brent. He's too big, too tall, too broad-shouldered."

"That brings us right back to Ellen. Motive—needs money. Means—we got anything for means?"

"Don't be snide. Why the hell haven't we found that murder weapon?"

"Ellen got rid of it someplace we didn't think to look," he said, then went back to laying out the evidence against her. "She was at hand to find Vicky's body with a thin story about a phone call. She found Taylor in her own kitchen, decorated with her own knife."

"Why didn't she use the gun?"

"Didn't think she'd need it again, disposed of it, had to improvise."

"Why didn't she get rid of the raincoat?"

"We don't know that she didn't. Isn't that what we're going out there to ask her about?" He leaned forward even more as wind edged the Bronco over the center of the road. When he got control, he eased back slightly. "Just before we read her her rights."

There is one other person, Susan thought, with just as much to lose.

Two cloud masses collided, and lightning streaked to the ground, bright, close. She braced herself for the crash of thunder.

THE RUMBLE seemed to go on and on. Ellen clasped the mug in both hands and sipped at the coffee. Marlitta hadn't touched hers. She sat across the table like a lumpy sack of old clothes. The ceiling light flickered, went out, then came back on.

"Marlitta," Ellen tried again. "Please drink some coffee. It has sugar in it. You look like you're in shock."

Marlitta seemed to stir herself like an old dog just coming awake. She blinked, looked at Ellen, rubbed a hand down her face, looked around the kitchen, and mumbled something.

Ellen leaned over the table to hear above the rain peppering the roof. "What?"

"Where's the knife?" Marlitta flicked a glance at the block of wood with one empty slot.

"The cops have it."

"Oh, yes, of course."

Fear prickled along Ellen's scalp.

Marlitta, elbows on the table, started to push herself up, then fell heavily back. "My purse." She looked around. "What have I done with my purse?"

"It's right there by the chair."

"Oh, yes." Marlitta reached down and lifted the brown leather bag to her lap, cradled it in her arms, then clicked it open and stuck her hand inside.

"Marlitta—"

"I have to stop this." Marlitta drew out her hand, black pistol in her fist.

"Marlitta, what—"

"The police have to have someone, so they'll stop."

"Where did you get the gun?"

"It's yours."

"It isn't mine."

"I'll tell them you just had it. I have no idea where you got it. They have been so stupid."

Ellen stared witless at her sister. Marlitta with a gun in her hand. Ellen felt numb. Her own sister was going to shoot her. Her mind looked on in horrified detachment.

"You killed Dorothy," she heard herself say.

"I'll tell them you called me and asked me to come out here."

"Why did you steal Daddy's painting?"

Marlitta, confused, shook her head. "No. I don't understand about that. Why would I steal a painting? Dorothy told me to be there. At the house. Eight o'clock.''

"Marlitta, please put the gun down.''

"That meant she knew.''

"Knew what?''

"The Ackerbaugh baby.''

"What?''

"I'll tell them you tried to kill me.''

"Nobody will believe that.''

"Because I knew you had Daddy's gun. What have you done with it? I had to defend myself.''

Thunder crashed. They both jumped. The light flickered.

"Mistake,'' Marlitta said.

"Yes. It was all a mistake. Just—''

"Vicky,'' Marlitta said impatiently, as though Ellen were being particularly dense.

Vicky was a mistake? Ellen couldn't unstick her mind from the round hole at the end of the gun barrel.

"When she said that about the raincoat,'' Marlitta said. "I had to do something. I didn't realize she thought it was you. Then it was too late.'' Marlitta shook her head. "Somehow she just knew.''

"You took my raincoat.''

"I brought it back. And there was Taylor. Really quite a nasty man. Creeping up on me. Interested only in money. Standing there smirking.''

"Why?''

"Why what?''

"Why me?''

"The police need somebody.''

"You took Daddy's gun from me. You called me from Vicky's. Why me?''

"The first day of school.'' Marlitta's voice was clotted with resentment.

"What?''

"Your first day. When you went to school.''

First day of school?

"Mother took you. She walked with you to school on your first day."

"Marlitta, what—"

"You were the only one." Marlitta stood up, stepped away from the table, and took dead aim at the center of Ellen's chest.

She's going to blow me away. Ellen's mind was making frantic, shrieking noises, but her muscles just sat there. The funny thing was, she didn't even remember their mother walking her to school.

Thunder boomed. The light went out.

Ellen slid under the table onto her hands and knees.

The gun fired.

Heart beating so fast she couldn't breathe, Ellen strained to see in the dimness. Marlitta scraped a chair away. It fell. Ellen crawled to the far end of the table.

"Ellen!"

The table skidded as Marlitta shoved it. She was mumbling.

Ellen slid out and ran for the door.

It blew open just as Marlitta fired. Ellen rushed out. The door slammed behind her. The wind shoved her back against it, forced her mouth open wide, and rushed into her throat. Rain pelted down. She leaned into the wind. It caught her and sent her stumbling sideways. She tripped, fell, and rolled.

Lightning flashed. She saw Marlitta coming after her, mouth open in a yell, but the words were blown away.

Ellen scrambled to her feet. Bent forward, she slithered down a slope toward the trees, got blown in staggering side steps, corrected, got blown the other way.

She hugged a tree, pulled air into her tight chest. In a bright flash of lightning she saw Marlitta, gun in her hand, whipped around by the wind, struggling through the rain.

Ellen peeled herself from the tree trunk and moved on,

sliding around trees. She stumbled up a slope, fell to her knees, scrambled to her feet.

The wind carried Marlitta's voice, screaming her name. If I can hear her, she's too close. She crawled to a boulder. Kneeling, she clawed away small rocks around the base. Her fingers groped for the plastic bag. Rain ran down her face.

She shook out Daddy's gun, unfolded the oily rag she'd wrapped it in. Would it fire?

"Ellen!" Marlitta's voice, high and thin. "Stop this. We're getting soaked."

Ellen curled her finger around the trigger. Lightning flashed. Thunder cracked.

THUNDER ECHOED away, followed by another crack and a rolling rumble.

"Ellen has a visitor," Parkhurst said as the Bronco's headlights picked out a dark car through the blowing curtain of rain.

Susan squinted, trying to identify the make. "You recognize it?"

He brought the Bronco to a stop behind it. "Marlitta's Plymouth."

Oh, shit. The one other person who had just as much invested in Brent as he did.

When she slid from the car, the wind caught her, nearly hurling her off her feet. The force of it shocked her. It snapped her hair against her face, stinging her cheeks. It pressed her pants legs tight around her; the cuffs fluttered against her ankles with a rippling sound.

As Parkhurst came around the Bronco, a gust slammed against him, pushed him back. He took several running steps before he recovered.

In just the few feet to the front door, they were drenched. He pounded on the door. She heard a rhythmic *bang bang, bang bang bang.*

Staggering, leaning forward, buffeted by the wind, they went around to the rear of the house. Ellen's Mustang sat nose in. The kitchen door blew open, banged shut, blew open.

It was dark inside. Flashlight held high and to one side, Susan eased in and moved quickly right. Parkhurst, gun drawn, moved left. The light beam spotted an overturned chair, the pine table shoved askew. She listened, trying to hear over the howling wind. Parkhurst flipped the light switch up, then down. "Power's out."

A sharp pop came from outside. They looked at each other.

"Gunshot," he said.

She was already moving.

"Where?" Stance rigid, constantly adjusting for the wind, pants legs whipping around his legs, he stared into the rain.

A shot, followed quickly by another.

He pointed. They took off, running into the wind. Susan stumbled uphill. Wind seemed the only thing keeping her on her feet.

"Parkhurst!" His name was scattered by the storm. She wanted to tell him to be careful. The trees gave them some cover, but they were floundering right into range of a bullet in the chest.

He crouched behind a tree. A few feet away, she did the same. Thirty yards downhill, she saw Marlitta, a gun raised, step out from behind a tree. She yelled something Susan couldn't hear and fired.

The shot ricocheted off a boulder. There was a flash of return fire. Marlitta ducked back.

"Police!" Susan yelled. "Drop the gun! Drop the gun!"

In a running crouch, she moved closer and got behind a tree. "Drop the gun!"

Marlitta, open-mouthed, turned; startled, confused, she aimed at Susan.

Parkhurst shouted, "Put your hands in the air!"

Marlitta spun toward the sound of his voice.

"Put the gun on the ground!" Susan yelled. "Now!"

Marlitta turned toward her. A long second stretched by. Marlitta lowered her arm.

"Put the gun down!"

She knelt and laid it on the sodden ground.

"Step away from it! Step away from the gun!"

Marlitta stood up, took a faltering step back.

Susan and Parkhurst converged on her from both sides. He cuffed her. Susan grabbed the weapon.

"Ellen?" Susan called.

Like a drenched kitten, frightened and miserable, Ellen appeared over the far side of the boulder. "She was trying to shoot me." Gun in her hand, Ellen rubbed the crook of her elbow down her face.

"Lay the gun on the rock," Susan said.

"Yes. Okay." Ellen placed the revolver on top of the boulder. "It's the one— She shot Dorothy— I think—" Ellen froze.

The rain had slacked off. Susan heard a great rumble, like a freight train. It bore down on them.

"Storm cellar!" Ellen took off running.

Susan snatched the gun from the boulder and shoved it in her raincoat pocket.

"Go!" Parkhurst shouted at her. He unsnapped one cuff and clicked it around his own wrist. Linked together, he half-dragged, half-carried Marlitta down the hill. Susan pounded behind them. Her ears popped. She felt light-headed, had difficulty breathing. Beyond the roar, she heard hissing and screaming.

Dirt, rock, boards whirled around her. A tree bent; the root structure rose up with yards of soil and was carried away.

Ellen struggled with the cellar door. Parkhurst nudged her aside and wrestled it open. Ellen stumbled down the steps. Marlitta fell in, arm stretched out, pulling Parkhurst after her.

Wind caught the door, wrenching it from his hands. It banged against him, making him stagger. Susan felt his free arm grope at her. Tangled in a clump, they stumbled, slid, fell down the steps.

They sat on low wooden benches, their heads tilted up, and listened to the world being destroyed above them.

The wind screamed, the rain sounded like bricks hitting the door. Around the edges, gusts seeped in, creating small eddies of dust and cobwebs. For sheer terror, this beat anything she had ever experienced.

MINUTES DRAGGED BY for hours before the roar, shriek, and pounding stopped, leaving behind an eerie silence.

Dreading what she might see, Susan opened the door. The world was still there. Ellen's house was intact. Battered trees, bare of limbs, lay scattered around. Parkhurst's Bronco was nowhere to be seen. Ellen's Mustang had been turned upside down and blown downhill. Marlitta's Plymouth, one wheel gone, had a barn sitting on it. A cow stood in the open doorway mooing plaintively.

THIRTY

JEN, PROPPED UP in the bed, looked at pictures of tornado devastation in the *Hampstead Herald*.

"Wow. You were right there," she said with awe in her voice, peering at Susan as if making sure she was real and not a cunning trick of light and mirrors. "You could have been smashed."

Two days had passed since that night in the storm cellar, an unforgettable night when cops, villain, and potential victim all waited together for the end of the world.

The northeast corner of the county was the only spot where the tornado had touched down. Hampstead itself had been spared a direct hit but had suffered severe storm damage from high winds, hail, and lashing rain: trees down, windows broken, roofs ripped off, streets flooded, power out.

Parkhurst's Bronco had been located undamaged in a wheatfield two miles away. The barn squashing Marlitta's car belonged to Harlen Dietz. The cow inside was unhurt, although it had taken some doing to get her down.

Marlitta had been arrested.

She'd known about the porphyria. Brent, not being a complete shit, had told her. This inherited disease kept them from having children.

Before the two married, Dorothy, being the woman she was, looked into her mother's old medical records to find out what Brent's father had died of. She simply wanted to know Brent's family medical history.

Marlitta wasn't as blind about her husband as the rest of them assumed. Foolishly in love, for sure, but she'd suspected the affair with Linette Ackerbaugh. Once in his office, she had, without his being aware of it, seen him stroke the back of Linette's hand. She'd turned away, knowing this would end, as had all the others.

When Dorothy got worried about the baby, started delving into medical texts and coming up with porphyria, Marlitta realized what must have occurred. Brent was the father.

She also knew Dorothy would not tolerate a physician's betrayal of a patient like that. Beautiful Brent was on his way out. Except Marlitta got her timing wrong. It was the stolen painting Dorothy had meant to deal with when she'd called her siblings together on that Saturday night.

Brent claimed he didn't know his wife had shot Dorothy or killed the others. If Beautiful Brent was to be believed, he also didn't know he was the father of the Ackerbaugh baby. Personally, Susan had her doubts, but the matter was now out of her hands and in the hands of DA's and defense attorneys.

There was talk from Carl and Ellen of tracing the stolen painting and getting it back; that too was none of Susan's concern, since no charges had ever been filed.

Earlier this very day, Jen had been moved from intensive care into an ordinary room.

"Should she be sitting up so long?" Susan asked Dr. Adam Sheffield.

"If she wants," Sheffield said. "She's a strong kid. She's going to be all right. She'll figure out her limits."

Susan wasn't so sure. It was only eight in the evening, and Jen looked more pale and fragile and tired than Susan could bear to see. Suddenly, she loved this little girl so much she had to bite the inside of her cheek to keep tears from slopping over.

"Ben Parkhurst was just here," Jen said. She agreed to have the head of the bed lowered, bunched the pillow, and snuggled into it.

"Yeah? What'd he say?"

"You're celebrating."

Right. Dinner maybe. "You're almost as good as new. That's something to celebrate."

"Don't forget the ballet," Jen said drowsily.

"I promise." Susan sat by the bed and watched Jen sleep, watched her eyelashes against her pale cheeks, watched her chest rise and fall. When Jen's mom came, Susan quietly left.

Driving home, she felt tired and feverish. She poured a glass of orange juice for her scratchy throat and carried it up to the bedroom, where she caught sight of her face in the mirror. She stared.

Dropping onto the side of the bed, she picked up the phone and punched in a number.

"Yeah," Parkhurst said.

"It's Susan. Listen, I'm afraid—"

"Afraid?"

"Well, that too, but I'm afraid I have the measles."

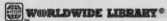

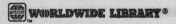